Under the Coconut Tree

A Chupplejeep Mystery

MARISSA DE LUNA

Murder, mayhem and Goan village life

For Dad

Author's Note

In 2011 while on vacation in Goa I visited the village where my father spent his childhood. Zosvaddo, a small village near Porvorim along with two other villages, Maina Armina and Vaddem, make up an area called Socorro. They have a combined population of around nine thousand people.

Captivated by Zosvaddo's rural charm and idyllic settings, a refreshing contrast to Goa's more popular tourist destinations, I was inspired to write *Under The Coconut Tree,* the first in the series of *The Chupplejeep Mysteries.*

The villages where *Under The Coconut Tree* is set are fictitious. However, Zosvaddo has hugely influenced my descriptions.

In reading *The Chupplejeep Mysteries* you will come across the occasional word of Konkani, the local Goan dialect, and Hindi which is spoken almost throughout India.

For more information on the location that inspired this fictitious world and a gallery of photographs please see www.marissadeluna.com

CHAPTER ONE

Lavita found his body at dawn on her way to clean out the chicken coop. At first she didn't notice poor Sandeep lying there. She was just going about her usual business, humming along. His body lay limp, camouflaged by the thick, hairy, discarded coconut husks piled high under the tallest coconut tree in Utol.

It was the whites of Sandeep's eyes that eventually caught the young woman's attention. She took a step back, dropping the *kapai,* brush, and the bucket of water that she had painstakingly drawn from the well. The soapy water seeped into the dry earth underneath the hardened soles of her feet, wetting the hem of her petticoat. Granny would be angry, having washed the hem only yesterday, but Lavita put her thoughts of Granny Monji to the back of her mind; Sandeep Shah was dead.

A single trickle of blood from the gash on his head had congealed into the shape of Sri Lanka just above his brow. His eyes were wide open – glazed and lifeless. Finally, the graveness of the reality brought out a sharp shrill sound from Lavita's mouth, piercing the morning birdsong and springing the usually dormant cockerel into action. Lavita gaped down at the body again before closing her eyes and shaking her head in horror. Was this really Sandeep? She opened one eye and peered down, taking a closer look at the face. Yes. Most definitely, the face belonged to the man who lodged in their outhouse.

'Lavita, Lavita. What on earth has gotten into you?'

The girl turned around, looking towards the house, to see Aunty leaning out of her bedroom window, her orange and green shawl wrapped tightly round her face to protect her from the cold morning air. 'What's all this noise? Be quiet, na. We're trying to sleep. You'll wake Baba with all your commotion. You know he gets terrible indigestion if he wakes up in the cold.'

Lavita stared at her aunt, annoyance rising in the pit of her stomach. She wanted to tell her aunty what she had found but when she opened her mouth no words came out.

'What is this behaviour?' Mrs Lalji said, scowling at her niece. She squinted at Lavita. 'Standing there with your mouth open like that – flies will go in.' She closed the window carefully, trying not to wake up her husband, tutting to herself at the incompetence of the child.

Lavita stood frozen to the spot for a minute before she heard the squeaky cycle horn from Bala, the *pau wallah*, in the distance.

'Bala *bhaiya*, Bala *bhaiya*!' Lavita shouted at the top of her lungs for the baker's attention. Immediately she heard his cycle brake and skid on the gravel outside.

~

Bala would have heard just a whisper from Lavita. He often lingered outside the Laljis' house hoping to catch a glimpse of the woman he wanted, so desperately, to marry. He walked around the side of the house to where the woman of his dreams was standing. She looked beautiful with her big, brown, almond-shaped eyes and soft black hair that Bala could imagine running his fingers through. Lavita caught hold of his arm and squeezed it. Bala couldn't believe his luck. Not only had she called out to him, but she was holding on to him as well. He sucked his teeth and smiled. Today was going to be his lucky day. He briefly looked up to the sky and thanked Parvati, the goddess of love.

'Look, look,' Lavita cried, pointing her finger at the pile of discarded brown coconut husks. 'Sandeep is dead.'

Bala did as he was told. Women were so dramatic. A drunk must have taken a nap in the garden. But making out the whites of the man's eyes, he screeched. 'Aye-yah!' he said, jumping back. He remembered Lavita and immediately stood in front of her, placing his hand over her eyes.

'What are you doing?' she asked, pushing his hand away.

'Protecting you. You shouldn't be exposed to such…such…horrid things. Why is he naked?'

'I've been looking at his body for the last five minutes,' Lavita said, as tears began to fall. She lifted up

3

her *dupata* to her face and started to wipe her eyes. 'I don't know why he's naked.'

'He looks so young. Who was he?' Bala saw his chance to put a comforting arm around her.

'Sandeep. He is young, just a few years older than me.'

'Sandeep who? I've lived in Utol my whole life and have never once come across this fellow. This is suspicious in itself, let alone the poor chap's passing.'

'He was the new driver at the Da Costas' house on top of the hill,' she said, between sobs.

'What was he doing here?' Bala asked, one eye on Lavita and one eye on the corpse. There was no doubting that this man was attractive, even in death.

~

Mrs Lalji could hear the mutterings and wailing from outside. 'Those chicken coops are not going to clean themselves,' she said a little too loudly.

'Eh?' Her husband made a noise. She could smell last night's *daal* on his breath. 'Who's there?' he asked, half-asleep.

'No one, no one, Baba. Go back to sleep.'

'Hmpf.' Baba made another noise, scratched his hairy chest, rolled over and let out a fart.

Mrs Lalji sighed. Now he would be gassy all day. 'Thank you Lavita, seriously-good-for-nothing child.' She pinned back her recently dyed, jet-black hair and grabbed her shawl from the grandfather chair as she walked to the kitchen.

The air was cool, a typical November morning. She could hear the drongo cuckoo but her eyes could only find the vibrant blue kingfisher that was perched in his usual spot on the mango tree, shitting on everything below. Mrs Lalji found her *chappals* on the red stone steps that led to the garden. She slipped her feet into the soft rubber, finding her imprints.

She wrinkled her nose. Her *chappals* were wet with dew. She was not happy. This was what happened when one woke so early in the morning. Her body was not young anymore like Lavita's, she thought, as she made her way towards her niece. She needed time to rise, and it was her prerogative now that Lavita was around.

CHAPTER TWO

'Ohhhhh!' Mrs Lalji let out a gasp when she saw the dead body lying on the ground next to her niece and Bala.

'Mrs Lalji, madamji please close your eyes. It is not for women to see,' Bala said.

'Shut up, man. I'm the lady of the house, no? I have to see what terrible happenings are taking place in my own backyard.'

'I'll get Baba,' Bala protested, 'It really is no place…'

'You'll get Baba, will you? Ok-ay, be my guest.' Mrs Lalji crossed her arms and smiled.

Bala weighed up the options. He had woken Baba up before, and the sight was not a pretty one. The baker certainly didn't want a repeat of that belching man's anger. Who knew how he would react to a dead man under his coconut tree? And what was the harm in Mrs Lalji dealing with the death in the first instance? After all, she had already seen the body.

'Who would do this?' Mrs Lalji asked Bala, and then eyed her niece suspiciously. She suspected that Lavita had a thing for the driver and it suddenly crossed her mind that perhaps Lavita wasn't on her way to clean out the chickens this morning.

'I don't know, Auntyji. I just found him. Tell her, Bala.'

'*Ji*, it's true. She called and I came running.'

'I'm sure you did,' Mrs Lalji said under her breath. She walked around the body, taking in the surroundings of the dead man. 'Okay,' she said, after she had walked twice around the coconut tree, 'firstly we cover the body. Lavita, go get an old towel from the cupboard.'

Lavita stood motionless, her feet welded to the spot.

'Go,' Mrs Lalji urged.

Still the girl did not move.

Mrs Lalji walked up to her niece and slapped her across her cheek.

Bala stood in front of the two women, his eyes wide and his mouth open. He had only ever seen women in the fish market hit one another. He didn't expect this type of behaviour from the Laljis and he wondered whether it was appropriate for him to intervene. But he didn't have to think for long. The slap had brought Lavita to her senses. The girl scampered back up the garden path, past the tamarind tree and into the house.

'Bala,' Mrs Lalji ordered, 'take your bike and cycle as fast as you can to the police station. This is a serious matter. We have a death in our village. In our back garden, in fact.'

'Madamji, why don't we telephone them?'

'The telephone is not working since last month,' Mrs Lalji said, wrapping her shawl around her shoulders. 'Quick, now go.'

Bala wanted to protest. He didn't have time to cycle all the way to Little Larara Police Station to report the man's death. He had bread to sell whilst it was still hot. How else would he have enough money to replace his cycle tyres, which were as bald as the underside of a cooking *handi*?

'Are you going or what?' Mrs Lalji asked.

He knew better than to say no. Bala turned and started walking away, but as he did so he heard Mrs Lalji mumble something.

'You know, I never liked Sandeep.'

Bala stopped in his tracks.

'He had a wandering eye.'

He turned around and tilted his head to get a better look at the dead man.

'He had a soft spot for Lavita, you know.'

The baker's pupils dilated for the second time that morning.

'I think she too liked him.'

A familiar feeling spread across his chest. 'I don't think Lavita would entertain – ' he started, but Mrs Lalji interrupted him.

'I was not sure on how to advise my niece,' she said, shaking her head from side to side. 'You know parenting is new to me. Drivers get paid well. But there was something about this fellow I just didn't like.'

Bala was silent.

Mrs Lalji sniffed the air and wriggled her nose. 'I wonder how long he has been dead for?'

'You never told me,' Bala said, scratching his chin.

Mrs Lalji shrugged.

'It would have been nice if I had known that you were considering him as a prospective suitor. But tell me, how could you consider a man you didn't like as a husband for Lavita?'

'I was weighing up his good points and bad points. No decisions had been made.'

'Why was he in your garden? Lavita said he was renting this place from you.' Bala pointed to the outhouse, as jealousy stabbed him again. What had Mrs Lalji put on this list she was making? A baker would never have as much respect as a driver.

'Bala, you know that already.'

'You never told me.'

'Stop acting all clueless just because I don't gossip extra with you.'

Bala winced.

'Who would have done this?' Mrs Lalji said. 'Sandeep was an honest fellow. Paid his rent when he was supposed to, and his working references were fine. Plus he was working with the Da Costas. They are a *pukka* family.' She looked at the lifeless body and shook her head. 'He must have done something to spite Lord Shiva to land up this way.'

The baker sighed. How could this respectable woman, who he knew so well, rent a room to a man that a) she hardly knew, and b) who was making eyes at her only niece? A worrying thought crossed his mind and he started to bite his fingernails. 'Lavita's a pretty girl, and there must be several suitors out there who wanted her for a wife. Do you think someone heard this Shah was making moves on her and got jealous?'

'What nonsense you talk, Bala!' Mrs Lalji scolded. '*Chalo*, go now. Stop time-wasting.'

'I heard the other day on the radio that seven out of ten murders in India are motivated by passion,' Bala said, as he turned to leave.

Lavita walked towards them with a pink towel.

'Not the good towels, *beta*,' Mrs Lalji shouted at her niece. 'Get that old green one from the pantry.'

Lavita turned around and disappeared again with the towel.

Mrs Lalji heard Bala's squeaky cycle move away from the house. As she looked intently at the dead body, she couldn't help but wonder: why on earth was Sandeep Shah naked?

CHAPTER THREE

The telephone rang just as the detective was booking a houseboat in Kerala. Agatha Christie's *Death on the Nile* had been his inspiration for a romantic getaway with Christabel on a riverboat. He was certain that this experience would make him more like the Belgian detective Poirot.

'Stupid slow government machine,' Chupplejeep grunted as he tapped the yellowing computer monitor, hoping for a response.

Rinnnnng, rinnnnnng.

'Pankaj?' Chupplejeep shouted, flicking his eyes between the half-loaded picture of the wooden boat and the kitchenette.

'Sorry, sorry, sir,' Pankaj said, carrying a tray with two cups of *chai* and two *batata wadas*. Pankaj put down the tray and answered the telephone.

Chupplejeep returned his full attention to his holiday planning.

'Ha. I see…Yes, of course…Oh, I see,' Pankaj said into the green handset as he scribbled furiously on his notepad.

Chupplejeep raised his head towards Pankaj. He could see the excitement in his face. Crime was rare in this sleepy part of the world. Chupplejeep looked at his watch. He clicked on the print button and picked up the greasy *batata wada* as he waited. The printer in the corner of their office coughed and spluttered as it contemplated doing something.

'Sir,' Pankaj said, replacing the receiver.

Chupplejeep looked up at Pankaj. They had only been working together for just over a year, yet Pankaj had become like a son to him. The boy was smart, if a little distracted at times. 'Tell, tell,' he said lifting the *wada* to his lips.

'A crime has been committed.'

'What crime? Don't tell me Ashok has had his mangoes stolen again,' Chupplejeep shook his head from side to side. 'I tell you, I couldn't – '

'A murder, sir,' Pankaj interrupted, suppressing a grin. After all, a murder was a grave crime.

'A murder?' Chupplejeep said, almost choking on the spicy potato. 'Who was it?'

'The victim, sir? I don't know.'

'The person who reported the crime!'

'A man called Bala.' Pankaj opened his book and read his notes aloud. 'He lives at house no.5, Utol, opposite the church. He stopped at a house with a telephone on his way here because his cycle's got a flat.'

'And how does this Bala know it is murder and the victim didn't die of natural causes?'

Pankaj was silent.

'You know these villagers. Anything for a bit of *naatak*, drama,' Chupplejeep said, taking the last bite of his deep-fried *wada* and wiping his hand on a paper napkin. He paid no attention to Christabel's voice at the back of his mind, telling him that fried potato would eventually cause the fatal heart attack he had been warned about. But Christabel couldn't tell Chupplejeep what to eat any more, especially after he caught her eating *bhajiyas* for breakfast yesterday. And from whom had this heart attack advice originated? Christabel's no-good elderly *Maausi*, aunt, who had decided to learn medicine in her free time.

'Sir, if you don't mind me saying, regardless of the cause of death, we should leave at once. In this heat, the body…'

'Of course,' Chupplejeep said. 'We must go now.' It had been a long time since he attended a suspicious death and despite what he had said to his officer, he couldn't help but feel excited at the prospect of a real crime. In Utol, Chupplejeep had resigned himself to solving petty village crimes like pilfering and the occasional case of graffiti. But this case, if it proved to be a homicide, could work in his favour. It could smooth over the whole Panaji fiasco, the reason for his move to sleepy Larara, and once again he could shine in the Inspector General's eyes.

Chupplejeep lifted the blind to peek outside. The sun was already high in the sky. The morning air was generally cool in November, but it was still warm as far as dead bodies were concerned. Chupplejeep put on his police cap and rose to his feet. He would have liked to call for a driver, but remembered that the drivers had been the first to go in the budget cuts that happened just as the last of the rains had passed. Had it been that long since someone had reported a crime they had to attend to?

'I'll drive,' Chupplejeep said, as Pankaj pulled the bolt across the station door and padlocked it.

'Shall I call Kulkarni?' asked Pankaj.

'Huh? Oh yes, yes. Quickly call him.' Usually, Chupplejeep would attend the crime scene first and then call in the forensic pathologist. However, since a body had already been identified as dead, they could make an exception. 'I hope this Bala fellow isn't making this up.'

'He sounded scared, sir. I don't think it was a lie.'

Chupplejeep nodded. Prank calls were a general pastime in the villages, and as the highest officer in charge at Little Larara, he didn't want the local kids to think he was gullible. If they thought that he was, then they would be prank-calling the station endlessly. It would be difficult to know when to attend to a report or not.

Pankaj unlocked the office door to make the phone call. Chupplejeep walked to his car.

'Kulkarni will meet us there,' Pankaj said two minutes later as he hastily climbed into the blue Maruti four-by-four.

'Could have used your mobile, na?' Chupplejeep said as Pankaj fastened his seatbelt.

'No signal, sir.'

Chupplejeep started the car and tutted. No mobile reception at their police station. What hope did they have?

~

Fifteen minutes later, after a quick stop at the *gado* to buy some Chicklets to freshen their breath, they arrived at the Laljis' house which was painted a milky green. Word of the body had spread and a small crowd was standing outside the compound wall.

'Eh, these villagers!' Detective Chupplejeep exclaimed, 'You fart in Panaji and people in Utol will immediately know what you had for breakfast.'

Pankaj laughed. 'All Goans, sir,' he said. 'Not just villagers. It's in our blood to want to know what is happening everywhere.'

Chupplejeep smiled. 'One hundred per cent correct.'

The two men walked through the small gathering. Pankaj looked around for familiar faces and spotted the Goa Dairy man, identifiable by grey and black tufts of hair that protruded from his ears and the large mole on his forehead. Pankaj didn't see anyone else that he could recognise and he was glad. Up until now he had only been involved in smaller, low profile crimes. A suspicious death in Larara would be big news and could be difficult to solve if he knew any of the people concerned. Local people would continually pester him for details that he wasn't allowed to share.

'Give them half an inch…' Pankaj muttered to himself. The last case he worked on involved Ashok and his stolen mangoes. Both his mother and aunty continually harassed him throughout the case and the result was that he almost lost his job.

'Tell me, na?' his mother had said. 'What is the use of having a police officer as a son when you don't give us any information?'

'No, Ma,' Pankaj protested, 'you just want to tell all your friends so you feel important. That's not how it works. The *Good Practice Policing Handbook* says that we are not to tell anyone about confidential information relating to cases we are working on. This applies even to relatives.'

'Bah! I'm your mother, not some relative!'

Pankaj had resisted at first but his mother had more persistence than he knew. He reasoned that perhaps by just telling her one piece of information, she would go away. She didn't. Jyotsana pestered him until he told her the full story. He found it, printed word for word the next day in the *Larara Express*. Thank Krishna that Detective Chupplejeep had just been assigned to the station and had proved to be an understanding boss. Chupplejeep didn't expect a *feni* bribe from Pankaj like his old boss would have wanted. Instead he had looked at the article and said with a knowing smile, 'You make a mistake like this once, you'll never do it again.'

Pankaj looked away from the Goa Dairy man with his protruding tufts of hair as he followed Chupplejeep into the Laljis' house.

~

The house was cool and decorated to Chupplejeep's taste. A charm of one lime and seven chillies hung in the archway leading into the hall, instantly telling Chupplejeep that the Laljis were superstitious. He nodded his approval at the red stone flooring and the minimalist whitewashed walls, similar to his home in Greater Larara.

A lizard darted behind the wooden pelmet where the lace curtains hung. A shiver ran down his spine. He hated lizards. They stopped in the kitchen where the Lalji family had already gathered.

'Please, Detective,' Mrs Lalji said, 'let me introduce you to my family before you go out to the garden.' She immediately introduced herself, her niece, her husband and Granny Monji before telling the detective where the body was.

Chupplejeep and Pankaj hastily introduced themselves and walked out of the kitchen, down the steps and into the garden, savouring the aroma of the *daal* simmering on the stove.

~

'How can they make food when there is a dead body in their garden?' Pankaj said casting a suspicious eye on the Laljis as soon as they were out of earshot. 'And who

17

does such formal introductions when there is a dead body in the garden?'

'Food can be very comforting,' Chupplejeep said.

Pankaj nodded. Chupplejeep was right. He was always right. Of course they were making comfort food. His mother often made him *daal* and rice when he was tired or anxious about an exam or a case. 'But what about the introductions?'

'It's habit for some people, especially as we're guests in their house. Formalities are hard to break.'

'I don't think I could make introductions if there were a dead body in my house.'

Chupplejeep smiled. 'Ah, Kulkarni!'

'About time,' Kulkarni said, raising his head from the body towards the two men.

'You got here fast!' Pankaj said. His eyes widened as he caught a glimpse of the corpse. It looked bloodless, like it had been doused in bleach. He gritted his teeth and tried to swallow the nauseous feeling rising in his chest.

'I was just across the bridge next to the circle when you called,' Kulkarni said. He smiled, exposing his brilliant white teeth that stood out against his pink gums and his dark Southern Indian skin.

'The Utol circle. Good timing,' Chupplejeep said, towering over Sandeep's body. 'The body was like this when you found him?'

''Es. I've not touched him. I've taken the photographs and scanned the area.'

'And the family, they've not touched the body?'

'Mrs Lalji said she placed this towel on the body. That's all,' Kulkarni said, pointing to a green towel next to the body.

'Of course, of course, she would have wanted to cover his dignity,' Chupplejeep said, looking at the victim's shrunken penis. 'Cause of death?'

'I'll need to examine his body first, eh, but from the gash to his head I'd say he was struck with a blunt instrument.'

'Once, twice…?'

Kulkarni bent over the body. 'One laceration would suggest he was hit only once. No defensive wounds.'

'Homicide?' Chupplejeep looked up at the coconut tree, where just a couple of tender coconuts hung. He could just about make out their green skins by squinting against the sunlight. 'That's a tall coconut tree.'

'The tallest in all Utol or so the *pau wallah* told me.'

'You spoke to him also?'

'He heard the niece call for help when he was delivering his bread.'

'So it could have been a coconut?' Pankaj said, as he peered out from behind the tree like a Bollywood actor, glancing upwards.

Chupplejeep raised his eyebrows. It was the most plausible explanation. He had got his hopes up before, but he knew murders were rare in such small villages.

'That's what I thought,' Kulkarni said, 'at first.'

'But there is no coconut around.' Chupplejeep scanned the area with his eyes. The garden was well maintained with thick shrubs and flowerbeds. He was

19

impressed. It was difficult to maintain a garden given the heat and soil in Larara. They must be using chicken manure and watering at least twice a day, he thought, remembering Christabel's advice on how to maintain his own garden. He recognised some of the red and yellow flowers from her garden. He himself did not have green fingers, unlike Christabel. His own garden was bare apart from the pink bougainvillea that grew of its own accord around his compound wall.

'I have searched and nothing. There are no coconuts lying anywhere in the garden. Just the pile of husks and they couldn't kill anyone.'

'Unless they were on fire,' Pankaj added.

''Es. Husks are superb for getting a fire going,' Kulkarni said.

'But a coconut seems plausible to me,' Pankaj said, again from behind the coconut tree. 'People don't just go around killing people here.'

Chupplejeep shook his head. 'And I suppose the coconut grew legs and walked off?'

'Come out from behind that tree. The body won't bite. You look like one *Zarbadast* hero standing there,' Kulkarni said to Pankaj. He turned to Detective Chupplejeep, shaking his head. 'These young officers, eh.'

Pankaj moved around the tree but still leaned against it, keeping his distance.

Chupplejeep screwed his lips together. 'I suppose a falling coconut is an option. We can't rule anything out at this stage. Take a good look in the shrubs, Pankaj, and we'll check with the family about it. They may have taken it inside unknowingly.' Detective Chupplejeep looked towards Kulkarni. 'Time of death?'

'Hmm, pallor mortis, algor mortis, rigor mortis,' Kulkarni looked up at the blue sky, 'given the time of day and the temperature last night, I'd say the vic has been dead nine or ten hours max, but it is hard to say.'

Since the budget cuts, Kulkarni's job description now not only encompassed his existing role as Greater Larara's most experienced medical examiner and coroner, but a forensic pathologist as well.

'I need to do a full autopsy, eh, but by looking at the rate of rigor mortis I would say that this poor fellow died somewhere between eleven last night and five this morning. Mrs Lalji's niece found him at six this morning.'

'Ah, so the niece found him? We must ask her what she was doing out here.'

'She was going to clean the chicken coop,' Kulkarni said.

'So you've also turned detective, Kulkarni?'

Kulkarni grinned.

'You never miss an opportunity to speak to a young woman.'

The medical examiner looked at his watch. 'The charlies from the morgue will be here soon. I want to get the body out of this blasted heat as soon as possible. I don't know what's taking them so long.'

Chupplejeep took a closer look at the dead body, swatting the flies away as he bent over Sandeep's face.

He noticed a bruise near his right eye. It had faded but it was definitely a bruise. *So Mr Shah had upset someone.* Chupplejeep straightened his back. Maybe the case was not as simple as he first thought. Maybe it wasn't a falling coconut after all.

~

Pankaj's hands shook as he looked around the garden hoping to find a stray coconut, one that looked like it could do some damage. He had never seen a dead body like that before. Sure, he had seen them in the morgue or behind a glass screen, when he was at the Police Training School, but never in someone's back garden. It made him feel nervous. He squatted near the rangoon creeper and poked around under the shrubs.

Suddenly the smell of a fresh simmering curry pricked his nostrils. Pankaj smiled. He stood up, grabbed a handful of curry-pak leaves and held them to his nose. He felt calm again.

CHAPTER FOUR

'Chup-ple-jeep?' asked Granny Monji, carefully pronouncing each syllable.

'Yes,' he responded. He knew where this was going.

'Chupple as in *chappal*?'

The detective smiled. Granny Monji was one of those typical Indian grannies who rarely left the house, but had something to say about everything and everyone. She would either be a help or a hindrance to this case. Which of these, only time would tell. Granny Monji's right eye was noticeably larger than the left. A milky film covered both irises giving her a ghost-like appearance. She didn't look kind or approachable like a typical granny, but she smelled of *ladoos* and had a comforting voice.

Regardless of what Chupplejeep thought, Nana had brought him up with manners and he was at work so he had to be professional. 'Yes, Chupple as in sandal,' he said, and gave a polite laugh.

'And jeep as in *motor gaadi*?' Granny Monji clenched her hands into fists and twisted them upwards as if she was revving a motorbike.

Chupplejeep nodded. He knew what she meant. 'Yes, Mrs Monji. Jeep as in a vehicle.'

'*Haan*, I have not come across this surname before.'

He braced himself for a fresh tirade of questions.

'Are you Gujarati then?'

'No, Goan through and through.'

'But I've never heard of Chupplejeep being a Goan surname. Who is your father?'

The detective had been right in his initial assessment. By the time he left the Laljis' house, Granny Monji would know more about him than he would know about Shah.

'My parents died a long while back.'

'I've been around a long time, son. I know of everyone. What is your good name?'

Who's the detective inspector here? Chupplejeep thought. So far he had not asked a single question. 'Arthur.'

'Arthur?' Granny Monji asked raising the eyebrow above her smaller eye, making her old features look sinister.

'Correct.'

'Are you sure?'

'No disrespect, Mrs Monji, but I know my own name.'

'Of course you do. But I've never heard of you. Your parents must have died when you were very young. You must have been brought up in that orphanage.'

Chupplejeep nodded, averting his eyes from the old woman.

24

'*Aacha*. Very well. Arthur is a good Catholic name.'
Granny Monji softened into a smile as she shook her
head from side to side. 'You're Catholic, no?'

Chupplejeep wondered if he should just say yes or
explain what an atheist was. It was never an easy term to
explain in the villages. He was so focused on the woman
with the mismatched eyes and the typical Goan nosiness,
he did not notice Mrs Lalji had walked into the room.

'Mummy, leave the Inspector's good name and
religion out of it,' Mrs Lalji said. 'What will he think of
our family if you act like this? He's here to ask some
questions about Sandeep, not answer questions about
himself?'

'Please sit,' Granny Monji offered, pointing to a seat
by the kitchen table. 'I am making *daal* and *chapattis* for
lunch. You'll stay?'

Detective Chupplejeep sat at the kitchen table but
politely declined the food. No matter how tempting it
was, he had a suspicious death on his hands and he had
work to do. He couldn't sit around making small talk.
'Mrs Monji.'

'Yes.'

'Tell me your version of events from the time you
woke up today.'

'I woke at around six o'clock when I heard my
grand-daughter screaming. I didn't get out of bed
though. Detective, at this age it takes some time to move
my bones. My joints are so stiff.' Granny Monji ran her
hands through her recently oiled grey and black hair. She

made a show of effort as she twisted her hair into a bun and secured it with a pin.

'Did you hear anything else after that?'

'I heard my daughter telling the child to be quiet. Then I heard some talking outside between my daughter and Bala.'

'Yes, that is exactly what I did,' Mrs Lalji confirmed. 'I heard a scream and I thought, as usual, Lavita was making a fuss for nothing. The girl is scared of frogs and in our garden they're everywhere. You know, when Lavita first came to live with us, Baba spent a full morning killing the wretched little things to avoid her treacherous screams. For a week our garden had no frogs, then more arrived. I said to my husband, you can't keep killing them, Lavita will have to get used to them. But no, it's been a year and nearly every day I hear her screaming because she has seen a frog. What to do?'

Chupplejeep didn't agree with the woman's instant dismissal of her niece's fears. After all, he was scared of lizards and in Goa they were as common as having rice and curry for lunch. He looked back at Granny Monji. 'Bala, the *pau wallah*?'

Mrs Monji smiled, making her smaller eye even smaller. 'Yes.'

'Does Bala often visit the house?' asked Chupplejeep, thinking of the baker with the wide-set eyes.

Granny Monji pursed her lips and looked at her daughter. 'Now and again, when he gets a chance. He may make a suitable husband for Lavita. She's almost nineteen, you know. If she leaves it any longer, she'll be *zoon* like an old vegetable.' Granny Monji closed her eyes. 'A spinster in the house could bring bad luck on all of us.'

Chupplejeep was silent. It seemed that bad luck had already arrived at the Laljis' house. Villagers felt strongly about marrying their children off young, but he himself didn't quite understand it. He had met Christabel at thirty-eight and he was a strong believer that you couldn't put an age limit on love.

'So what does Lavita think of Bala as a prospective suitor?'

Granny Monji's eyes darted towards her daughter as fast as a lizard's. They shared a conspiratorial look.

'She's busy with her household chores. Lavita has little time to think of men in that way. Anyway, I'm sure you're not here to talk about the non-existent love life of my niece,' Mrs Lalji said.

Chupplejeep scanned the kitchen. It was well kept; the floors had been mopped and the trinkets on the shelves had been recently dusted. He noticed two old school sports day certificates had been framed and hung on the wall.

'Mummy was a keen sportswoman back in her day,' Mrs Lalji said, looking at Granny Monji.

Chupplejeep smiled and then looked at his notebook. 'Were Lavita and Sandeep friendly?'

'You'll ruin the name of my only grandchild,' Granny Monji snapped, her tone quickly changing. 'If you go

27

around asking questions like that, people will think there was something.'

'So you don't know if there was a relationship between them?'

Granny Monji picked her fingernails whilst Mrs Lalji focused her eyes on a plate hanging on the wall behind him.

'I'm asking only you, Mrs Monji, and your daughter. Not the whole village, unless you give me reason to.'

'I've seen them talking,' Mrs Lalji said with a sigh. 'They're both young. I suppose they have things in common.'

'He *was* young, Mrs Lalji,' Detective Chupplejeep said, writing in his notepad, 'sadly he will not grow old. Can I ask why Lavita lives here and not with her parents?'

Granny Monji stared at the detective. 'Because they are dead.'

'Oh, I'm sorry to hear that.'

'The fire in Soco village.'

'I've heard of that case,' Chupplejeep said, making a note to ask Lavita about her relationship with the deceased. Of course he had heard of the fire in Soco. The whole house went up in smoke because of a cooking accident. The daughter, out with the buffalo at the time, survived. It had been talked about for days back when it happened. 'What a terrible accident.'

Mrs Lalji walked to the stove and turned off the gas burner. She moved the pot of *daal*. 'Can I get you a drink, Detective?' she offered. 'With all this commotion I forgot my manners. A Limca? *Nimbu pani?*

'Don't worry, water's fine.' He wondered if Pankaj was having better luck talking with the villagers. Mrs Lalji returned to the table with a jug of water, glasses and some *channa* snacks. Granny Monji took a handful of the snack and started popping the grams one by one into her mouth.

'Mrs Lalji, tell me, you didn't move the body?' Chupplejeep asked.

'Like I said to the other man, I sent my niece to get a towel and Bala to fetch the police. I then woke my husband up and told him about the incident. We waited in the kitchen till you arrived.'

'Did you move anything from the garden?'

'Like what?'

'Coconuts? Any objects, stones even?'

'*Chya*, of course not. I've seen detective shows. We're not backwards in the villages – we have Star and Zee in this house. I know you should not move anything.'

'We know about Star television,' Granny Monji said. 'All these youngsters are watching American shows and now they are even talking like them.'

'You are intelligent women, I can see that, but it's my job to ask,' Chupplejeep said. He knew that charm and flattery usually won people over. For some reason, the people he dealt with often opened up to him once he paid them a compliment, especially women. Chupplejeep made a note to tell Pankaj this later. It was essential for his protégé to know the importance of public relations.

If he gained people's trust it would make his job a whole lot easier, because people in Goa were good at pretending that everything was okay on the surface. Meanwhile everything was in fact all *ulta pulta*, upside down, underneath.

'Do you know how Sandeep came to be in your garden?' Chupplejeep asked.

'Oh yes. That much I know. Sandeep was renting a room from me, the outhouse at the back of the main house.'

'We'll have to investigate that room so please make sure no one touches anything.'

Mrs Lalji shook her head from side to side in agreement.

'You said he was working for the Da Costas?'

'Yes.'

'For long?'

'Three months now.'

'And he lived here during this time?'

'Yes,' Granny Monji responded, 'too little time to get to know about someone's family. I didn't learn much about his family and I didn't like that. I used to ask him questions. You know how it is, Detective. But he always gave such vague answers.'

'You took references when he asked to rent a room?'

'From his previous employer in Kukurul, Mapusa. They said he was a decent fellow. Good manners.'

'I'll need to see that reference. Do you normally have lodgers?'

'This was the first. Just for a little extra cash.'

'She didn't want to send her niece out to work,' Granny Monji said. 'Even though Lavita has been of working age for some time. They're spoiling that child. She'll be fattened and no use to her husband. I was married at sixteen.'

'We don't need Lavita to work,' Mrs Lalji said. She looked towards the detective. 'The price of produce has gone up considerably in the last year. My husband makes enough money. We're doing well.'

Granny Monji scowled. 'I told her there was enough money and no lodgers were needed. Bringing shame on her husband by telling people he could not provide for his family.'

'I didn't tell people such things.'

'But you did – simply by renting out the outhouse.'

'And you didn't benefit from the extra money his rent brought in? You didn't buy any extra chikoos or mangoes at the market?'

Granny Monji looked away. 'So it was murder and not an accident?'

'We're investigating that now. The body will be at the morgue soon and an autopsy will be carried out.'

'But you know how he died. He was hit on the head,' Mrs Lalji suggested, 'I could see a cut on his head and blood.'

'We are looking at all possibilities,' Detective Chupplejeep said, 'all possibilities.'

CHAPTER FIVE

Pankaj opened the door to the outhouse. Sniffing the air, he recognised the smell of Palmolive soap and stale fish curry. He looked around the bare four walls. There were no posters of Aishwarya Rai and no calendars of foreign girls. It was unlike any other driver's room he had seen before. His suspicions stirred.

There was a red and yellow checked mattress in one corner of the room with a small statue of Lord Ganesha on an adjacent shelf. A khaki sheet lay haphazardly over the bed as if Sandeep Shah had just got up to pee in the night when he met his untimely end. Pankaj stood over the bedding. It was possible that someone who knew his routine could have been waiting for him. After all, the toilet was outside in a sheltered spot next to the shower tap in the garden.

Pankaj's mind began to wonder, as it often did. Perhaps Sandeep Shah didn't want to pee, perhaps a lover lured him outside. He scratched his head. He needed more clues.

He found some stale curry and two green mangoes next to the stove and smiled nostalgically. The mangoes reminded him of his childhood. All through his school life, a hawker had sat with his *pato,* woven basket, outside the bus shelter selling green mangoes. Every evening as Pankaj descended the steps of the bus, he would give the vendor two rupees for chopped green mango smothered in salt and chilli powder. His mouth began to water at the memory. He returned his attention to the curry. It was covered in old newspaper. 'This must have been Sandeep Shah's last meal. The rest he must have been saving for breakfast.'

Pankaj put on his latex gloves. This new glove rule part of the *Good Practice Policing Handbook*: *The revised edition* made his palms all sweaty.

He started looking through the victim's possessions. There wasn't much to go through; a few shirts and a pair of trousers, a pile of underwear and a small green soap in a little dish by his mattress. There was nothing suspicious, but still he ordered the officers from Kulkarni's office to bag up the victim's possessions. Pankaj squatted near the mattress and then lifted it up. Underneath was a small chit of paper with a phone number on it. On the reverse was written a single name: *Sanjog.*

~

Lavita opened her bedroom door just a fraction so that she could hear what the detective was saying, but thanks to the labourers hammering the hard laterite stone outside her window, she couldn't hear a thing.

Clouds of red dust floated past the glass, reminding her of the washing she had to do. 'That blasted red mud,' she moaned, 'it won't come out of any of the sheets. When will they finish their works?'

She sat at her dressing table resting her chin on her right hand, and pinched her arm to stop the tears which were forming behind her eyes. The labourers reminded her of Sandeep.

Now he was gone, no one would care about her. When she had complained to Baba about the red mud, her uncle had simply stated that the labourers had to finish their works for some water pipe. Refusing to speak with them, he had told her to hang the washing on the other side of the house. That had been a useless suggestion – what was the point in making up a new washing line directly under where the kingfisher did his business? Luckily Sandeep had come to her rescue – well, sort of. She had heard him asking the workmen to hang some wet cloths up where they were digging so that the red dust would not blow onto her laundry.

'Do you know who I am?' Sandeep Shah had asked the labourers after they told him where to go.

'No,' said one labourer, eyeing Sandeep's footwear and bringing his pickaxe down hard on the stone in front of him, 'and I don't care who you are. This is government work.'

'Hmpf,' Sandeep had snorted, looking at the labourer's broken *chappals*. He spat at the base of the large banyan tree. 'You should know your place,' he said adding '*Daasiro,*' bastard, for effect. But his words fell on deaf ears.

Lavita had seen and heard this entire conversation but pretended she hadn't. Instead she thanked Sandeep, claiming she was in his debt for his help because Sandeep was the man she wanted to marry. She was of marrying age, Granny had told her so a million times. And if Granny had mentioned it then she had to move quickly. There were not many men like Sandeep around Utol. With his dark, dreamy eyes and floppy black hair, he was quite easily the most handsome man she had ever met and much nicer than Auntyji's first choice, Bala.

Lavita's friend Sonali had advised her that pretending to be in a man's debt was the best way to get a man to propose. 'Bat your lashes and pretend you know nothing. Be grateful to him for anything,' Sonali had told Lavita after her own wedding ceremony. 'It's the only way to get a man. If you make him feel important, he'll want you as a wife. All men want to feel important.' Lavita couldn't argue with that. It made perfect sense.

She let go of her arm, exposing a red bruise. Now that Sandeep was dead, she didn't care how she looked. She glanced over at the door. It wasn't just her lover's death that was bothering her. Lavita was worried about what the detectives would say when they found out about her affair. Would they talk? Would the gossip spread? And worst of all, would they accuse her? They were sure to ask questions and the truth was bound to come out. It always did in such circumstances. A single tear rolled down her cheek, streaking the talcum powder she had only just applied to her face. The knot in her stomach tightened. Aunty would send her to Belgaum if she knew that she had been having an affair with their lodger.

'You've ruined your reputation!' Aunty would say. 'You've brought shame on this family.' She would propose a visit to the Mukherjees to formally meet Bala's parents. Aunty and Granny had constantly been dropping hints about the baker for months now and this would be a perfect excuse for them to arrange a ceremonial meeting. She shook her head, Bala was all well and good for Utol's standards but he was no Sandeep Shah.

Lavita had done well to hide her relationship with Sandeep from her aunty and uncle but she was sure Granny Monji knew something. Granny knew everything, but if she did know something, she had kept quiet about it. Then again, it was not unusual for Granny to sit on information before making her move.

Granny Monji was cunning like a fox – one of those red and grey sorts, which often crept around the village at night. These foxes would spend their time gathering information, like where the chickens slept, which houses confined the fattest chickens and so forth, all the while keeping their presence hidden. Then when you least expected, the fox would pounce, killing as many chickens as possible in one swoop.

Granny was exactly like that. She had seen it with her own eyes when Granny suspected their maid, Archana, of stealing. First, she saw her take a tablecloth from the cupboard but didn't say anything. Then she noticed two pillowcases being taken out of the house under the girl's blouse. Finally, Granny saw the maid help herself to a five-rupee note, which Baba had carelessly left next to the fruit bowl. That's when Granny had attacked. It hadn't even been Baba who had left the note there, the sly fox had marked the note and planted it next to the fruit bowl herself. Oh, there had been a big showdown in Archana's village that evening.

That was the worst part. Granny had not confronted the girl at the house and sent her packing quietly like Aunty or Baba would have done. Granny Monji bided her time until she was good and ready to make an example out of the poor girl. Lavita sighed, was Granny planning the same end for her?

A black mass hovered over her heart and a nauseous feeling filled her belly. She wanted to cry and scream – she had lost the man that she loved, but at the same time she had to act as if Sandeep had just been lodger, someone she spoke to when she fed the chickens. Lavita walked to her bed and buried her face in her pillow as the sobbing began.

Two minutes later, she heard a knock on the door. She looked up just as the door opened fully. It was too late to pretend to be asleep.

CHAPTER SIX

'The *pau wallah* is definitely suspicious.'

Chupplejeep thumbed through his notepad. 'Bala Mukherjee?'

'*Haan,* yes.' Pankaj looked out of the station window, admiring the red hibiscus.

'Explain. Don't just start a conversation and stop halfway through,' Chupplejeep complained. If it was one thing that annoyed him about Pankaj, it was his incessant daydreaming; staring at flowers as if they were girls in mini-skirts. Chupplejeep threw his notepad at the officer, wondering how he had managed to pass his tenth standard let alone graduate from Police Training School.

Pankaj looked at his superior with a start as the book clipped him on his ear. He walked over to Chupplejeep and handed the book back to him. 'Sorry, boss. Bala claims that he went running into the Lalji garden when he heard Lavita screaming.' He shuddered, remembering the sight of the decomposing body under the coconut tree. 'This much is true. He confirms what Lavita told us.'

Chupplejeep narrowed his eyes. 'Go on.'

'He said he didn't know that the driver was living there. Odd, don't you think? Everyone I spoke to knew the Laljis had taken a lodger.' Pankaj looked at the large yellowing clock that hung on the wall. The rusty hand pointed at one, which meant it was two. He retrieved his tiffin box from under the desk. 'If the man delivering bread doesn't know who is living where, then village life is not what it used to be.'

He stopped to think of his own community. Like Utol, it consisted of just a few houses. He could tell you every going on in each household if he was asked, irrespective of his policing skills. It was part and parcel of village life. Everybody knew everybody's business and everyone knew their baker. In fact on most Sunday afternoons, Pankaj played Carrom with his village *pau wallah*.

~

Chupplejeep wrinkled his nose. Pankaj may have been a dreamer but he had good instincts. They had been working together for some time now and the boy was improving with each case. On the last important case they had worked on together, Pankaj had been the one to suggest that they look for the missing child in the old boathouse, when everyone else believed that the girl had been kidnapped. They had found her there, playing with her imaginary friend, oblivious that half the village was looking for her.

39

'A neighbour confirmed that Bala knew that Sandeep was a lodger. He went as far as to say that Bala and Sandeep had been in the same class together when they were in school. They completed their fourth standard together.'

'Fourth standard for someone of Bala's age is a long time ago. He must have been how old? Only nine. Now he must be at least twenty-something. He may have easily forgotten whom all he went to school with. I certainly don't remember all my classmates.'

'Twenty-seven, sir,' Pankaj said, checking his notes. 'This may be the case, but it's still suspicious, don't you think? Too much of a coincidence. And if what the villagers are saying is true, then Bala had a motive.'

'What are they saying?'

'That Bala's in cahoots with Mrs Lalji to marry Lavita, but we suspect that Lavita was more than friendly with the deceased. You said yourself, Granny Monji definitely knows that something was going on between Lavita and Sandeep. See how defensive she was.'

Chupplejeep nodded. If Pankaj was right then there certainly was a motive. 'We need to discuss this whole affair business with Lavita, away from the prying eyes of her aunty and grandmother. There's something she's not telling us. Get the case files from the Soco fire – the fire that killed Lavita's parents. I want to make sure the police didn't miss anything there.'

'Very good, sir. I'll call Soco police station today and ask them to send them over. When you were talking with Mrs Lalji, I went to speak with Lavita who was crying when I first entered her room. She looked me in the eye and said that Sandeep was just a lodger. Nothing more. She stuck with her story of going to clean the chicken coop when she stumbled across the body. When I asked her why she was crying, she excused it as stomach ache after eating sausage bread from the cart near the circle yesterday evening. But you know what spoilt sausage bread is like. No chance she would be able to clean the chicken coop so early in the morning if she had food poisoning. She should have said she was crying with shock of having seen a dead body. That's more believable, no?'

'Perhaps.'

'Bala was the one to call in the murder. I read about this once. In murder cases the culprit often calls the police station because he thinks that by doing so he'll not be suspected.'

'Did the Da Costas have anything to say?'

'They're visiting their daughter in the UK.'

'The staff at the house?'

'Shah had just started work there, three months back. The gardener didn't know much, he said Sandeep kept to himself. But the cook said once she caught him flirting with her daughter and told him if she ever caught him again she would cut off his – '

'Okay, I get the picture,' Chupplejeep said, grimacing. These villagers could be so crass sometimes. Poirot never had to deal with such filthy-mouthed people. 'What does the cook's daughter do at the Da Costas?'

41

'Mopping and the ironing,' Pankaj said, referring to his notes.

'It sounds to me like Sandeep liked the ladies.'

'I questioned the cook's daughter, Utsa. She had high hopes of marriage but she'd heard rumours that Lavita was in a relationship with Shah.'

'Mrs Lalji had plans for Lavita to marry Bala. If I had a daughter, I too would want her to marry a baker not a driver,' Chupplejeep said.

'Sir, really?'

'Would you want your daughter to marry a driver over a baker?'

'A driver surely is one up in society.'

'How do you figure that? A baker has his own business. A driver is always a driver for someone else.'

'I didn't think of it like that, sir. You're always one step ahead.' Pankaj rested his chin in his hand. 'But sir, in our village drivers are better respected than the *pau wallahs.*'

'Never mind,' Chupplejeep said.

'Did you speak to the man of the house, sir? He could have suspected something between his niece and Sandeep.'

'Mr Lalji? Yes. He came home from work late last night and went to sleep after dinner. He didn't hear anything until his wife woke him up and told him about the body. His wife confirmed this. I also questioned if they knew why Sandeep Shah was naked. Neither of the Laljis could provide me with a reason. I find it odd that the man was completely naked. No underwear even, that's strange.'

'Perhaps he slept that way, sir.'

The green telephone on Chupplejeep's desk started to ring for the second time that day. Chupplejeep answered the phone as Pankaj lifted the metal lid of his tiffin. The smell of *bhaji puri* filled the room and made his mouth water. Pankaj's mother, Jyotsana, was a world-class cook. She often sold portions of whatever she was cooking that day from her kitchen window. Perhaps if he managed to leave the station in time, he would get a chance to swing by and pick up some *bhaji puri* for dinner. Christabel would like that.

'Hallo…ah Kulkarni,' Detective Chupplejeep said, playing with his old medal for excellence which was on his desk. He looked over at Pankaj who was busy scooping up spicy potato with a piece of puri. His mouth began to salivate. Twenty minutes later when Pankaj had swallowed his last mouthful, Chupplejeep replaced the receiver back in its cradle.

'Kulkarni needs authority to start the autopsy and we need to get the body formally identified,' Chupplejeep said, picking up the victim's details he had obtained from the Laljis. 'If we get permission by sunset, he can have the results for us tomorrow morning. Get up, Pankaj, because now we must do the worst part of the job.'

A worried look spread across Pankaj's face.

'Don't worry. We'll do it together.'

Pankaj instantly regretted his heavy lunch. 'What exactly do we have to tell them?'

43

'Obviously that the man is dead and at the same time we need to ask for permission for the autopsy and ask for someone to come and formally identify the body.'

Pankaj put his hand to his mouth. He couldn't imagine what would happen to his parents if someone were to tell them that he was no longer in this world. Clasping his hand tightly around his mouth, Pankaj ran to the toilet.

Chupplejeep rose to his feet. 'It's going to be a long drive to Mapusa.'

CHAPTER SEVEN

Neeraj sat cross-legged with his eyes closed in the middle of the garden, wondering what to do next. '*Che,* what was I thinking?'

'I don't know what were you thinking,' came his wife's response.

Neeraj opened his eyes with a start. He turned and saw the round of Paavai's stomach before he saw her face. His wife's tummy, which made her look perpetually pregnant, protruded over her green and red sari.

From the time Neeraj and Paavai had started dating, people would occasionally stop Paavai in the street and ask if she was expecting. 'When's it due?' some long-lost relative would ask, or they would smile at her belly and ask 'Boy or girl?' Neeraj was never bothered by the rudeness of their so-called friends; he loved the comfort of resting his head on the soft mound of his wife's stomach. Paavai never got used to the questions hurled at her, but neither did she do anything to eradicate the problem like go for brisk walks in the village or eat fewer *mithai*. All she did was mutter expletives in Konkani as soon as the offender was out of earshot and criticise their bad taste in clothing.

Neeraj looked up at his wife's face and saw her piercing eyes. It wasn't the time to be thinking of her soft belly. He had much bigger things to worry about.

Paavai stood with her hands on her hips, staring at her husband, her eyes popping out of her round face. Shaking her head from side to side, her long plait followed her movement. Now wagging her finger, she tutted as loud as she could. 'What are the neighbours going to think?' she whispered, 'Why are you sitting in your shorts in the garden talking to yourself like a mad man? Did you marry me only so you could embarrass me?' She offered him her hand to help him to his feet. 'Now, what were you saying?'

'You're back!' Neeraj said as he took her hand and stood up. His tall frame towered over his short wife.

'Of course, I'm back. I told you, na, I would be back from Diwar before sunset.'

'How's your sister?'

'Never you mind how my sister is. You tell me why you're talking to yourself.' Paavai eyed her husband with suspicion. 'Yave you been gambling again?'

'Of course not,' Neeraj said. His eyes focused on a gecko sitting motionless on the garden lamp.

'Why can't you be like your son-in-law? He's so sensible.'

Neeraj was silent. He loved his wife, and her occasional mispronunciation of words beginning with the letter H when she was angry made him love her even more. He didn't want to break her heart by dismissing what she was saying, even if he did know it to be untrue. Paavai may have been strong on the outside, but inside she was soft like her round belly. He wanted to put his arms around her. She smelled of Ponds cream and he couldn't help but want to touch her when she smelled like that. But he held back. It wasn't the right time.

'Where's Gita?' Paavai asked, as they walked together back into the house.

'She's out with Ashu,' he mumbled. 'Before you ask me, I don't know where she has gone. She said she'd be returning home anytime now,' Neeraj said as they entered the house.

Paavai shook her head at the one-eyed cat that was meowing in the hope of some scraps of food. She shooed it away and pulled the back door shut with force, causing some of the faded blue paint fall to the ground. 'She's living in our youse or not? She should tell us where she's going, no.'

'*Che*, let her be. Here, let me help you with dinner.' Neeraj looked into the jute bag that Paavai had brought back from Diwar. Her sister cooked food better than any restaurant he had ever eaten at. Then he took the crockery from the side table and started setting the table. As he did so there was a knock on the door.

'Your daughter is knocking now in her own yome? I tell you she must be watching these Western dramas somewhere. Next she'll be calling us Mr and Mrs.'

Neeraj laughed. 'Paavai, relax. Of course it's not Gita. It must be some other person.'

47

~

Paavai raised an eyebrow from the kitchen where she was heating up the chicken biryani. 'Who?' she asked as Neeraj walked to the door.

He shrugged and she silently prayed that it wasn't those *goondas* from the neighbouring village. How much her husband owed she didn't know, she didn't want to know. She made a quick prayer to Laxmi, the goddess of luck, and to Hanuman of course so he didn't feel left out.

'This is Detective Chupplejeep and Police Officer Pankaj,' Neeraj said.

She felt faint. Neeraj walked over to his wife's side and squeezed her shoulder.

'Come in, come in officers. Please sit down,' she said walking over to them with a forced smile. 'Can I get you a drink?'

'Water,' Chupplejeep said.

Pankaj motioned for the same.

Paavai went to the kitchen, poured two glasses of water and prepared a bowl of grams. What had her husband done now?

~

'You must be wondering why we're here,' Chupplejeep said, twirling one end of his moustache. Lately he had been trying to get it to look more like Poirot's thin, black facial hair, but with his thick, wiry

Indian hair he was having no such luck. The detective found that by occasionally twisting it, not only did it make him look as if he was contemplating something intelligent but it also made the hair on his face less unruly.

Paavai and Neeraj looked at him expectantly.

'You are the parents of Sandeep Shah?' he asked.

'No,' Neeraj said quickly.

'No?' Chupplejeep retrieved the address from his shirt pocket and squinted at it.

'We know Sandeep Shah though,' Neeraj said.

'He gave his employers this address as his family home.'

'What is this?' Paavai said. 'Sandeep lives yere with us.'

'Lodger?' Pankaj asked.

'No. Look, is there a problem?' Neeraj asked.

'Where does his immediate family live?' Pankaj asked.

Neeraj and Paavai exchanged a look.

'He has no immediate family,' Paavai said.

Pankaj let out a small gasp. 'No immediate family?'

Chupplejeep sighed. Why this alarmed his colleague, he had no idea. Orphans did exist, after all he had once been an orphan. Lavita Lalji had been orphaned. It wasn't an uncommon occurrence. 'He told the Da Costas and the Laljis this was his immediate family.'

'What's happened to Sandeep?' Neeraj asked.

49

'We are as good as his immediate family,' Paavai said. 'His parents died in that bus crash three years ago. You know the one between Mumbai and Goa.'

'The Ghats are terrible,' Neeraj said with a shake of his head. 'They make treacherous driving conditions. Winding roads down almost vertical cliffs, *che*.'

Chupplejeep nodded his head in understanding.

'So you knew his parents well?' Pankaj said.

'We never met them,' Paavai said.

Pankaj scratched his head. 'So why then was Sandeep Shah living with you?'

The door opened and halted their conversation. A young woman with a dark birthmark to the left of her face walked into the sitting room. As soon as she saw the detectives, she stopped in her tracks. With a hesitant look, she slowly stepped forward.

Chupplejeep noticed the woman was holding a small child in her arms.

'Gita,' Paavai said with a look of relief on her face. 'This is my daughter. She is the reason why Sandeep was living here.'

CHAPTER EIGHT

Utsa made her way from the Da Costa house, down the hill into the village. The thorny shrubs scratched her legs as she walked, but she didn't mind. It was something she had grown accustomed to. She had been born and brought up in Utol and occasionally stopped on her way home to pick and eat the small blackberries hidden beneath the colourful flowers of the wild lantana shrubs. Occasionally, if she was lucky, she would find some fallen tamarind. Today she didn't stop though. She was in a hurry. Utsa had heard the news of Sandeep's death from the officer who had visited the Da Costa house and she had unintentionally diverted the attention of the police to her best friend. Now she had to go and warn her.

Utsa hadn't spoken to her friend in at least a month. It was a sad state of affairs because at one time they had been inseparable, but recently they had fallen out. Over what, she couldn't recall, but they seemed to have the same taste in men and that hadn't done their friendship any favours, especially in Utol where young men were in limited supply. Lavita had snubbed her when she was buying fish the other day and hadn't told Utsa that she was dating someone. Instead, she heard the gossip from Sonali who had asked Lavita about her new man but she had denied the claims, saying she was free and single, all the while shyly smiling like the cat that had got the cream.

Utsa weighed up the consequences of what she had told the police officer. It wasn't far from the truth. There *had been* rumours that Lavita and Sandeep Shah were dating and if she combined this information with what Sonali had told her, then it could have been true.

As Utsa fought her way through the prickly bushes, she thought about her last meeting with Sandeep. It had been a mistake to get involved with the man. Now if she wasn't careful she could easily become part of the police investigation and she could lose everything.

She was sure that she had been the last one to see him alive, so there was little chance of the police ruling her out. Although the police didn't know this fact yet, but Utsa knew that once they found out, they would come for her. She bit her nails at the thought of it and hoped it wasn't the case. What had she been thinking, going to see Sandeep Shah so late that night? She knew the reason. Three months ago, she didn't have a man in her life, she knew she was going to be a spinster forever. It was lucky the driver arrived on the scene when he did. He had saved her. But now her life was different. Sonali had been right. The minute one boy turns to look at you, other boys also want to see.

She felt guilty. She knew she shouldn't have told the police the rumours about Sandeep and Lavita. But her guilt disappeared no sooner than it appeared. It served Lavita right for making moves on Sandeep Shah at the same time that Utsa had been getting friendly with the driver. It wasn't as if Lavita didn't have any other options. Everyone in the village knew Mrs Lalji was going to make her a match with the lovelorn Bala Mukherjee. Lavita shouldn't have been making eyes at anyone else. She bit her bottom lip. She couldn't be held responsible for what she had said to the police.

Arriving home, Utsa hastily dropped her bags. She quickly changed out of her uniform and walked across to the Laljis. 'Lavita!' she shouted as she entered the hall.

'What's the hurry, child?' Granny Monji asked. 'You'll have an accident if you go about your business so fast.'

Utsa hadn't noticed the old woman until she heard her. Granny Monji was always sitting in some dark corner waiting and watching.

'Good evening, *naani*. No rush. Is Lavita home?'

Granny Monji pursed her lips as if she were about to say something, then stopped. Instead she pointed to Lavita's room. 'She's in there. Been in there all day,' she said with a hint of bitterness.

Utsa wanted to get away from Granny Monji as fast as possible. The old woman was giving her the creeps by staring at her with her cloudy white eyes. She wondered if, even with such poor eyesight, the old woman would have seen her on Saturday night. Had she seen her climb over the part of the wall where the broken glass deterrent had weathered over the years, so much so that it was now as smooth as the outside of a tender coconut? She hoped not.

Utsa flashed a smile at Granny Monji and headed to Lavita's room. She could feel the old woman's eyes on her until she was safe behind the door. Then she saw her friend lying face down on her bed. She sat next to her and stroked her hair.

Lavita looked up. Her eyes were red and puffy.

'What's this crying? What will your granny think?'

'What's it to you?' came Lavita's reply.

'I know we've not been the best of friends recently. But I am still your oldest friend in Utol. That must count for something.'

Lavita was silent.

'I heard the rumours. I know you were friendly with Sandeep Shah. I came here today to be your friend, to give you some support.'

'I loved him,' Lavita said.

'Who?' Utsa asked. Lavita's response was not what she expected.

'Who do you think? Now he's dead.' Lavita lifted herself up from the mattress and sat cross-legged on the bed.

'You didn't tell me,' Utsa said, her cheeks flushed as her guilt mounted.

'I haven't seen you in ages.'

'I saw you just last week at the Goa Dairy and the week before buying fish near the circle. I live right next door, you could have told me at any time.'

'Sandeep wanted to keep it quiet. And I didn't want to tell anyone. You know how people talk. If Aunty and Uncle found out, it would have been terrible.'

'I heard the rumours. I didn't know it was love though.' Utsa folded her arms across her chest. 'You know I worked with Sandeep and at one time I too liked him and he liked me. I thought he would have told me something like this. We spent a lot of time together up at the Da Costas. We told each other things.'

Lavita narrowed her eyes. 'He told me he loved me every morning when I went to his room before cleaning out the chicken coop.'

'You went into his room?' Utsa stared at her friend.

'Don't tell anyone,' Lavita pleaded. Her eyes widened as she realised what she had confessed to.

'It's terrible then, what I've done,' Utsa said suddenly feeling the weight of what she had said to the police. 'You should have told me you were in love. I wouldn't have told the police...' She trailed off although she wasn't sure if this was strictly true.

'What have you done?'

'I didn't think it would cause you any harm. A police officer came to interview me at the house. I told him I heard the gossip about you and Sandeep. I'm sorry. I'm so sorry. I didn't realise.' Utsa reached out to Lavita but she took a step back.

55

'You just said you too were friendly with Sandeep and that he was your good friend. I bet you didn't tell them that.'

'It was the only way to get them off my back. I didn't want them telling Mom anything. You know what she is like.' Utsa changed her tone. 'Nothing happened between Sandeep and me, unlike you two.'

'Backtrack now all you like.'

'What are we going to do?'

'What am I going to do, you mean. The police have already asked me about him once, but now they are sure to come back.' Lavita buried her head in her hands. 'When did you see him last?'

'Yesterday as I was leaving work. He normally gives me a lift home but he had to take the Da Costas' dog to the vet,' Utsa said, avoiding her friend's eyes.

'Mmm, okay then I was the last person to see him alive.'

'You saw him in the morning today?'

'No,' Lavita said, fresh tears streaming down her face. 'I saw him yesterday evening.'

Utsa grabbed Lavita's wrist. 'At what time?' This could change everything. But before Lavita could answer, the door opened.

'Lavita, don't cry so much,' Granny Monji said, poking her head around Lavita's bedroom door. When Granny Monji tilted her face like that, her larger eye seemed bigger than usual. 'You'll get used to death. At my age I have seen many deaths. I was the one who found your papa's body.' Granny Monji looked up to the ceiling and smiled as she always did when she spoke about her late husband. 'Have some *karela* and rice. It will make you feel better. Utsa, you will stay for some?'

Utsa wasn't hungry, but she accepted anyway. She could never say no to Granny Monji.

CHAPTER NINE

'Bloody hell!' Pankaj quickly put his hand to his mouth. 'Sorry sir, but I can't believe Sandeep Shah had a wife!'

Chupplejeep smiled. 'Now we are getting somewhere. People just don't die out of the blue like that. If Kulkarni tells us it is murder then there will be a motive, and most often that motive is love.' He thumbed through his notes. 'Gita Shah, wife of the deceased. Daughter of the deceased, Ashu.'

'Murder,' Pankaj said, his eyes lighting up. 'I feel bad. It's not right to get excited about murder, but I've never worked on a murder case before.'

'It happens.'

'Shah was living with his in-laws. He had a baby and still he was doing this *mazaa*! Incredible, sir.'

'Outhouse,' Chupplejeep said.

'Huh?'

'Shah was living in the Laljis' outhouse at the time of his death. Not with Neeraj and Paavai Dhaliwal.'

'Did you see the outhouse, sir? You cannot call that a home — one mattress on the floor and a stove in the corner. That was temporary accommodation whilst he worked.'

'Still, he was living there.' Chupplejeep put his notepad down and looked at Pankaj. 'Don't you find it odd that he wasn't working closer to home? Or that he didn't move his family to Utol?'

'His wife explained that, sir. Here, I have it in my notes. He couldn't get a job in Kukurul, she said, "Sandeep was going to move us out to Utol once he was settled."'

'But let me guess, at the last minute something came up and he postponed the move to the next month.'

'Yes.'

'I enjoy Christabel's company. I can't imagine living somewhere that is over an hour away from her.'

'Sandeep Shah wanted to have his fun.'

'*Aacha*, but the wife would have been pestering him to move there, no? Especially with a young daughter to look after.'

'But her parents are in Kukurul. They can help her with her daughter more than a husband who's on call ten hours a day. And Sandeep had only been in Utol for three months in total.'

'Something in my gut tells me otherwise,' Chupplejeep said, rubbing his round belly. 'I think Gita didn't want to go to Utol for another reason.'

'Maybe she knew about her husband's behaviour – chasing after other women. He was making eyes at the cook's daughter, Utsa, and the Laljis' niece.'

'We have no proof that he actually did anything with these women. To look at other girls is sometimes okay.'

'Really, sir? I've never had a girlfriend. I don't know.'

'Yes,' Chupplejeep said.

Pankaj leaned in closer to his boss.

'When you start going steady with Shwetika, you too will find other girls attractive. It's normal, don't worry about it.'

'Would you say that in front of Christabel?'

'Hmm, don't you worry about Christabel. I'm just telling you so when you finally get together with Shwetty you don't turn into a woman.'

Pankaj blushed. He had almost forgotten about Shwetika since the death of Sandeep Shah was reported. Now that his boss had reminded him, he remembered how desperately he wanted to ask her out. If only he was like his friend, Sailesh, who had a way with pretty girls. Pankaj wiped his hands on his trousers; just thinking about asking her out made his palms sweat.

'Hearsay counts for a lot in small communities,' he said, trying to steer the conversation away from his love life, or lack of it. 'There's no smoke without fire. I don't care what you say, but to have a wife and child and still be looking at other women is wrong.' He was silent for a moment, while he contemplated what Chupplejeep had said. His boss was never usually wrong. Then another thought crossed his mind. 'I don't think Sandeep Shah was just looking. And if he was making eyes at Utsa and Lavita, who else was he trying to get friendly with?'

'We'll interview Lavita again. Get to the bottom of their relationship.'

'If Lavita was having an affair with Sandeep Shah, she too is a suspect. You see, Lavita could have found out about his wife Gita, and in anger she could have waited outside the outhouse for him to go for a piss in the night and then *phataak*, she could have hit him on the head. Some girls will do anything if they believed they have been wronged.'

'In my opinion, love is one of the biggest motives for murder, after money. But really you cannot call it love when a death occurs. It is more like frenzied passion.'

'You're right, sir.'

'Of course I'm right,' Chupplejeep said, mumbling something about grey cells.

Pankaj scratched his head. 'You know, sir, there are quite a few people who had motive to kill Sandeep Shah. Bala claims he didn't know Sandeep, but he went to school with him so it proves he is a liar and that there is some history between them that he's not telling us about. Also he wants Lavita as a wife. That is a super motive if you ask me. If what Utsa said is true, everyone in the village must have known about Lavita and Sandeep.' Pankaj paused. 'I think Bala knew about the affair and wanted Sandeep Shah out of the picture.'

'Bala is not as stupid as you think. If Bala is cunning as you say he is, he would have looked into Sandeep's past. He would have found out that that he had a wife and child and blackmailed him. He could have got rid of him that way.'

'Maybe he was blackmailing Sandeep, but Shah refused to go away. So Bala went to visit him in the dead of night and killed him in anger. Perhaps it was a spontaneous reaction to Sandeep's indifference about the situation.'

'It's good that you let your mind wander, Pankaj, but don't you think Sandeep Shah would have put up a fight if that was the case?' Chupplejeep stood up and walked towards Pankaj's desk. 'Kulkarni said there were no defensive wounds. So if Bala went to see Sandeep, the visit had to have started off as a friendly one and the attack must have come out of the blue. Also the Laljis didn't hear any commotion in the night so it would have had to have been a surprise attack, without any raised voices.'

'He could have been poisoned,' Pankaj offered.

'Kulkarni reported that the blood tests showed no evidence of poison in Shah's bloodstream so no sedatives were used. He would have fought back, wouldn't you?'

Pankaj nodded. 'You said Gita Shah didn't want to go to Utol, sir, and you may be right. I think Gita should also be a suspect,' he said with enthusiasm. It was the most exciting case he had ever worked on and he wanted to take full advantage of airing his views whilst he had the Detective's full attention. In Police Training School, Pankaj had achieved ninety per cent in Criminal Psychology, but that was all based on case studies. This was a real life crime. He simply had to take advantage of the situation.

'You've been doing a lot of thinking, Pankaj. Did you see how Gita Shah wept when we told her that her Sandeep was dead? And it's not just that. She allowed the autopsy. Most villagers are against autopsy, something about dividing and intruding on the complete human body. She could have easily delayed it if she were hiding something. It would take weeks to get a court order for a post-mortem.'

'Anyone can pretend to cry, especially if they are prepared. She didn't cry when we took her to the morgue and she saw the body.'

'Maybe she was in shock. How would you feel if you saw someone close to you dead? And how many times have you seen a family member identify a dead body?'

Pankaj frowned. He didn't want to think about having to identify the dead body of someone he loved. That would be too horrific to imagine. Chupplejeep was right though, he was inexperienced when it came to dead bodies. Sandeep's body was the first corpse he had seen. Previously, he'd only ever been exposed to cadavers. 'Never, sir.'

'Even once is too much. I've seen people cry, faint, vomit, even laugh.'

'Laugh, sir?'

'A lady whose husband's body we thought we had found. She cried all the way to the morgue. Then when she saw the body and realised it wasn't her husband, she laughed.'

'I suppose you would.'

'Her husband's body was found the next day. Turns out she was the one who had stabbed him.'

'Serious?'

Chupplejeep walked back to his desk and sat back down on in his chair.

'Still, sir, if you don't mind me saying, there was something wrong with the way Gita Shah was crying. It looked fake to me. I think she's hiding something. You saw the look she gave us when we asked for a hair sample Kulkarni had asked for?'

'But she gave it.'

'Eventually.' Pankaj was silent for a moment. 'I still think the wife is suspicious.'

'You should be in the Wizard of Oz.'

Pankaj tilted his head to one side.

'You're a heartless fellow just like the tin man.'

'You said that as a police officer it is better not to have any emotions.'

Detective Chupplejeep smiled.

~

'So what you're saying is that time of death was between eleven in the evening and five in the morning and that you can't narrow it down further. The vic had relieved himself before he died due to the lack of excrement at the scene. Also you're saying that the vic died from a blow to the head caused by some blunt instrument,' Chupplejeep said.

Kulkarni stepped forward towards Chupplejeep and hit him on his head with a metal spoon.

'Ouch!'

'Blunt force trauma, eh. That is where the instrument hit the victim. You see the laceration to the front right of the skull?'

'What kind of instrument do you think?'

'Something like a baseball bat or a rounded stone. Nothing sharp,' Kulkarni said, playing with the spoon.

'Nobody plays baseball in the villages. Perhaps a cricket bat?' Pankaj asked.

'The force was tremendous but roundish or conical, not angled like a cricket bat.'

'Do you think a woman could have done this? A woman say about this high?' Chupplejeep put his hand against his shoulder to show the height of the woman.

Pankaj instinctively thought of Gita. Chupplejeep was shorter than him at about five foot eight. Gita was about that height he was indicating, but then both the cook's daughter, Utsa, and Lavita were of a similar height. They were all short, like most of the women he knew.

'No. I don't think so. She would have had to be taller because the victim was hit from above,' Kulkarni said confidently. 'And Sandeep was taller than Pankaj.'

Pankaj suppressed a smile. Gita and Sandeep Shah must have looked very odd standing together.

'So that rules the women out. They're all short,' Chupplejeep said.

65

'Unless they had an accomplice,' Pankaj said. 'Someone could have helped them.'

Pankaj and Chupplejeep looked at the corpse that was now almost white. A thick purplish colour was visible at the back of the body.

'What's the bruising?' Pankaj asked. He rubbed tiger balm under his nose to dilute the smell of the rotting flesh. It didn't help.

'The body was flat after death so the blood settled at the base of the body. That's why you can see the bruising,' Kulkarni answered. 'It's helpful. It shows Mr Shah died this way and was not moved post-mortem. The blow was so strong it caused an extradural hematoma where bleeding occurred between the inside of the skull and the outside of the brain. The victim could have been saved, but he passed out and was not found until it was too late. The blood pushed the brain towards the skull and crushed it.' Kulkarni drove his fist into the palm of his other hand to show the police officers the force of the blood.

'It's a terrible way to die,' Pankaj said. He felt sorry for the victim and hoped that when it was his time to pass, it would happen painlessly in his sleep.

'That's why there was not much blood splatter at the scene, eh,' Kulkarni continued.

'Anything else suspicious?'

'There were no other internal or external traumas and like I said, the livor mortis suggests that the body was not moved. He died where you found him. Also no poisons were found in his bloodstream like I told you on the phone, so no chance of sedation. Because of the lack of external bleeding, the person who did this would not be covered in blood and therefore could have easily gotten away without anyone noticing.'

'Did you check for all poisons?' Pankaj asked.

Kulkarni put his hands on his hips and narrowed his eyes at Pankaj. 'Sorry, which poisons were you after?'

'Well, you know there are new ones coming out all the time.'

Kulkarni raised his eyebrows at Pankaj and then looked away.

'Can't you give us a more exact time of death?' Chupplejeep asked.

'It's a tough one. I know that his evening meal was only partly digested so it was not long after he ate.'

'Fish curry?' Pankaj asked.

Detective Chupplejeep and Kulkarni both looked at Pankaj.

'I saw it in the room.'

'*Aacha,*' Chupplejeep said.

'Fish curry, chapatti and pickle.'

'Mango?' Kulkarni asked.

'There were green mangoes at the scene, but no they were not made into a pickle. The pickle was *brinjal,* aubergine.'

'Each to their own I suppose,' Chupplejeep said.

'Given the temperatures and the extent of rigor mortis, you are looking at a window from eleven in the night to five in the morning. I can't pinpoint it any more than that.'

'Sometimes on *CSI* they get the exact time of death,' Pankaj said.

''Es, and this is not *CSI*. This is real life.'

'He must have eaten late,' Chupplejeep said.

'Any other evidence?' Pankaj asked, averting his eyes from the body.

'We've checked the body for trace evidence and we bagged the husks for checking. We need this evidence to check for fibres, hair and nail samples. A lot of coconut fibres were found on the body and head, after all he fell onto a pile of husks. There was only one hair which we found not belonging to the victim.'

'And?'

'Long, black hair.'

'Ah I see, that's why you asked us to collect a hair sample from Gita,' Pankaj said.

'Ninety per cent of the Indian population must have long black hair. Not just Gita Shah, but Lavita and Utsa as well,' Chupplejeep said.

'Are you looking for a DNA match?' Pankaj asked.

'Chemical analysis,' Kulkarni said. 'It will be the quickest way. For DNA, I would need saliva samples and that would need to be sent off to Mumbai. We have no DNA testing facilities here.'

'So what you are saying is that all the evidence points to murder?' Chupplejeep asked.

'From what I have seen so far it's pointing to unnatural death, yes,' said Kulkarni, 'unnatural death indeed, unless the birds in Utol were shitting stones!'

Chapter Ten

'*Aye, aye*. See who it is. Big-shot has arrived.'

'*Bhendaa*! We're over here.'

Pankaj walked over the to the back of Joe's Taverna in Little Larara. It had been a long day at work and he craved a glass of *feni*.

'Bhendaa, tell this man what you want to drink,' Sailesh said, pointing to a short man with a grey moustache and dirty shorts.

'Get me a glass of *aarrak* and a plate of chicken *xacuti*.'

'*Xacuti*? *Arrey wah*, Bhendaa. Here we are in a recession and you want chicken *xacuti*. They must be paying you well in the police. Or are you getting *baksheesh*?'

Pankaj laughed. Minutes later his drink arrived, with a tin plate heaped with the thick spicy chicken curry and a roll of bread. Pankaj took out a fifty-rupee note but the small man declined.

'On the house,' the waiter said, looking in the direction of Joe who was grinning behind the bar. He retrieved a bottle of water and a glass from the bar and placed it next to Pankaj's meal.

'See, *baksheesh*!' Sailesh exclaimed to the rest of the table. 'You police get it so easy. Tell me Pankaj, is that why you joined the police force? To get free chicken *xacuti*?'

Pankaj put the fifty-rupee note under the ashtray on the table.

'This is why we call you Bhendaa – long and green like an okra and full of goodness inside!' Sailesh said, ruffling his friend's hair.

'So tell us about this murder in Utol?' Raja asked.

'You fellows probably know more than me,' Pankaj said.

'Oh yes, policy 412, na? What was it?' Raja said with a grin, looking at Sailesh.

Pankaj narrowed his eyes at his friends but carried on eating. He stopped, briefly, to pour himself a glass of water. The *xacuti* was exceptionally spicy today, just how he liked it.

'A driver who had his eye on half the ladies in Utol, died. That's all we know,' Raja said.

Pankaj was silent.

'So Pankaj still hasn't asked Shwetty out, huh? Jealous of this Sandeep guy?' Raja asked. 'He seemed to know how to ask women out.'

Pankaj wiped his hands on a paper napkin and took a large gulp of water.

'Seriously, Pankaj,' Sailesh said, his eyes fixed on his bottle of beer, 'you really think this fellow was murdered because he was fooling around?' He raised his drink to his lips.

'Pankaj!' Joe shouted from the bar. 'Come here one moment please.'

Sailesh looked at Pankaj, but he didn't answer. He rose to his feet, took a sip of his *aarrak* and walked over to Joe.

'I heard something this morning,' Joe said in a whisper, 'about this suspicious death.'

Pankaj refrained from rolling his eyes. Everybody wanted to know what was happening. Everybody wanted to be part of the drama. 'Listen to everything because you never know when you'll hear a whisper of the truth,' Chupplejeep said when they worked on their first case together. Dutifully he leaned into the bar to hear Joe better. 'What did you hear?'

'You need to speak to Manoj.'

'Manoj, the Goa Dairy man?'

'He's often up during the early hours of the morning. He'll be here soon. He comes everyday about this time for his glass of *aarrak*.'

'I see.'

'He's what you call…insomniac. Is that the correct word for someone who doesn't sleep?'

'Yes. An insomniac,' Pankaj said.

'He goes to his stall, washes up and goes early to get the milk.'

'And he knows something?'

'Here he is now,' Joe said, signalling towards the door.

71

A man with grey and black tufts of hair in his ears approached the bar. He greeted Pankaj and looked around the room.

'Tell him what you saw,' Joe said.

'Oh, oh what I saw was nothing,' the Goa Dairy man said with a chuckle. 'You know Joe. Always making everything into a drama. He likes to grind the masala. Isn't that right?'

'Anything you saw that night could be a clue,' Pankaj said encouragingly.

'Here,' Joe said pouring a glass of *aarrak* from a glass bottle and sliding it across the bar. 'Perhaps this will jog your memory.'

The Goa Dairy man smiled a toothless grin. He took a sip of his drink. 'Okay, I saw something that morning. The morning the body was found,'

'What time?' Pankaj asked.

'At around one in the morning I saw a stranger in Utol. You may be wondering how I remember this. Let me confirm. I'm not a drinker. I have one glass every afternoon, that is all. Joe, tell him.'

Joe shook his head in agreement.

'Two reasons why I noticed this man. One, there are never strangers in Utol at that time of night or should I say morning. Two, if anybody is out in the village at that time they are *tho* most definitely not in their senses. Occasionally you'll get a drunk villager stumbling home. Usually the older people are home by eleven-twelve, maybe three-four in the morning if they have been for wedding. The kids are never back from parties so early.

Normally they come home at three-four in the morning, minimum. One o'clock in Utol is the most deadliest time of night.'

'Do you know who this man was?' Pankaj asked.

'If I knew him, he wouldn't be a stranger. How you became a policeman by asking such stupid questions?'

'What was this stranger doing?' Pankaj asked.

'Walking near the church.'

'Near Bala Mukherjee's house – away from the Laljis?'

'Or towards the Laljis – he was near the church.' Manoj looked around the bar again. 'It could have been nothing. He could have been going to pray.'

'At one in the morning?'

'What men, I'm not the detective. That's your job.' He put his little finger between the tufts of hair coming out from his ear and started rooting around as if searching for something.

'Could you describe him?'

'I could try.' He pulled his finger out of his ear and looked at the end of his appendage, then wiped it on his shirt.

Pankaj took out his notepad and wrote as Manoj spoke. The description was of an average-looking Goan male, with a wide brow and nose. The description, though bland, was familiar and there was one particular feature that stood out; this Goan, if he was a Goan, was tall, nearly six foot, and that was what Pankaj underlined in his notebook.

CHAPTER ELEVEN

Christabel took the white tablecloth with the red and yellow flowers from the cabinet and placed it over the wooden table. The tablecloth was one of the few homely items Chupplejeep possessed, but she would soon change that. She enjoyed coming to his house after work and preparing dinner for him. It gave her great comfort that she had a purpose in life other than her work, which she cared very little for.

She laid out the plates and cutlery before stirring the *sorpatel* that was simmering on the cooker. The table was almost set but something was missing. 'Ah, candles,' she said. Walking towards the dresser in the hall, she opened each drawer in turn until she found what she was looking for. Placing two long yellow candles in brass candlesticks on the centre of the table, she stepped back to admire her work. 'Perfect,' she said. It was ready for the romantic dinner she had in mind.

By Christabel's calculation, she was certain that tonight would be the night. The signs had been there for months. Arthur was being exceptionally kind to her of late, considering her needs when he went to the market or to the hardware store. He had even taken her to dinner in the fancy new restaurant in town, which had opened next to Mandovi Bridge. And on this occasion he had needed no cajoling from her, he had thought of the dinner all by himself. Yes, something was definitely up.

But as the minutes passed, Christabel was beginning to lose faith. Most evenings she had been sorely disappointed when she had her hopes up like this. And if she *really* thought about it, tonight was most definitely not going to be the night. It was a weeknight. Arthur had some big case on and he had planned nothing. It was she who had planned the romantic dinner at home. This irritated her. Now she wanted to fling the candlesticks across the room, but instead she made a face and lit the candles in preparation. She would have to hold on to her hope, it was all she had left. Anyway, why couldn't it be today? Just because it hadn't worked out last week, that wasn't to say tonight's dinner wouldn't be in her favour. It would be a defeatist's attitude to give up now. Christabel was many things, but she certainly wasn't a quitter.

She had been dating Arthur for over a year now. But despite his recent show of affection, she was becoming increasingly dissatisfied with their relationship. There were several reasons that made her feel this way. The most important was that they lived separately. They ate dinner together most nights but Arthur had still not asked her to move in with him. Yet he didn't mind being cooked for. Typical man, she thought. She shook her head as she played out an imagined conversation in her mind.

'Christu, your cooking is first class. You rarely stay over but I like having you here. Why don't you just move in?' Christabel often fantasised about what Arthur might say. She would, of course, look coyly from under her lashes at him while he spoke.

Then he would beg her. 'Please Christu, I need you in my life.'

Christabel imagined shaking her head with dramatic effect. 'I couldn't possibly do that,' she would say, averting her eyes from her lover. 'What would people think? You know how your neighbours love to gossip. They would say "Eee, look at that woman. Has she no shame moving into the Detective's house." I couldn't have that. My poor mother, she wouldn't be able to leave the house. She would die of humiliation.'

Christabel then imagined herself waiting patiently, perhaps doing some embroidery or cross stitch on a cushion. Then the moment would come. Christabel couldn't contain the smile spreading across her face.

'Oh Christabel,' she imagined Arthur saying, 'my life is not complete without you. Please...' At this point he would bend down on one knee. She would put down her needle and thread and shake her head like they did in those shampoo adverts. Arthur would say, 'Christabel, please do me the honour of being my wife.' At this point she would swoon, but Arthur would catch her. He would open a red velvet box to reveal a gold and ruby engagement ring.

She held up her plump hand, imagining the ring. A ruby would most definitely be the best stone for her. Firstly, it was her birthstone and secondly, she loved pink. She wondered if Arthur had picked up on her hints about this. She had mentioned it several times already, and she had been careful to wear red at every possible opportunity. She knew it was important to emphasise her point through all mediums. She had read this in a marketing magazine, which had been left lying around at work.

But Christabel didn't have much hope for her boyfriend's ability to pick up on such clues, even though it was said that he was a top-notch detective inspector. Since June she had been dropping hints to Chupplejeep about marriage, but still she had no luck. Where had she gone wrong? She didn't even touch that last *rava*-fried *shinaneo* yesterday when they were passed around at her friend's house. She wasn't going to be left a spinster just because she failed to pay attention to that old Goan wives' tale that said if you ate the last canapé, you would die an old maid. She had duly honoured this tradition for some time now. Christabel's mouth began to water just thinking of that last juicy fried mussel coated in semolina. Then she shook the thought away. Jean had been the one to eat it, but Jean didn't have to worry about such things because she was already married. Life was unfair.

Now that Christabel had finished her daydream, back in reality her 'glass half empty' side was beginning to take over. She sighed. It was foolish to think that

Chupplejeep was going to propose today. She had tried to convince Arthur he was ready for marriage, but he was as stubborn as an ox. Even her mother had tried. She couldn't help but laugh remembering Arthur's difficult conversation when her mother had cornered him one day after dinner.

'When are you going to make my daughter an honest woman?'

'Soon, don't worry,' Arthur replied sheepishly.

'I'm in my sixties. Of course I have to worry. Who's going to look after my poor Christu when I am gone?'

'I'll always look after your daughter. You know I love her.'

'Prove it. What are you waiting for? Neither of you are young anymore. Time is ticking if you want to see a baby Chupplejeep.'

Christabel had seen the little beads of sweat forming on Arthur's brow. He had not been quite right for the rest of the evening. He had even skipped the pudding of *bebinca* saying that he had to get back to the station on an urgent call.

Later he blamed the Goa sausage but Christabel knew that Arthur was afraid of commitment. Why? She had no idea. Her mother had been quick to harass her about it.

'If he won't marry you now, he never will,' she said.

Was her mother right?

'You're already old. If he keeps you hanging any longer, you'll be too, too old. You'll have to wait for a divorcee. You want someone else's damaged goods?

Divorcees come with too much baggage – children, ornaments…'

Christabel gritted her teeth. Her mother was backward in her thinking, but the old woman had a point. Christabel didn't want someone else's wedding gifts littering her home. If she was honest, she didn't want someone else's kids either. With that in mind she had made a foolish promise to her mother: she would have a ring on her finger by Arthur's fortieth birthday or she would kiss their relationship goodbye. But now she was scared. She had no intention of leaving Arthur but time was running out. His birthday was just around the corner. She put her head in her hands. Arthur's attitude began to niggle at her and by the time he arrived home, she was well and truly worked up.

'Christu!' Chupplejeep said as he walked through the doorway. He kissed his girlfriend on both cheeks and wandered over to the stove. '*Arrey, sorpatel*,' he said stirring the pot, 'and…'

Searching the kitchen with his eyes he spotted a plate covered with a tea towel. '…And s*annas*!' he said with a grin. 'What is the occasion? It's not Sunday.'

'Why not?' said Christabel sulkily. 'It's not like we're getting younger. We should enjoy our meals. We don't have any children to spoil.'

Chupplejeep opened his mouth to say something but stopped himself. Instead he decided to tell her about the case he was working on. He would save his surprise for later.

'This suspicious death I'm working on is taking up so much of my time. I spoke to Kulkarni today. Most definitely, it's a murder.'

Christabel raised her hand to her mouth, 'In Larara? Murder?' she asked, momentarily distracted from thoughts of marriage.

'In Utol, not here.'

'Utol is not far,' Christabel said, quickly walking over to the front door and locking it. Something she rarely did. 'Have you caught the culprit yet? Do you have any suspects?' she asked, walking back to the kitchen and attending to the *sorpatel*.

'Give us some time,' Chupplejeep said, letting out a sigh. 'We don't have a murder weapon yet, usually that's a key ingredient in solving any murder. And solving a murder is like making a curry. You have to have all the right ingredients: the body, the motive, the opportunity and the murder weapon in order to get it right. Similar to the garlic, onions, all the spices and coconut you needed for curry. Not having a murder weapon or any definitive suspects with a motive, is like making a curry without spice.'

Christabel ignored Arthur's analogy. 'You're not at risk, are you? Is this man dangerous?'

'I didn't say it was a man.'

Christabel gasped. She stopped ladling the *sorpatel* into a bowl and looked at Arthur. 'What are you saying? That a woman could have been involved?'

'We can't rule it out.'

80

'This is not the West. Women are respectable here. They don't do things like that.'

Arthur shrugged.

'You have a female suspect? *Che.*' Christabel walked to the table with the plate of sannas and sat down. 'Still,' she said, 'this may be a good case for you to be leading on. You can prove your worth to the Inspector General.'

'In Panaji I refused a bribe, that is all. But you're right – it will show the Inspector General.'

'Would he post you back to Panaji if you solve this case? I wouldn't move from Larara and I couldn't handle the long distance,' Christabel said. Panaji was the last place that she wanted to raise children.

Chupplejeep walked over to his girlfriend and started rubbing her shoulders. 'All this talk of murder and moving, let's stop it. I'm not going anywhere, Larara is my home now. I shouldn't bring my work home.'

Christabel waved her hand at Arthur. 'Don't worry about me. It was a long day at work.' She paused. 'I'm beginning to sound like my mother. Women too can be vindictive. I know that. It was just a shock to hear.'

Arthur Chupplejeep laughed. 'Office was busy?'

'Same, same. Never mind. Let's eat.' She stood up to get the bowl of the thick, spicy pork stew, but Arthur took her hand.

'You may've noticed I've been acting a little different of late.'

Christabel took a deep breath and nodded. *Was this it?*

'I think it's time to tell you my surprise.'

Christabel steadied herself. She sat back down and shook her hair. Crossing her legs at the ankle, she gave her boyfriend a seductive smile and fluttered her eyelashes.

'I wanted to do this after dinner, but now seems like the right time. It will give us something to enjoy with our *sorpatel.*'

'Oh Arthur,' Christabel said. She wasn't sure if she could contain her excitement and she was certain there would be some swooning later.

Chupplejeep sat on the chair next to her. He held her hand. 'Can I ask you something?'

Okay, so he wasn't on one knee but she would settle for this. She didn't want to ruin the moment by asking him to kneel. No, this would do nicely. 'Of course, ask me anything.'

'I've booked a trip on a houseboat. Will you come away with me?'

'What?'

'In Kerala...a-a holiday for us,' he stammered. 'For my fortieth.'

Christabel frowned. 'A holiday, is that so?'

'I was watching Poirot in *Death on The Nile* and I got the idea.'

'You and that programme. You're not Poirot, you'll never be Poirot. Take Poirot on a bloody houseboat in the backwaters of Kerala. Who wants to go there? It's the same as Goa.'

Christabel narrowed her eyes at her boyfriend and stood up. She smoothed her red satin dress and walked to bathroom, slamming the door behind her.

Chupplejeep got up from his seat. He looked at the closed door. 'What about dinner?' he shouted after her.

Chapter Twelve

'Why are you being so difficult?' Mrs Lalji asked. She was squatting in front of the large *daanten,* pounding the red chillies and spices into a thick masala in readiness for the fish Baba was out buying. The monotonous noise of the granite made Lavita's eyelids droop, but she didn't have the luxury of stopping for a nap. She had to grate the coconut for the curry.

'Look at the girl's eyes,' Granny Monji whispered to her daughter, taking her usual seat in the corner of the kitchen.

Lavita concentrated on the coconut in her hand.

Granny Monji wiped the plastic-coated tablecloth with her wrinkly hand, pushing the crumbs to the corner of the table. 'She's not sleeping well. I could hear her twisting and turning in her bed all night.'

Mrs Lalji looked over to her niece as she put another handful of chillies in the stone pot. 'Mummy, you hear too much. You should be concentrating on sleeping yourself, and not listening to other people.'

Granny Monji shrugged.

'She's not sleeping because of the death, Mummy,' Mrs Lalji said. Then turning to her niece, she said, 'It is a shock for all of us, na, *beta*. Don't worry. The shock will wear off eventually. These things take time.' Mrs Lalji turned back to her mother. 'If not, I'll take her to see doctor by the end of next week.'

'It's not the shock,' Granny Monji said defiantly. 'We all know why she can't sleep. And now look at her being so stubborn.' Granny Monji turned to Lavita. 'Just like your mother, you are,' she scolded. Then she looked at her daughter. 'Remember, how stubborn your sister was? All the trouble she caused. That cannot happen again. I won't let it.'

Mrs Lalji was silent.

Lavita didn't look up from the coconut. She held the hard white flesh steady against the blade. Piercing the coconut, she pulled it towards her before she pushed it away again. She soon got into a rhythm of grating the coconut on the blade. Usually it irritated her when Granny spoke badly of her mother, but today she didn't mind being compared to her mother.

'Mummy, enough!' Mrs Lalji shouted over the noise of the grinding and grating.

'It's true and you know it,' Granny Monji said, her larger eye focusing on Lavita.

'Leave my poor dead sister out of this.'

Granny Monji made a face. 'The whole village knows that Lavita was carrying on with that driver.'

Lavita carried on with her grating, looking intently at the coconut.

'You should listen to your aunty,' Granny Monji said. 'She knows what's good for you. Bala Mukherjee is a good man – a thorough Goan.'

'Maybe I don't want a thorough Goan,' Lavita said. 'Maybe I want someone with a little more ambition.'

'You think we would have allowed you to marry someone like Sandeep Shah?' Granny Monji asked, sucking her teeth. 'Your aunty may have been contemplating the match but no, sorry. That Shah would never have done. He had no proper family. We didn't know the first thing about him. We only knew that he liked more than one woman in Utol. That's not what you want in a husband: a wandering eye. *Che*, you don't want a husband like that.'

'Granny's right. There are rumours,' Mrs Lalji said. She stopped her grinding and looked up at Lavita. 'Baba was kind enough to buy a small television, but I don't want you watching it anymore. Life is not like *The Bold and Beautiful*. Don't get big Western ideas. You can't go from one man to the next. You can't pick and choose who you want. You'll get a bad name. You'll end up an old spinster like Dipthi *Baapulbain*. You want that?' Mrs Lalji didn't wait for an answer. 'See Baba and me. Our parents arranged our marriage. We listened and see how perfectly it worked out.'

Lavita stopped her grating. Aunty had never before spoken about her relationship with Baba.

'You think I loved Baba when I first met him? Never,' Mrs Lalji said, shaking her head. 'I thought he looked like a *langur*!' she laughed. 'But after some time I got used to him. Eventually I fell in love with him.'

Lavita went back to grating the coconut.

'I'll be speaking to Baba about Bala asking formally for your hand.'

Lavita sighed. She didn't want to be a simple villager's wife spending the rest of her days in Utol. She wanted to travel and see the world; see the rest of Goa if nothing else. But her family were doing everything in their power to make sure she had the same miserable existence as the rest of them. She would be stuck in Utol forever.

Sandeep had promised to marry her and take her away. He was saving but he was also expecting a payment, he had said. When he received this, he would take her wherever she wanted to go. It would be just the two of them. She felt a lump rise at the back of her throat. Sandeep was no longer around.

'An engagement will stop the rumours. You're lucky Mr Mukherjee and his family don't listen to rumours,' her aunty said.

She tried to ignore them. She had finished grating one half of the coconut. She put the empty shell on the stone floor and lifted the other half up to the blade.

'*Beta*, don't act as if you can't hear me. Listen, if word of this gets out people will think you are a *chedi*, prostitute. Then no one will want you as a wife. You'll be spoilt goods. Bala is willing to overlook this. You should take his hand now whilst you have the chance.'

87

The old wooden door at the front of the house creaked. The three women stopped what they were doing and looked up as Baba walked into the kitchen carrying a parcel wrapped in newspaper. '*Bangde,* Mackerel,' Baba said as he placed the package near the sink. 'Despite the weather, I managed to get some mackerel.'

Mrs Lalji clapped her hands. She stood up from her position behind the grinder to fetch the package. 'Well done,' she said pulling open the string and the newspaper. She stuck her finger under the gills of the fish and prised them open. 'Fresh.' She kissed her husband on the cheek. 'You're my *langur*!'

'I'm not a monkey, you mad woman,' Baba said. He picked up the day's newspaper and headed towards the veranda.

Mrs Lalji smiled at her husband as he went. Then taking the mackerel from the newspaper, she pointed to an article in the *Larara Express* under the slimy head of the fish. '*Aieee!*' she exclaimed, stepping back.

'What?' Granny Monji asked, straining her neck and her good eye to see what her daughter was looking at.

'Sandeep Shah…' Mrs Lalji said, trailing off.

Lavita looked at her aunty.

'What about Sandeep Shah?' Granny Monji asked, as if afraid it was something she didn't already know.

'Sandeep Shah…' She looked at Lavita this time. '…had a wife.'

~

88

Bala Mukherjee pulled the shovel out from the large clay oven by the front of his house. There was a queue outside. Customers stood gossiping with their plastic bags and twenty-rupee notes as they waited for the fresh bread.

'Bala, can we talk?' Detective Chupplejeep asked as he and Pankaj approached the *pau wallah*.

Bala motioned for a man standing next to him to take over at the mouth of the hot stove. He wiped his hands on his blue apron. The evening was warm and standing next to a hot oven didn't help. The baker rubbed the sweat from his brow with the back of his hand and smiled politely. Taking two hot bread rolls from a *pato*, woven basket, he handed one each to the detective and the police officer. 'For you, for keeping this village safe. Since that tragedy I've started praying every day for protection.'

Chupplejeep and Pankaj shared a look.

'We need to ask you a few questions,' Pankaj said, taking the *pau*. He looked at the baker's clothes. There was a suspicious-looking brown stain on Bala's shirt.

'What?' Bala said, following his eyes.

'Nothing,' Pankaj said.

'This stain?' Bala said scratching at the mark. 'It's grease from the oven. I was having problems with it today.'

Pankaj looked at the baker. 'Defensive, *haan*?'

'Am I a suspect?'

Pankaj was silent.

'Smell it if you want.'

89

Pankaj raised his hand indicating it was not necessary. 'The oven is made of stone.' He paused for a moment. 'Surely no grease is needed.'

Bala hesitated. 'I was talking about the small oven inside. Used for cooking, not baking.'

'Two ovens – rich man,' Chupplejeep said.

Bala smiled. 'One is for business. The other for my mother.'

'I see,' Chupplejeep said. 'Please, I don't want to waste your time, I'm sure if you had killed Mr Shah in that shirt you would have had the sense to wash it by now, no?'

Bala smiled.

'Let's get to the point,' Chupplejeep said.

'You're after some information about that Shah,' Bala said. 'I didn't know him. I only saw him when Lavita called to me.'

'That's exactly what I want to talk to you about,' Chupplejeep said. 'You see, in your earlier statement made to Officer Pankaj you said that you didn't know Sandeep.'

'That's correct,' Bala said, shifting his weight from one foot to the other.

'And in Lavita's statement she said that you also confirmed this to her.'

'Yes, yes. I just said I didn't know the fellow.'

'And yet you went to school with Sandeep Shah.'

Bala looked at the line of people outside his house. The baker tugged at his collar and scratched his neck.

'Come inside,' he said, ushering the two men towards the wooden door.

Inside, the house was cool, with tiled floors. Low ceiling fans hung amidst the rafters of the roof. The house was full of old stone and wood carvings; a grandfather chair with a large hole in the seat was strategically placed in front of a brand new television. It looked out of place in such a traditional home, but it was to be expected. Everybody had a television these days.

'My father's,' Bala said. 'The chair needs re-weaving but he won't send it to the furniture man. You know how old people get. He wants a new television but he won't repair his old chair.'

Bala led them to the kitchen table where a small paraffin lamp was burning. Apart from what remained of the late evening light and the lantern, no other lights were on in the house. They sat at the table and Pankaj and Chupplejeep put down their bread rolls.

'You live here with you father, mother and siblings?'

'I have only one brother. He lives around the corner with his wife and daughter. Ma and Pa have gone to temple.'

'So Bala, I'm going to ask you straight. Are you lying to me? If you knew Sandeep Shah, why did you pretend you didn't know him?'

'I finished my schooling after fourth standard. Someone needed to help at home. My father suffers with his back.'

'So you didn't remember Sandeep?'

91

'No I didn't…' Bala stopped himself, he made a sour face before he continued. 'Okay…I knew him.' He paused. 'I knew him, just slightly.'

'I think you knew him well,' Chupplejeep said.

Bala was silent.

'Do you want me to bring you proof of this and come back with a warrant for your arrest?' Chupplejeep asked.

Bala looked to the floor, then looking back to Chupplejeep he said, 'No, sir. I'll tell you everything.'

'Tell then. We're not leaving until you have.'

Bala's eyes flicked to a gecko that cast a large shadow on the kitchen wall. His eyes moved up to the rafters. Not long ago they had seen a rat snake up there. It had caused his mother a great deal of stress even though it was not poisonous. He had to pay two hundred rupees to get a snake charmer to lure it away. He looked back at the detective. 'I remembered him well. Who could forget a bully like that? He used to rag me at school.'

Pankaj opened his notebook and started writing.

'Once Sandeep made me strip myself bare, to my *chuddies*, poured water on them and then made me stand in my wet underwear next to a coconut tree for the full break time. All the children were pointing and laughing at me.'

'So you had reason to want him dead?' Pankaj said. 'Under a coconut tree just like how you were made to stand?'

'After seventeen years? Please. Don't think that I've been bearing a grudge for so long.'

'So why pretend you don't know him?'

'Utol is my village. I've been here my whole life. Sandeep Shah moved away years ago. When I saw him at the *gado* leaning against that Honda City he drove for the Da Costas, I remembered him. I stared at him. And you know what? He looked back at me as if he didn't know me at all. At first I thought maybe this is a good thing. I mean who wanted to know him anyway? And now I'm a karate black belt. I could have made *bhaji* of him if he tried any stunts.' Bala smiled before he continued. 'But then I realised Sandeep Shah pretending not to know me was a bad thing, a very bad thing. He must've thought he was some hero or something and that I was a nobody. So I decided that I too would not know him.'

'And you pretended you didn't know he was renting the outhouse at the Laljis' also?'

Bala shook his head from side to side in agreement. 'If that bastard didn't want to know me then why should I want to know him, or anything about him?'

'You didn't have to pretend that you didn't know he was living there. You could have admitted to that and said you just didn't know him well. Tell me Bala, why did you lie? Why did you say that you didn't know the Laljis had a lodger? I've heard it mentioned that everyone in the village knows each other's business. I find it strange that you felt you had to deny that you knew this.'

'It's complicated.'

'I'm a detective inspector. I like complicated,' Chupplejeep said.

'It has to do with the Laljis' niece.'

93

'Tell me,' Chupplejeep said.

Bala looked down at the old wooden table and blushed. 'I'm hoping to marry her.'

'Marry? That's a big step. Are you friendly yet?'

Bala looked at the two officers. 'She's coming around.'

'Did you know there were rumours that Lavita was having a relationship with Sandeep Shah?'

Bala narrowed his eyes at the officers. 'It's not true. I heard rumours. But you know what these JVs are like?'

'JVs?' Chupplejeep asked.

'Jolly Villagers. They say anything to get their cheap thrills. You know, small people – small minds. Gossiping for their own entertainment. Paying no attention to whose good name they ruin.'

'But it's obvious to me from what I've heard that Lavita really liked Mr Shah,' Chupplejeep said purposefully rubbing salt in the wound. They hadn't spoken to Lavita again about her relationship with Mr Shah as yet, but from looking at Bala's pained expression, it was clear that she and Sandeep Shah definitely were an item.

'So how did pretending not to know Sandeep benefit your relationship with Lavita?'

'It's silly,' Bala said.

'We have time,' Chupplejeep said to Bala. Then to Pankaj he said, 'You're getting all this?'

'Yes, sir,' Pankaj said, his hand moving furiously along the page.

Bala cleared his throat. 'I thought if I didn't acknowledge Shah's presence, neither would Lavita.' He looked at the floor.

'If you want to marry this girl, your feelings must be pretty strong,' Chupplejeep continued. 'Plus the fact that Mr Shah made your schooling days a misery suggests to me you had a motive to put an end to his life.'

'I could never do anything like that,' Bala said, rising to his feet. His fists were clenched. Chupplejeep stood up as well. He started at the baker until Bala sat down. Then he too sat down.

'But you just said that you were ready to make mincemeat out of Sandeep if he hurt you again. Wasn't he hurting you by taking all the attention from the girl?'

'It's not like that. I didn't mean it like that.'

'These stone figures, you collect them?' Pankaj asked Bala as he looked around the kitchen. He noticed a ring of dust that had been created on one of the shelves closest to him, any further and he wouldn't have noticed it in the dimly lit house. What else was Bala Mukherjee hiding? A stone statue could have easily have caused the fatal blow to Sandeep Shah's head. 'There appears to be one missing.'

'I suppose that's why you're an inspector,' Bala said.

Colour rose to Pankaj's cheeks. 'Just an officer,' he mumbled.

Pankaj stood. He walked over to shelf with the missing statue and lifted up another one.

'My mother collects them – buys them from the flea market. She was dusting the other day and...' Bala paused and looked up at the roof space before continuing, 'Her eye caught sight of the tail of a rat snake in the rafters. She got scared. The statue fell from her hands and broke.'

Chupplejeep followed Bala's eyes. A shiver ran down his spine. 'Where were you on the night of the tenth November?'

'At home asleep,' Bala said, looking away.

Pankaj looked at the brown stain on Bala's shirt. 'Can anyone vouch for that?'

'No,' came his response.

'Stay in Larara for now,' Chupplejeep said. He rose to his feet again and motioned to Pankaj that their interview was over. Pankaj picked up their bread rolls.

'Where would I go?' Bala asked as he walked them to the front door.

Chapter Thirteen

Lavita read the article again. She had managed to get the scales off, but the newspaper still smelled of fish. 'Sandeep Shah, twenty-seven. Husband to Gita, and father of Ashu…' Lavita read the words aloud then she slammed her fist into her pillow.

'He lied,' Utsa said. She put her arm around Lavita. 'He told me he was twenty-two. Utter pervert.'

'Forget his age,' Lavita said, 'what about the wife and kid? I've been so stupid.' She had forgiven Utsa and Utsa had forgiven her. Realising that they only had each other for comfort, they were best friends again. 'He told me that he had to wait to marry because he was saving money. Also he said he was getting some big payout. He didn't want me to have to worry about a dowry.'

'These are old-fashioned laws,' Sandeep Shah had told her one afternoon whilst he was picking chikoos from the tree outside Da Costas' house, 'and I'm not an old-fashioned man. I don't want you to have to come to my house laden with jewellery.'

'But it's part of the tradition. Aunty will like doing all the wedding shopping. It's part of the fun,' Lavita had said.

Sandeep had smiled. 'If you insist,' he had said with a grin.

Now Lavita realised just how modern he was. He was modern enough to have a wife and child at home and a girlfriend on the side. Maybe even two girlfriends if he had been trying to get friendly with Utsa like she had implied.

'We were both stupid,' Utsa said. 'I wonder how many other women he was fooling with?'

The girls were silent as they contemplated this question.

~

Thank goodness for Mr Krinz, Utsa thought to herself. She silently thanked the goddess Lakshmi for bringing this man into her life before she managed to totally screw it up by committing to that swine, Sandeep.

'Everybody in the village knew about us,' Lavita cried. 'My name will be ruined,'

'*Shhh*, not everyone knew. You didn't tell anyone, did you?'

'Only you.'

'Then there is no fact. Let people talk. You just deny it. Don't worry, I'll take your side one hundred per cent and back you on this.'

Lavita rubbed her eyes. 'I want to see his wife.'

Utsa let out a nervous laugh. 'What are you saying?'

'She lives in Kukurul, Mapusa, no? It says here in the papers.'

Utsa shifted on the bed. 'You know the papers get everything wrong.'

'Will you come with me?'

'Lavita, you are not listening. It's a foolish idea. You can't just barge in and force his wife to see you. She didn't know about you. It wasn't her fault. It was your fault – you were the other woman!'

'I was the other woman. You were not so innocent yourself,' Lavita said, suddenly wanting company for her guilt.

Utsa pressed her big toe onto the stone floor, killing an ant. She scratched her arm. Nerves made her itch. She comforted herself with the knowledge that Lavita was unaware that she had climbed over the wall into Sandeep's room the night before he died. Utsa decided she would never tell a soul about her last visit to see Sandeep Shah. She would take this information with her to the grave.

'I'm going even if you're not coming. I just want to see her face. I won't say anything,' Lavita said defiantly.

'Mapusa is a big place. You'll never find her.'

Lavita smiled. 'I'll find her, don't you worry about that.'

~

Sailesh bit his fingernails as he thought about Sandeep Shah. His lunch was going cold in front of him as his hangover caused a feeling of nausea in his stomach.

He heard his mother's voice behind him. 'You haven't gone to work today, *beta*?' Should he tell her he had drunk too much at the Shack last night and chance getting his ear bent? Or should he just play to his mother's maternal instinct and tell her he was not feeling well? He sighed, fed up of all the lies.

He was twenty. He had finished his studies three years ago and now successfully ran his own auto-shop. Why then, like every other charlie in Larara, did he have to abide by his mother's antiquated rules? Sailesh let his mind drift. Perhaps he could be the leader of a new generation of young Goans. He could leave home and get his own place. Then no one could tell him what to do.

Sailesh stuck a piece of his *roti* in the *keema*. That would never work, he thought. Indians couldn't cope without being intricately involved in each other's lives. If he tried it, his mother would probably leave their family home and move in with him. 'Soon,' Sailesh said to himself. As soon as he was married to the love of his life, he would be able to move out of home.

'Out with your friends again?' Meenakshi asked, as if reading his mind. 'The Shack, na?'

Sailesh's frown confirmed it.

'You see, I know everything,' his mother said with a smile as she took a plate out of the cupboard.

'By talking to Raja's mother!' Why did his friends have to tell their mothers everything?

'What happened to the music laws, no loud music on the beaches after ten?'

'I thought you knew everything?'

Meenakshi laughed a deep laugh that made the fat around her stomach jiggle. There was something about her laugh that was infectious and even Sailesh smiled at his mother, despite his worries.

'It's moved off Baga beach to one of the side streets. The cops don't come there. The owner is the son of some government member, an MLA.'

'I went for my morning walk today,' Meenakshi said.

'Were you walking or gossiping?'

Meenakshi smiled. She looked at her empty dish. 'You know Raja's mother was telling me about Lipi's son. Have you heard?' she asked, putting some okra, rice and *keema* on to her plate.

Sailesh stopped chewing. He looked intently at his mother but she didn't give anything away. He swallowed his mouthful with a gulp of water and stared at his plate. His mother knew. How could she have found out? His palms started to sweat but he wasn't about to let her know that he knew that she knew. Instead he braced himself. 'Tell me,' he said.

'*Arrey wah,* what shame the boy has brought on the family,' she said, looking at her son from the corner of her eye. She pushed a loose strand of hair behind her ear. Smoothing her sari with her plump hands, she removed her bangles before delicately making a ball of rice and *keema* with her fingers. She held the food to her lips and looked directly at her son. 'Lipi's son ran off with the maid!' she said her eyes widening. She popped the tiny rice and mince ball into her mouth without taking her eyes off her son. 'Terrible, na?'

'Maybe they were in love.'

'*Che*, what nonsense. The boy is only nineteen. What does he know about love?'

'You married Pops at nineteen.'

'That was different,' she said, shooing away a fly that had landed on her rice. 'This thing he has done – what shame on poor Lipi. I would hate to be in her position, but then I have nothing to worry about.'

'You don't even know Lipi. She may be happy for them.'

'Why are you being like this?' she said, making a face.

Sailesh often wondered if his mother had ever taken acting classes. She could change her facial expressions in a blink of an eye. And they always looked so convincing.

'Too many young maids are getting above their station. Where are they meeting young men outside their class? Do they go to places like the Shack? Maybe your father and I should go there one night and see where the youngsters are hanging out.'

Sailesh was silent.

'I heard one of the Da Costas' maids has her eyes set on a young man from a much better class. Is it true?'

'You hear everything. You tell me,' Sailesh said, dipping his *roti* in the bowl of mince.

'Take some on your plate. Don't dip your *roti* in the serving bowl,' his mother scolded.

Sailesh put a spoonful of the *keema* onto his plate.

'I heard this news from the horse's mouth!' Meenakshi continued. 'Mrs Da Costa came in to the dentists today. She has a wisdom tooth that is paining her. I overheard her conversation.'

'Good for Mrs Da Costa,' Sailesh said, rolling his eyes. 'Anyway, I thought they were abroad.'

Meenakshi hesitated. 'Well, they're back.' She paused. 'The shame, the shame of it,' she repeated the word shame for effect. 'If it happened to me, I would do the honourable thing and burn myself.'

Sailesh shifted in his chair. 'Drama queen.'

'*Tut*. I would.'

Sailesh was silent. He wiped his dish clean with the remaining *roti*.

Meenakshi smiled and took another spoonful of *keema* onto her plate.

CHAPTER FOURTEEN

'*Yaar*, of course I am knowing Gita Shah. The short sturdy girl with the marking on her face who was married to that murdered fellow?' the man said, shaking his head from side to side whilst looking at Lavita's legs.

Lavita looked at Utsa in her *shalwaar* and was jealous. She had made the wrong decision this morning when she chose a skirt. But perhaps it wasn't so bad. Maybe the sight of her legs would encourage the man to tell them what they wanted to know.

The drink-seller stuck his fingernail between a gap in his teeth and started picking at something. 'She works part time in that Bata,' he said as he pulled his fingers out of his mouth. He pointed at the shop with the big red and white Bata sign across the road. 'Terrible thing, na – what happened with her husband. How the poor woman is coping, God only knows. You know rumour has it that that husband of hers never sent any money home.'

Utsa tutted under her breath – she had a lucky escape indeed.

'Is it now?' Lavita said, wondering where Sandeep Shah's salary was going every month. He had told her he was saving for their wedding but she had her doubts about this after she found out about his wife. Perhaps he was saving so that he could run away with her. This made her feel much better. But she also felt sorry for Sandeep's wife. Not only was her husband cheating on her, but he was making her work as well – and they had a child to look after. She shook her head. She didn't know what to think anymore.

'But then maybe she deserved it,' the man said, offering his wooden stool to the two girls. They politely declined so he sat down, slipped his *chappals* off. He crossed his legs and started playing with his toes.

Lavita's ears pricked up. 'You think she deserved it?'

The *gudkhi*, vendor, was silent.

'Tell us,' Lavita encouraged. All these gossips were the same, putting their price up unnecessarily.

'It seems like Gita Shah was having, how you call it?' He looked around to check that no one else was listening. 'An affair.'

'Really? Never!' Utsa's eyes widened.

'Yeally. It is true. But then I am only hearing things from customers. It's not often someone gets murdered in a small village. Here in Mapusa, maybe murder is possible. Panaji, also possible. Margao, definitely murderings are happening. But somewhere like Utol. No, you have to be a suspicious bugger if you get murdered.' The *gudkhi* put his fingers back in his mouth and began picking between his teeth again. This time he pulled out something small and black.

Lavita stared at the man in front of her who, only moments ago, had been playing with his toes with the same hand. The shop keeper put the black item back in his mouth and swallowed it.

Lavita wanted to retch but she refrained from doing so. Instead she smiled politely.

'The whole of Mapusa is talking about Shah,' the man continued. 'You think Mrs Shah would have the senses to kip her *chuddies* on when the murder is being investigated, but no.'

'How you know this?' Utsa asked.

'Mr Desai came in yesterday. Said he was driving by the cross on the Mapusa hill and saw Mrs Gita Shah and that fool Vasudev. And they say that this Vasudev was Mr Shah's best friend. If my friend did something like that to my lady friend, oof, I would bloody...' The man shook his head as he started playing with his toes again.

'Dirty fellow,' Utsa whispered to Lavita.

Lavita tucked her hair behind her ears. She wondered whether she could push the shop owner for more information or if he would start asking her questions if she did so. They had already been standing there long enough.

To Lavita it was now obvious. Sandeep was in an unhappy marriage and wanted to leave his wife and be with her. He must have been pushing his wife away so that it would be easier to leave her. The more she toyed with this idea, the more she believed it to be true. 'Come on,' she said taking Utsa's hand.

'Thank you, sir. You have been so helpful telling us where our old friend is,' Utsa said.

The *gudkhi* nodded and waved the two girls off. 'Before you leave, who should I say was looking for Mrs Shah?'

'Don't worry. We're going to see her now,' Utsa said pointing towards the Bata shop.

'But I must know, na, who you are, in case she is naat inside,' the vendor persisted.

'Her old classmate, Sandu,' Lavita said as she turned on her heel and headed towards the shop.

~

Lavita and Utsa stood in the alleyway opposite the shoe shop. A dead rat in the drain made Utsa jump. 'I hope she arrives soon. I hate these big cities. I want to get back to Utol.'

'And waste our bus fare by going back so soon? No, there are things to do here. I want to see Sandeep's wife.'

Utsa scrunched her face and applied some tiger balm under her nose.

'Come on.'

Utsa looked hesitant.

'Don't you want to know what he was married to? What she looks like?'

Her friend shrugged.

'I know a good Chinese cart nearby. My treat if you keep quiet.'

Utsa considered her friend's offer. Eventually she smiled, thinking about a large portion of vegetable chow mien with chilli sauce. 'Okay, so long as you don't make a fool of yourself.'

'What do you mean?'

'I'll stay if you promise not to go and speak to her.'

Lavita pressed her lips together. 'Promise.' She let out a gasp. Grabbing her friend's arm, she pointed to the shoe shop. 'That must be her.'

A short and slightly stout woman with a dark mark on her cheek stepped outside the shoe shop with a broom. She started sweeping the pavement outside.

'She doesn't look happy,' Lavita said. She tilted her head to get a better look.

'Would you if your cheating husband was dead and you had to support a child on your own?' Utsa asked dryly.

Lavita narrowed her eyes. 'I look better than her, don't I?'

'*Puh-lease*. Are you really asking me that? Is that why you dragged me to this godforsaken place?'

'Fine, come on let's go,' Lavita said with a scowl.

'You do,' Utsa said, 'you look much better than her. Happy?'

Lavita turned to leave but Utsa caught her by the hand. 'Wait, see that man.'

Lavita turned. A tall, well-built man approached Gita as she swept the pavement outside the shop. The women stood still and watched.

'Looks like he's telling her something private,' Utsa said.

Lavita squinted. 'This must be Vasudev. He must be the murderer.'

Utsa took a step back and looked at her friend. 'What are you saying? You don't know that. Don't go making up rumours that could get people into trouble. It's one thing to make up stories of everyday nonsense, but this is something else.'

Lavita bit her lip. 'What about Gita? You think she could have been the murderer?'

'Nah, look at her man. She's half Sandeep's height.'

'But look at her size – she must have some strength. It's fat not muscle. Look, you can see by the way it's wobbling,' Lavita said, laughing at her own joke.

'She's hardly fat.'

Lavita grunted.

'Anyway, you're not a policeman. Leave it to the detectives.'

'Both of them could have done it together,' Lavita said, ignoring her friend's remark. 'Gita wanted her husband out of the way so she could carry on with his best friend. And Vasudev wanted Sandeep out of the way to carry on with Gita.' She smiled, happy with her deduction.

'Stick to grinding masala rather than making it! I don't think they did it. If you ask me, Sandeep's wife knew about his affairs and found her own lover because she was lonely.'

Lavita took one last look at the couple outside Bata. Her Sandeep was betrayed not only by his wife but by his best friend as well. No wonder he turned to other women. Gita Shah and Vasudev's relationship had driven him to cheat. Satisfied with her conclusion, she gave in to the whines of Utsa and started walking towards the Chinese cart.

Chapter Fifteen

Pankaj knocked on the dusty brown door. The two halves of the door didn't quite meet in the middle. There was a gap, as if the door was open. But it must have been locked by some kind of bolt or chain across the inside, because when Pankaj tried the door it just wouldn't give. He pushed the old door again. No use. He scratched his head. It was extremely odd in a village such as Utol for someone to lock their front door during the day.

Pankaj walked around the side of the house. He heard a rustling noise coming from the bushes and stopped in his tracks. He crossed his fingers, hoping it wasn't a dog, then he took a few steps forward. The last time he entered a suspect's garden, a dog had jumped up and bit him on his behind. He was lucky that it had been just an old Lhasa Apso whose teeth were blunt. He was even more fortunate that he had been wearing jeans pants at the time. The dog's teeth didn't quite get through the material of his trousers and he had been saved from having rabies injections in his stomach.

He quickly checked his attire. 'Eh,' he grumbled, 'who designed these police uniforms?' A dog could easily get his teeth through the flimsy material of these government slacks. He bent down and picked up a small stone he could easily warn a dog off with.

The rustling grew louder as Pankaj cautiously approached the rear of the house. The garden was larger than the standard rectangular mud patch most villagers in Utol maintained. It was beautifully landscaped with all the shrubs in one corner, a rock garden in the other and a marble statue of a girl with a butterfly sitting in the palm of her hand right in the middle. What was most surprising was that the garden had a lawn; good quality, soft lawn like the kind he had only seen in five-star hotels, not the cheap, easy to maintain crab grass that was used everywhere else. He let out a low whistle. These people had money.

Cluck cluck cluck, rustle, rustle.

Pankaj heard the noise from an allamanda bush, its bright yellow flowers in full bloom. He looked curiously at it, only then did he notice a large rear backing out towards him. The bottom was clad in a pale green cloth with pink flowers. He couldn't help but stare at the enormity of it. Suddenly, he noticed that the rear was turning around. He quickly looked up at the tender coconuts hanging from a nearby coconut tree.

'Who are you?' said a squeaky voice. 'And why are you in my garden?'

Pankaj looked at the woman, her voice didn't match her figure. It was what he could only describe as nasal. 'Sorry madam, I didn't mean to disturb you.'

A round face looked back at him intently. 'Disturb me? You're trespassing in my garden. I could have you arrested.'

'But, madam…'

'What do you want?'

'I *am* the police, madam.' Pankaj pointed to the logo on his shirt. He hoped that this would act in his favour.

The woman shook her head from side to side. 'You are from the police. You should know better than to trespass. What if I'd been in my nightie? *Haan*? Then what – how would you explain yourself to your superiors?'

Pankaj thought it best not to respond. The woman took a step closer – she smelled of ghee and jasmine.

'Where is Prashant? We normally deal with that officer,' she said.

'He no longer works at the Little Larara Police Station, madam.'

The woman's lips curled downwards. 'Why? What happened to him?'

'Transfer, madam.' Pankaj refrained from elaborating on the detective's move. Good-for-nothing Prashant had done nothing but spread corruption. His transfer to a small fishing village was the first blessing that came out of the Inspector General. Prashant had not been moved because of his corrupt ways, but rumour had it he had been fooling around with the Inspector General's daughter. Inspector General Gosht had therefore sent him to some back-end village in Canacona, as far away as possible from Larara.

'So, it is you that we have to deal with now.' She shook her head as if a very bad thing had happened. 'I can't help, I'm afraid. My husband deals with police matters.'

Baksheesh, thought Pankaj. This woman and her husband were used to getting their way by paying a bribe. He wondered how much they used to pay Prashant just to keep him off their backs. Never mind. It wouldn't happen under Chupplejeep's watch. The thought made him smile. Just last month some hero from Daswali had tried to offer Chupplejeep one thousand rupees to turn a blind eye to the brothel he was running. Chupplejeep had turned down the offer and had closed the place.

Pankaj shook away the thought and tried to focus on the task in hand. When he started making his enquiries about the name he found on the chit of paper under Sandeep's bed, the local villages only had one thing to say, and that was that Sanjog was an illegal moneylender. Pankaj was sure that the rumour was true. How else could he afford *pukka* grass and a marble statue such as this? Had Sandeep Shah borrowed money from Sanjog? He had learned in college module 274, *Criminal Psychology,* that money was definitely a motive for murder.

'Detective Inspector Chupplejeep is in charge of the Utol area now and I'm Police Officer Pankaj.'

'I've never met with him. What's his good name?'

'Arthur.'

'Catholic good name and Hindu last name?' She held out her hand and twisted her fingers signalling that she wanted to know the reasoning behind this. 'Should I trust a man with one Catholic name and the other Hindu?'

'I'm here about the Sandeep Shah case,' Pankaj said, ignoring the woman's question. Why was everybody so concerned with his boss's name? Pankaj pulled out his notepad.

'I see. You're investigating that terrible business. But what do you want from me?' Her face softened and she fluttered her eyelids as her downturned lips changed direction and turned into a smile.

'I was told I could find Sanjog Viraj here.'

'Who told you that?'

Pankaj thought about it for a second. He could tell her the truth and get a neighbour in trouble or he could hide behind the need for discretion. He chose the latter. He didn't want to stir up any further tensions in the village.

'My job requires me to be silent about how and where I get my information, madam. A woman like you would understand, of course.'

'Of course, of course.' The large woman in the green and pink *shalwaar* assured him that she knew all about his profession in her nasally voice. 'Discretion is a good attribute to have in a job like yours.' She tilted her head back and looked down her nose at him.

'So, Mr Sanjog Viraj does live here?'

The woman looked from side to side and then peered over the fence into her neighbour's property before she responded. 'I am Mrs Sanjog Viraj. Call me Kamana.'

115

Pankaj smiled. 'If you don't mind, I just need a couple of minutes of your husband's time. I need to ask him a few questions.'

The woman quickly glanced over the fence again and waved at someone Pankaj could not see. Then she smiled and quickly ushered him into the house. Once he was seated with a bowl of chips and a glass of water, he questioned Sanjog's whereabouts.

'Is the water okay?' Kamana said, ignoring the question.

Pankaj shook his head. 'Should it not be?'

'New water purifier,' she said with a smug smile.

'So, Kamana, can I ask again where is Mr – '

'Out on business,' she interrupted.

'On a weekend?'

'You're working, na?'

'There has been a terrible crime. We have to work all hours until this criminal has been caught. What time do you expect your husband back?'

'I'm not sure.' She smiled again.

Pankaj looked at his notepad, unsure if she had winked at him or if she had something in her eye. Nevertheless, it made him uncomfortable. He pulled at the collar of his shirt. It was warm inside the house. Kamana had plump lips and he couldn't help but wonder what it would be like to kiss them. As soon as he realised what he was thinking, colour rose to his cheeks. He tugged at his collar again and cleared his throat.

Kamana crossed her legs at the ankle and looked at him intently.

What am I thinking? Pankaj thought. This woman was old enough to be his mother and she was not in the least bit attractive. If anything she was being evasive in her answers. Her pink fleshy lips had formed into a wry smile, like the fisherwomen near Pato Bridge trying to sell off their day-old *thesreos,* cockles. If you were foolish and ate them, they were guaranteed to send you running to the toilet. Pankaj was certain only bad things could come of him thinking about this woman in such a manner.

He tried to compose himself. What about Shwetika? Chupplejeep said it was natural for him to look at other women, but Kamana Viraj? It felt wrong – very wrong. He was certain that Shwetty wouldn't approve. Thinking about Shwetika did not help. It made him feel even more flushed. He took a deep breath.

'Are you okay, Officer? Kamana asked.

Pankaj looked up. She winked again. This time he was certain that it was a wink. Was it because her name meant desire that she felt the need to flirt with him? Or did she think her flirtation was as good as *baksheesh?* He wondered what else Prashant had received from the Viraj household.

'I'll come back when your husband's here to ask some questions,' Pankaj said, standing up to leave.

'Don't leave just yet. Maybe I can answer some of the questions for him.' Kamana shifted her chair closer to his.

'I don't think so,' Pankaj said, desperate to leave her company, but the lady was staring intently at him.

117

'Erm…okay then,' he said, flustered. He sat back down. 'Can I ask where you were the evening of the tenth?'

'This month? That was the date, no?' Her eye's widened. 'The date of the terrible thing.'

'Yes, madam.'

'Let me think,' she said. She stood up and walked to an old wooden cabinet. She opened the drawers and started looking through them one by one. 'I'm looking for my diary. It has everything in there.'

Pankaj was silent whilst Kamana searched. Every so often the woman stopped and looked meaningfully at the ceiling.

Pankaj looked up. He noticed a gaudy gold and glass chandelier. This was no ordinary villager's house. With a proper lawn, a water purifier and an expensive light fitting. This was the house of someone wealthy. He made a note of this.

'I cannot locate my diary, but the date rings a bell. I'll find it, don't worry. I put everything in there.'

'It was only last weekend, madam.'

'Hmm, you are right,' she said hitting her forehead with the palm of her hand. 'I was visiting my daughter. She's moved Panaji-side – just had a little *bachha,* baby. So cute. Yes, most definitely I was there.'

'And your husband?'

'Oh Sanjog.' Kamana paused. 'No, he didn't come with me. I don't know what he was up to. But the date, it definitely rings a bell. He must have been doing something. I'll have a look for my diary later and tell you.

No point asking my husband. His memory is like a bucket with a hole in it – useless.'

'Maybe the date is memorable because it was the day Mr Shah died.'

Kamana nodded in agreement. 'It's not every day someone drops dead in your village.'

'Can I ask what your husband does for a living?'

'He deals in antiques.'

'Antiques? In Utol?'

'I can show you a room full of old wooden items he's trying to sell if you don't believe me.'

'There have been murmurings in the village that he lends money.'

Kamana raised an eyebrow.

'Well, does he?'

'He lends money to people. Not much. He gives them a long time to pay back. You know if you just gave Mr Prashant a call he would explain everything,' Kamana said, stroking the arm of her chair.

Pankaj shifted. He was certain the temperature was rising in the house. 'Charging high interest and making sure they pay?'

'No, no. You think we would be living in Utol if he made charges like you say. No, we would be living in one of the big cities. He should be like that, no? Then maybe we could buy a bigger house. He is too *sharif,* honest, for this business. You'll see when you meet him. He couldn't hurt a fly.'

Pankaj stood up to leave. 'One more question. Why is your front door locked shut?' From inside the house,

Pankaj could see the thick bolt across the door. The bolt looked old and well-used.

Kamana hesitated before she responded. 'There is a murderer on the loose, Officer. You cannot be too safe even in a small village like Utol.'

Chapter Sixteen

'I don't think you have been entirely truthful with us,' Detective Chupplejeep said.

Lavita picked at her fingernails.

'Don't lie to us. It'll only make it more difficult for you. It's our job to find out the truth when someone is lying. We've been asking around. Several witnesses say you were having relations with Mr Shah.'

Lavita was silent. She didn't know where to begin.

'I can call your aunty or your granny if you would feel more comfortable talking with them present. Would you like that?' Chupplejeep said, looking at her across the table. He already knew the answer to the question. But in this line of work there was never any harm in veiled threats.

The woman's face fell.

'I think it is best if we wait for your guardians.'

'No. I'll tell you what you want to know.'

'Okay then,' Chupplejeep said with a sigh. He'd forgotten how difficult youngsters could be. And it made him think about children for a brief moment. How much patience one required with them. A shiver ran down his spine. If Christabel wanted marriage then she most definitely would want children as well. Although he saw children in his future, he never saw them as babies. He only saw them as young adults who could have reasonable conversations. He didn't know the first thing about babies – babies scared him. How did mothers interpret their cries? He wouldn't know where to begin. Poirot never married and he never had children. He was a wise man. Chupplejeep wiped the beads of sweat that had formed on his brow with his white handkerchief.

Thinking of Poirot made him think of the houseboat he had booked for his fortieth birthday, but remembering the look on Christabel's face when he had mentioned it to her made him flinch. The problem was not going away. Christabel was becoming increasingly irritable and it had all started when her best friend got married.

The ultimatum would come soon. He had seen the signs. It had happened with his last two girlfriends. First, they had wanted to move into his house. Then they were upset whenever he took them for a fancy meal and no engagement ring was produced. Finally, they just spelled it out for him. Of course he had known already that these ex-girlfriends were hankering after marriage, but he could never bring himself to commit.

Christabel was different though. She wasn't like his recent ex-girlfriends, Lavinya or Atika. He didn't want to lose this one. But she was growing increasingly impatient with him. And she was noticeably cranky also. The Kerala trip tantrum was a sure sign that she was at breaking point. Although she had conceded to the trip eventually, he was sure that if no engagement ring was produced during their Keralan adventure, Christabel was likely to push him off the boat.

Chupplejeep looked at his suspect sitting before him. This was the main difference between himself and Poirot. Poirot never thought about his personal affairs when trying to solve cases, except for that one time. He cleared his throat. 'So Lavita, tell me, when did your relations start with Mr Shah?'

Lavita was silent.

Chupplejeep drummed his fingers on the table. He tried to be patient. His gut instinct told him that the young lady was innocent and usually his instincts were right. Lavita had simply got herself mixed up with the wrong sort of man.

Finally, she spoke. 'I started seeing him three months ago when he first moved into Aunty's outhouse.'

'Immediately?' Chupplejeep asked. Village life had changed over the years. When he was that age, he would have had to make eyes at a girl for at least one month before he could pluck up the courage to speak to her. It seemed that the whole of Goa was taking tips from Star TV; the whole of Goa apart from Pankaj who was stuck in his traditional ways.

'Not immediately,' Lavita said quickly. 'He asked me to be his girlfriend for some time, but I said no.'

'But eventually you said yes,' Chupplejeep said, trying to get to the crux of the matter. 'Did you know that he had a wife and child?'

Lavita shook her head vigorously. 'Of course not. The first I knew about his family was when I read it in the paper.'

He noticed her eyes had tears in them and he couldn't help but feel sorry for her. He couldn't imagine what it was like to suddenly realise that your lover had a significant other and child. Poor Lavita, she too had been a victim, yet she was getting no sympathy from anyone. Instead she had to suffer in silence. Although it would be better that way. The less people talked about it, the quicker they would forget about it and her reputation wouldn't be damaged. In a village as small as Utol, reputation was everything. 'He made no mention of his family? Mother? Father?'

'We talked about our own marriage. You think I'd have carried on with a married man? Sandeep said he was saving money so I wouldn't have to pay a big dowry. He said that his father was traditional and would expect a payment. But he didn't want me to have to buy extra jewellery. He was thoughtful like that.'

Chupplejeep wondered if he should bite his tongue, but he felt that the girl ought to know the truth. It may make her forget him sooner. 'Sandeep Shah's parents died a while back. He had no father.'

Lavita bowed her head. 'He should have told me. I'd have understood. My parents are also dead.'

'He needed an excuse,' Chupplejeep said softly.

She questioned the detective with her eyes, but he said no more on the matter.

'And you used to visit his bedroom?' Chupplejeep asked. He didn't want to embarrass the girl but he had no choice.

'Yes,' she said, studying the tablecloth.

'Were you with him the night before you found his body?'

Lavita shook her head again. 'I wanted to see him early that evening. I walked to his room and knocked on the door. He answered, but then my aunty called. I had to do *puja* with Aunty and Uncle, so I had to turn and run back to the house. They wouldn't have liked to see me talking with Sandeep.'

'Did you often visit his room in the evening?'

'I saw him in the mornings before I cleaned out the chicken coop. The rest of the family don't get up till late, so even though it's light at that time it was the best time to see him.'

'Did you see him that morning?'

A tear slipped down her cheek. 'No. I was on my way to his room before I attended to the chickens. That was when I saw him there.'

'Hmmm.' Detective Chupplejeep pursed his lips. 'Did you ever hear him talking on the phone or mentioning any names?'

'I know that he used to play cards. He always said he was going to win big, he called it a big payment or payout, something like that. He said after he won he wouldn't have to be a driver anymore. We were going to get married and he was going to buy us our own house. And we would have servants.' Lavita touched her fingers to her lips as the words left her mouth. 'I was a fool,' she said.

Sandeep's deception was cruel. But Chupplejeep couldn't help but think of his own situation. Was he deceiving Christabel by not telling her that he wasn't ready to settle down? But then again, forty was fast approaching. He would have to bite the bullet soon.

'Are you okay, Detective?'

'Yes,' Chupplejeep said, shaking off his thoughts of turning forty. Thinking about his birthday always made him feel a little sad. 'I'll need a hair sample from you,' he said to Lavita.

She looked startled.

'We need to eliminate people from our enquiry. If you don't want to…'

Her hands shook as she plucked two strands of hair from her ponytail and handed them to the detective.

'Thank you.' Chupplejeep held open a small clear plastic bag for her to put them in. After she deposited them in the packet, he put it in his breast pocket and patted it. 'If you remember anything else, no matter how insignificant, please remember to tell us.'

Lavita cleared her throat. 'Detective, can I say one thing?'

'Go on.'

'I heard that Sandeep's wife was going around with a friend of his.'

'Oh!' Chupplejeep said, his eyebrows raised. 'And who told you this?'

'I needed to go to Mapusa to run an errand there. I started speaking with a local. He told me.'

'Mapusa is a long way for errands. Isn't that where Mr Shah's family live?'

Lavita shrugged.

'You should know gossips are not always the best people to believe.' Chupplejeep heard the shuffling of feet. He turned to see Granny Monji standing at the entrance of the kitchen carrying a large sack of rice. 'Can I help?' he asked.

Granny Monji shook her head. 'Nothing doing. I'm used to this,' she said, carefully placing the bag on the stone floor.

Chupplejeep wondered how such an old woman could carry such a heavy bag so effortlessly. She wasn't even out of breath.

As if reading his mind she said, 'You look surprised, Detective, but you shouldn't be. We village folk are stronger than you think. We haven't been softened by living in the city. We haven't had the luxury of having labourers to carry our loads for us.' Granny Monji picked up a small paper-wrapped parcel and a steel bowl and took her place in her usual corner. Opening the paper, she started to shell peas into a large stainless steel bowl. Despite her fiddly task, she didn't take her cloudy eyes off Chupplejeep. Occasionally she popped one of the little green vegetables into her mouth instead of the bowl.

Lavita bit her lower lip. Visibly concerned at how long Granny Monji had been standing at the kitchen door listening to their conversation.

'Thank you, Lavita. You've been helpful,' Chupplejeep said, finishing his glass of water.

'I can go?'

'Of course,' Chupplejeep said with a smile. He twisted one end of his moustache.

Lavita got up from the table and went to her room as he rose to his feet.

'Do you mind if I take a look upstairs? I want to get a bird's eye view of the crime scene,' Chupplejeep asked Granny Monji.

'Sure. Go ahead. You want me to come? My room is upstairs.'

Chupplejeep shook his head. 'Oh, I would have thought it was down to save you the stairs.'

'No, no. It's up directly above Lavita's room. I only go up to sleep. I don't like sleeping next to the kitchen so Lavita has taken the downstairs room. It's bad luck to sleep next to the kitchen.'

Chupplejeep could tell from the chillies and lime hanging at the front door that someone in the house was superstitious. Now he was certain it was Granny Monji by her reluctance to sleep near the kitchen. He thanked her and walked upstairs.

Granny Monji's room faced the front of the house. The Laljis' room faced the crime scene but a large mango tree obstructed it. Chupplejeep could only get a clear view of where Sandeep's body was found from the window on the landing. He stood at the window for a while before he made his way downstairs. Granny Monji was waiting for him in the hall.

'You know you should also ask that neighbour, Utsa, about her involvement with Mr Shah,' she said.

Chupplejeep looked at the mischievous old woman. 'You never said anything before.'

'I'm telling you now,' she said casually. 'Utsa jumped over our compound wall and went into his room the night before Shah's body was found!'

'How do you know this?' Chupplejeep asked.

'I saw her,' Granny Monji said. 'I saw her.'

Chapter Seventeen

'*Che*, this whole mess, it's all my fault,' Neeraj said to the one-eyed cat.

The cat meowed as he rubbed his side against Neeraj's hairless legs.

'At least you will always love me,' he said with a sigh. He knew that the police were going to pay him a visit that evening. They had telephoned his neighbour earlier in the day, asking for him.

Paavai would be annoyed that the neighbours knew their business. This would be her ammunition to get a phone line connected. Neeraj sighed. He should stop pretending that he could get by without modern technology and just buy his wife a wretched phone. But the phone issue was the least of his worries. He lifted the cat onto his lap and scratched him under his chin. Would the police know that he had been to Utol? Would the gods punish him if he made up a story to prove his innocence? Surely they would look kindly on him. After all, he was only trying to put right his earlier wrongdoings.

'I should never have introduced that rogue to my daughter,' Neeraj said to the cat. 'When I introduced Sandeep, I never meant for it to go as far as it did. But the whole business took on a life of its own. It spiralled out of control and there was nothing that I could do. You understand?'

The cat jumped off Neeraj's lap and found a sunny spot on the veranda to lie in. Neeraj slumped back into Paavai's rocking chair, thinking about what he had done.

It had been a hot evening in May. Everyone in the village had their windows open and were regularly splashing their faces with cold water to keep cool. Sandeep had come to the poker game as a substitute for Jonny who had finally got a sales position in Dubai.

That day it all changed. Neeraj had been winning nearly every hand, but after Sandeep joined the game his luck turned. He didn't see it at the time but he could see it now. He should have known then that Sandeep Shah was bad luck. Instead, he had duped him. My wife is right, Neeraj thought; I'm a fool, a stupid fool.

The cat half-heartedly lifted his head to look at his master and then swiftly dropped it back down again.

Neeraj had been taken in by Sandeep's sob story. How Sandeep had lost his parents at such a young age. How he had to get by driving the rich around in their air-conditioned cars. He had even felt sorry that in the winter months Sandeep had to suffer with their air conditioning full blast.

'Even if I have a cold I have to keep the air-con on. They like the cold,' Sandeep had said to Neeraj that day, 'they are from foreign where it is colder. What to do?'

Neeraj had taken pity on him, not considering that in the summer months Sandeep enjoyed the luxury of air conditioning, whilst he himself was usually stuck under the bonnet of some broken-down car in the midday sun, usually getting sunstroke.

Instead of pointing out the benefits of Sandeep's position, Neeraj had invited him over to his house for dinner. He was in awe at the way this new fellow played at the table. After all, he didn't know at this time but Sandeep Shah, the orphan from Belgaum, had crossed into Goa on the run from thugs from whom he had borrowed money. No, Neeraj had found that out later. Much later, in fact, when it was too late. As the *goondas* stood at Neeraj's door, Sandeep was nowhere to be found and Paavai and his pregnant daughter were in the next room. Neeraj had no choice then but to use what little money he had managed to save to pay them off. He never told Paavai then that the thugs were after her precious son-in-law. He had not told anyone about the matter – what a stupid decision that too had been. Perhaps they would not be in this mess if he had told Paavai everything from the start. But Neeraj was getting ahead of himself. The real problem started the night he introduced Sandeep Shah to his family.

That night Paavai had welcomed this tall stranger into their home and was her usual welcoming self. She had outdone herself with fresh *rava*-fried breadfruit, fish curry and fluffy, white basmati rice. Neeraj smiled when he saw that Paavai had even put out the lime pickle that her sister had sent from her village.

The evening had gone well. Sandeep had managed to charm his wife and daughter, so much so that he had returned every Friday after that for a meal at their house. Of course Neeraj had not mentioned to his wife that like him, Sandeep was a gambler. Instead, he said that he had met Mr Shah at his workplace and they had become good friends. That was the first lie of many.

Two months later when Sandeep asked for his daughter's hand in marriage, Neeraj nearly choked on his *chai*. 'This is not the way to propose, Sandeep,' Neeraj responded, irked that his new friend had not followed the correct procedures.

'You're forgetting that I'm an orphan,' Sandeep said. 'I've no family. No father to ask you. So I have to ask myself.'

Neeraj stroked his chin. He would have to consult with Paavai and she would be angry. He could hear her voice. 'We invite him into our home every Friday and this is how he repays us! All your friends are hopeless.'

'I don't think so. I don't want my daughter getting involved with…'

Sandeep raised his eyebrows. 'A gambler?'

'Gambling is evil. It gets into your blood and…' Neeraj was stuck for words. 'It won't be a good life for her. The life I want her to have. No, being married to a gambler is not what I want for my daughter.'

133

'I hear you owe four thousand rupees to Gonsalves,' Sandeep said.

There was a silence between the two friends.

'You've been kind to this orphan. Let me repay this favour to you.'

Neeraj didn't respond. What was Sandeep trying to do? His new friend had already been generous with his family. As Neeraj squandered money playing cards or the lottery, Sandeep bought gifts of speciality foods such as *para* and pickle with his winnings. Foods like this always made them forget there was not enough fish in the curry.

'Paavai mentioned that Gonsalves's men have already been to the house.'

'She did?' Neeraj asked, forgetting his doubts about Sandeep. His wife never normally spoke to others about his gambling.

'She's worried. She asked me to talk to you. You know how women think. She thought we could chat man to man. But lets cut the bullshit. I've an offer for you. I've some savings. What do you say I pay off your debts and in return you give up this terrible habit?'

Neeraj respected that Sandeep was looking out for him. And if his wife had trusted an outsider, she must have been desperate. He knew it was time he gave it up but he had no way of paying Gonsalves back, which was the main reason he had continued to gamble. But all it did was make matters worse. It was a vicious circle. Time was running out and he was getting too old to owe *goondas* money.

Sandeep Shah was offering him a way out without having to confess to Paavai how much money he owed. He could start again with a clean slate. If he had to tell Paavai, she would probably never speak to him again. She would pack her bags and move to her sister's. Neeraj couldn't imagine a life without Paavai. So even though he had been sceptical about his friend's offer, he had held out his hand.

Sandeep shook it. 'So no gambling?'

'Only Lotto,' Neeraj responded, breaking into a smile. 'But tell me what's in this for you?'

'If your daughter likes me and wants marriage, you can call this payment a dowry; an *ulta pulta*, upside-down dowry. After all, families help each other out,' Sandeep said.

Neeraj swallowed hard. He wanted to take back his handshake. The words were on the tip of his tongue but the offer was too good to pass up.

'And if Gita says no?'

'Then you still keep the four thousand. It's a gamble I'm willing to take.'

Neeraj smiled. There was no harm in this deal. He didn't have to force his daughter to do anything she didn't want to.

That evening as Neeraj walked home, he rehearsed what he would say to his wife. But after dinner as he opened his mouth to speak, Paavai, as usual, interrupted him with her own news.

'Gita has told me that she likes that boy,' she said.

'What boy?' he asked, his eyebrows knitted together.

135

'Your good friend Sandeep,' she said, looking at her husband from the corner of her eyes.

'Our daughter said that?'

Paavai relaxed in her chair. 'Don't be angry. We should be happy that Gita can tell us her feelings. Not many daughters are so close with their mothers.' Paavai blushed. 'I know my cousin-sister is having such problems with her daughter not telling her anything. Gita was wondering if you would talk to Sandeep, see if he's thinking of marriage, starting a family. You know he has no father or mother, no? So it's best to ask him outright. How else is it done when no parents are involved?' Paavai said. 'You shouldn't be angry with Gita. She respects us and she respects tradition. That's why she has come to us. Now we need your help in this matter.'

Neeraj kissed his wife on her forehead. 'I'll see what I can do,' he said with a grin. For once in his life, Neeraj believed he had the upper hand in their household. Even though nobody else knew it – it was his little triumph. He knew that opportunities like this were rare, so he would have to make the most of it.

'It will be a good match. That boy has no parents so they'll have to live with us. I won't lose my daughter. I'll be gaining a son,' Paavai beamed.

Neeraj had remained silent about the *ulta pulta* dowry and three months later, Neeraj's debts were paid off, just before the wedding ceremony. Tensions in their family evaporated and soon Gita had announced her pregnancy. But just as Neeraj was thanking the gods for bringing Sandeep into their lives, four men who looked like they spent the majority of their time lifting weights knocked on his front door, and in Marathi they asked for one thousand rupees which was owed to them from Sandeep Shah.

Neeraj had given up gambling like he had promised and so he had some savings. With this money he cleared Sandeep's debts. But he couldn't just stop there. Sandeep was now part of his family. After asking around, Neeraj soon discovered that Sandeep was on a losing streak in the gambling circle in Kukurul. This time it was Neeraj's turn to offer Sandeep a lifeline.

'I've paid your debts to the thugs from Belgaum. Now, like you did for me, I must do for you. I want you to promise me for the sake of my grandchild you'll stop gambling. If you don't, I'll have no choice to confess everything to my Paavai and Gita,' Neeraj said. 'They may kick me out of the house, but I cannot let you do this to my daughter.'

Sandeep agreed. Two months later, after several heated discussions with Neeraj, a promise was made. Neeraj was to clear a further one thousand rupees of Sandeep's debt in Kukurul. Soon after, Sandeep announced he was leaving Kukurul for a job in Utol.

'They don't gamble so much in the villages,' he said. 'In Kukurul I know where the temptation is. I want to stop for the sake of my family.'

Neeraj, happy with his son-in-law's reasoning, supported his move despite protests from Paavai and his daughter, and he gave Sandeep his best wishes.

'*Che*, it was my fault. I brought that man into our lives,' Neeraj said.

The cat rolled over and stretched.

Neeraj knew the story didn't end there. Initially, he believed that Utol was a change. Sandeep told him that he was making a new life and once he had a house, he was going to move Gita and their newborn out to the village. Neeraj was envious. Utol was beautiful with its greenery and rural location. He assumed most of the households there didn't have phones either.

But then Neeraj met an old classmate for a drink. An old *dhobi* who washed the sheets for big houses in various villages. Occasionally they met in the local taverna to talk about fishing, they never discussed any personal matters. The *dhobi* knew nothing of Neeraj's family and Neeraj laughed when the *dhobi* told him that the new servant, at a big house in Utol, was eyeing up the cook's daughter and several other girls in the village. There was nothing better than maid's gossip. But as soon as the *dhobi* mentioned that this new servant was in debt to a local loan shark, Neeraj's palms started to sweat. Finally the *dhobi* said, 'This Sandeep Shah is such a character and I think he comes from your village.' Neeraj had nearly choked on his *aarrak*.

That evening, the sight of Neeraj's first grandchild in the arms of his daughter brought a tear to his eye and in that instant he knew what he had to do.

CHAPTER EIGHTEEN

'So you jumped over the wall to tell Mr Shah you were in love with someone else?'

'*Yaar*,' Utsa said.

'You told him that you could no longer accept his advances?'

'Yes, sir,' she said.

'Did you enter his room?'

Utsa studied the floor. Her mother would be back any minute now and she was hoping the detective and the officer would leave before her return. Otherwise she would face further questioning from her mother.

'Mr Shah is not here to verify your story and you lied to us the first time,' Detective Chupplejeep said. 'You said he was having a relationship with your good friend Lavita.'

'I said that I heard *rumours* that he was having an affair with my friend.'

'You were not afraid to give us your friend's name.'

'I entered his room,' she said after a moment's pause, scratching at her elbow.

'Could you not have told him over the fence that you did not want any relationship with him?' Pankaj asked.

'He wasn't taking no for an answer. He was that type only.'

'You say you broke off your relationship with him because you were getting friendly with someone else?'

'I'm not getting friendly. I'm in love with someone else. I'm not that sort of girl. I don't just get friendly with anyone. Make a note of that,' Utsa said, staring at Pankaj's notepad. 'I don't want people thinking I am cheap.'

'How long were you in his room for? And what else did you discuss?'

'Less than five minutes. I told Sandeep that I wanted him to stay away from me. Also I asked him to stop making eyes at me at work. Then I left.'

'Who's this someone else you're in love with?' Pankaj asked. 'Maybe he can verify your story.'

Utsa was silent. Never before had the police questioned her in such detail. She felt nauseated every time they asked a question.

'You're confident enough to tell us you're in love, now you must tell us who the man is. Come on, miss. We'll need to check if what you are saying is fact or not,' Pankaj said.

Utsa's eyes followed a line of black ants that were making their way towards a cupboard.

'We haven't got all day. You want us to clear your good name or not?' Chupplejeep said.

She sighed and her shoulders dropped. She had no choice. If she lied and gave a false name, they would find out. It would make her look guilty. She had to expose who the real love of her life was. Her body itched with nerves and her palms were sweaty. She thought about the repercussions of what she was about to say. Her boyfriend's mother was like a devil. He would certainly feel the sharp edge of his mother's tongue if word of their relationship got out. His mother may even send him off to his uncle in Mangalore. And the very thought of her love leaving Goa made her feel faint. On the other hand, the detective had warned her that if she didn't co-operate they would have to take her to the station for questioning. She didn't want that to happen either, because everyone in the village would see and talk about it.

Utsa opened her mouth to speak but suddenly a new thought struck her. What if what she was about to say angered her boyfriend and he broke it off with her? What if his menacing mother gave him an ultimatum: to stay in Utol and leave Utsa or be moved to another village in the back of beyond? If Utsa were in the same position, she wouldn't know what to do. Would she be able to leave Utol? She didn't think she could. She had never left Utol for longer than a day. Her boyfriend was the same. He had his business here. All his friends were here.

'Come on, miss. What's taking you so long?' Pankaj urged the girl.

'We're not leaving here until you tell us,' Chupplejeep said decisively, 'and we'll need a sample of your hair.'

'Why?' she asked. Her hand trembled as she touched the top of her head.

Chupplejeep looked at the girl and shook his head. 'It's a police investigation. We've found hair at the crime scene that we need to identify.'

Utsa looked from Chupplejeep to Pankaj. She was certain she was going to be sick. Had they found her hair on Sandeep's body? Could they pin the crime on her with just one strand of hair? Perhaps they could. She didn't know the first thing about police investigations. She weighed up her options then reluctantly plucked a strand of her hair and put it into the plastic bag Officer Pankaj was holding open.

She looked at the door. She was running out of time. Her mother would be back soon. She hadn't thought about how her own mother would react to the news of her being in love. It could go one of two ways. The Dragon would either want to celebrate her daughter's social manoeuvring or give her a tight slap across her face and tell her she was grounded for life.

'Come on, miss, we haven't got all day,' Pankaj said.

Utsa looked at the two men. She pursed her lips. 'Sailesh.'

'That wasn't so hard,' Pankaj said, writing the name in his notepad. 'Sailesh who?' he asked.

'Krinz. Sailesh Krinz.'

Pankaj stopped writing and stared at the girl.

~

Pankaj Dashpande wasn't the sort of fellow who liked breaking rules. Ever since graduating from the Police Training School he had stuck by the *Good Practice Policing Handbook*. His peers had laughed at him. 'You'll never get far in the Larara Police Force by being so honest,' they had said. To a certain extent they had been right.

Whilst his other friends were gaining experience in the big cities, Pankaj had opted to work in the place where he grew up, Little Larara. 'Honesty can stay in the villages,' the Inspector General at the time had said, when he was assigned to his position.

But his choice paid off. It wasn't long before Chupplejeep moved to the area and he realised he would be learning from the best. But whilst Pankaj had recognised his boss's achievements, other higher-ranking officials had been quick to forget about Chupplejeep's award for excellence and that he had caught Goa's only serial killer to date. Instead, they concentrated on the detective's recent failing in Panaji. It seemed no matter what one's accomplishments were, nobody in Goa liked a straight-laced cop.

Pankaj was hopeful. If they solved this case the new Inspector General, who was considerably less corrupt than the last, would perhaps see that Chupplejeep and Pankaj were a good team. Pankaj knew that he and his boss could be one of the best homicide teams in India.

143

They could change the face of policing in Goa and eliminate corruption altogether. He smiled. His ex-classmates would not be laughing then.

What Pankaj was about to do would not please the Inspector General and would thoroughly go against the *Good Practice Policing Handbook*. Sailesh Krinz was his friend. The same fellow he had played Captain Cook with in the summer holidays and the same fellow who gave him his first Hot Wheels car. Speaking to Sailesh was definitely what was referred to as a conflict of interest.

But if anything happened to Sailesh then Meenakshi would hold him personally responsible. And Sailesh's mother was like family. Amongst a whole load of good deeds she had done for his family over the years, last summer she had taken it upon herself to deliver freshly cooked meals to Pankaj and his father for a full month when his mother was sick.

Pankaj pulled up on his scooter outside Sailesh's house. Detective Chupplejeep had been reluctant to let him question Sailesh, but he had put his neck on the line by agreeing to it, especially as Sailesh was now looking like a suspect. Pankaj had done a good job in persuading his boss to let him ask some questions.

'Sailesh is like a brother to me,' he pleaded with Chupplejeep. 'He may open up with me,' he added to justify his reasoning. He truly believed this, but at the same time he was afraid, afraid that his best friend was part of this horrific crime and that he would have to arrest him. Sailesh had a temper and everyone knew that.

Pankaj knocked on the door, hoping that his friend had a watertight alibi for the tenth November.

Meenakshi opened the door. '*Beta*, come in. Get out of this hot sun. So warm it is for this time of year.' She pulled Pankaj towards her and embraced him, almost suffocating him in her large bosom. 'I haven't seen you in so long. When was it last?' She didn't wait for a response. 'Must be at Sola's wedding, na?'

'That was only last month, Aunty,' Pankaj said.

'*Baap re baap*, only one month passed! With this humidity, time is going so slowly.' Meenakshi wiped her brow with the edge of her sari and led Pankaj to the kitchen. 'I know your mother makes the best *bhel* in Utol but I have some freshly made. You'll have some, na?'

Meenakshi piled a small bowl full of the puffed rice, onions and tamarind and placed it in front of Pankaj.

'Some *nimbu pani*? Sweet? Salty? I'll make it sweet and salty. You work so hard like my Silu. Working in the hot sun, you must keep hydrated.' She started massaging the limes in her hands.

'You get afternoons off? I make sure my Silu comes home for lunch and a siesta. There is absolutely no point working in the afternoon sun. He would get sunstroke, na? Not worth it. Not worth the trouble. As if his customers cannot wait. Fast, fast. These days, young, rich people have no patience. Everything quickly. I thoroughly blame technology. It is utterly no good. But Silu can't work in the hot sun. It's not like he has one of those fancy Western garages, all sheltered. You know some of them even have air-con.'

145

Pankaj smiled as Meenakshi passed him his drink. He took a sip of the sweet and salty lime-juice water.

'Better, na? I was meaning to call your mother to find out about this terrible murder business. Who would have thought a murder could happen here? But now you are here I can ask you direct, na?'

'You know I cannot discuss the case, Aunty' Pankaj said, trying to concentrate on eating the *bhel*.

'*Arrey*, I am not just anyone. I am your family, na, *beta*?'

'I haven't even spoken about the case to my mother.'

Meenakshi folded her arms. She sat next to Pankaj and looked at him out of the corner of her eye. 'I've known you a long time. You won't discuss this, will you?' She shook her head from side to side. 'Always worth asking, na? I said to your mother, what good is it having a son in the police force if he is not willing to share the information? She agreed it was useless. You would have been better off as a fisherman who worked by himself, out on the water all day, with no gossip to bring home.'

'Is Sailesh in?' Pankaj asked, seeing his moment to get a word in.

Meenakshi looked up at the kitchen clock. 'He'll be home any minute now. It's gone one o'clock. That's why I made the *bhel* – it's his favourite. Uncle will be back too.'

Pankaj ate the bowl of *bhel* in front of him as he listened to his friend's mother talk. She would be truly disappointed to know that her son was dating a servant girl. That's if what Utsa was saying was true. Although

Pankaj had to admit the girl didn't look as if she was lying. He could see why Sailesh had developed a soft spot for her. She was pretty. A typical Goan girl, with long black hair and almond-shaped eyes, but she had high cheekbones, which made her stand out.

'Bhendaa! What are you doing here?' Sailesh said as Pankaj finished the last mouthful of *bhel* from his bowl. He was standing at the back door of the kitchen. 'You can't be here for Mom's *bhel*, your mother's is much better.' Sailesh grinned.

'*Goonda!*' his mother said. She stood up from her chair and playfully tapped Sailesh on his head, then placed a large bowl of food in front of her son with a bottle of water from the fridge.

Pankaj smiled but said nothing.

'*Aacha*, I know when I'm not wanted. I'll leave you two boys alone.' Meenakshi left the kitchen, half-closing the door behind her.

'Sir, to what do I owe this visit? I don't get a big-shot policeman visit me everyday? Check out the uniform and everything.'

'I was here just the other day,' Pankaj said, pointing to the door Meenakshi had left open.

'Mom,' Sailesh shouted, 'I can hear you listening at the door.'

They both heard footsteps as Meenakshi walked away.

Sailesh laughed. 'Must be serious.' He looked back at his friend. 'You don't often visit in your lovely uniform with these small palm trees on the shoulders.' Sailesh playfully flicked one of the embroidered coconut trees.

Pankaj grimaced. He didn't like these trees on his uniform that made his work seem so frivolous. Chupplejeep had said that it was keeping in theme with the tropical state where they worked and no one else in the force had complained, so Pankaj held his tongue. He looked through the kitchen window. He could see Meenakshi dozing in a rocking chair on the veranda. He was certain that she couldn't hear them out there, but still he whispered. You could never tell with that woman. 'It's about Utsa,' he said.

Sailesh choked on his mouthful of food. He quickly lifted up the bottle of water to his lips and took a large gulp of the cold clear liquid. His eyes darted to the veranda and then back to Pankaj.

'You're going out with the girl?'

'Who told you?'

'Is it true?'

Sailesh pushed away the bowl of food in front of him.

'I'm not here to tell you who you should and shouldn't go out with,' Pankaj said.

'My mother…'

'Your mother's prejudices are not why I am here. This is a police matter. As a friend we can discuss how you're going to tell your mother about your girlfriend. But this is more serious. I persuaded my boss to let me speak to you first so your mother wouldn't get suspicious. You're my closest friend. Both my boss and I could get a firing from the Inspector General if this came to light.'

Sailesh waved his hand in front of Pankaj's face. 'Don't give me that corrupt bullshit. Grow some balls.'

'Really, Sailesh? I'm here trying to do you a favour and you are telling me to man-up.'

Sailesh bent his head. 'Sorry,' he said putting his arm on his friend's shoulder. 'You know what I'm like.'

Pankaj stared at his friend. He knew exactly what his friend was like, quick to fly off the handle. He had broken up many bar fights Sailesh had started over the years. Had his friend done something really stupid this time? He noticed that Sailesh's hands were trembling and hoped it was because he was worried his secret was out, not because he had anything to do with the death of Sandeep Shah.

'How is dating Utsa a police matter?' Sailesh asked.

'So you *are* friendly with Utsa?'

'We have been for some time now.'

'And did you know the late Mr Shah?'

'No,' Sailesh said. He pulled his bowl of food back towards him.

'But you knew of him? And that he liked Utsa?'

'Everybody knows *of* everybody here, you know that.' Sailesh shifted in his chair as he dug his spoon into the mixture and swirled the puffed rice about.

'Look Silu, if you're not going to be straight with me, then you'll have to come to the station to be questioned by my boss or Detective Chupplejeep can come here.'

'I knew Sandeep liked Utsa. He was pestering her. She told me a couple of weeks back,' Sailesh said. 'I was angry. I dropped her at the Utol circle and then I went home. Afterwards, I spoke to Utsa. She promised me that once she knew my feelings for her were true she was going to cut off all contact with him. I think she did as she'd promised.'

'Were you jealous that he liked Utsa?' Pankaj asked as he made notes in his book.

'What is this, man? What are you writing?'

'I'm checking to see if you had a motive.'

'I watch *CSI*, brother. Your first question should ask where I was that night?

Especially if you think I am a murderer. We have been friends for fifteen plus years. How could you think that?'

Pankaj took a deep breath. Couldn't his friend see he was just doing his job? Why was he being so defensive? 'Not everything you see on television is correct,' Pankaj said. Perhaps he should have let Chupplejeep deal with him. But then Sailesh would have had a go at him for that too. No, this way was better. 'Okay then. Tell me. Where were you Saturday night, Sunday morning? The tenth and eleventh?'

Sailesh rubbed his chin. 'Let me think. This was when this Sandeep fellow died?'

Pankaj shook his head from side to side in agreement.

'Saturday, Saturday...' Sailesh said, thinking aloud. 'Something must have been happening at the Shack, na?

'I was at home that night,' Pankaj said. It was tough socialising at venues that broke all the rules. He would have no choice but to shut the Shack down if he visited after ten and loud music was playing. But he knew the owner had some connection with a government official and he couldn't go against that authority. Not when he was merely a police officer. No, he would be litter picking in Anjuna for the rest of his days if he tried to make trouble for the son of a government minister. It was better to avoid these party places all together.

'*Haan*, yes it was the Blast at the heli-pad. I was there. Check with Raja if you don't believe me.' Sailesh grinned and slapped his friend on the back. 'I was there till at least six in the morning listening the latest tunes from the Channel V DJs. Mom had clipped me around the head as I stumbled to my bedroom that morning.'

'No Sailesh. I know very well the Blast was on the Friday night. I am talking about the Saturday.'

'Oh,' Sailesh said sheepishly. 'Saturday night I was still hungover. I was watching movies on Zee.'

'Aunty, Uncle were also at home?'

'They were out at some wedding. They didn't come back till after I went to sleep. Maybe midnight.' Sailesh looked at his friend. 'Okay so I don't have an alibi. You can't charge me with that, brother.'

'Did I say I was charging you?' Pankaj looked at his friend who he had known since the third standard. 'I have to report this to Detective Chupplejeep, that's all. We'll be in touch if we need to speak to you again.'

'We'll be in touch? What kind of language is this?'

'Sailesh, let me do my job,' Pankaj said as he headed to the front door.

Sailesh followed. They both stood in the hall. Sailesh opened his mouth, as if to say something.

Pankaj waited in anticipation but Sailesh just opened the door for his friend without another word.

CHAPTER NINETEEN

'Ah, Mr Sanjog Viraj, I was told I could find you here?' Chupplejeep said.

'By who?'

'Your wife.'

'Call me Sanjog.'

Chupplejeep held out his hand and introduced himself and Pankaj. 'Sanjog. Can I ask what you were doing in that house you just came out of?'

'No, no, you must be mistaken. I was just walking past.'

Chupplejeep shook his head. 'Most definitely I saw you leaving that house. There, that one.' Chupplejeep pointed to the house with the metal railings soldered into the shape of flowers.

Their suspect was silent.

Chupplejeep looked at Pankaj. 'Officer, did you see this gentleman leaving that house?'

'Yes, sir,' Pankaj was quick to reply. 'Just now I saw him leave that house.'

'Oh, now I see. Of course, yes, that was the house I was in,' Sanjog said, shading his eyes with his hand as he looked towards the house in question. It was midday and the sun was directly above them. 'I was just visiting a friend, that's all. It's so hot outside. Can we not talk somewhere cooler?'

'We can go to the office and talk there,' Pankaj said.

'Office? Why office? There's a good shop making cool shakes just around that bend. Surely we can just talk there,' Sanjog said, pointing towards the end of the road.

'Hmm, okay,' Chupplejeep said after a moment's hesitation. He took out his handkerchief and mopped his brow. He could do with a cool mango shake. 'It's closer than the office. Follow us. And please don't drive off, otherwise we'll have to chase you and you must know from speaking with your wife that we already know where you live.'

Sanjog put his hand to his chest and frowned. 'Detective, you must think badly of me. I would never – '

'That's your car?' Pankaj interrupted, pointing towards the black Skoda parked a few metres away from where they were standing. The metallic car shone in the sunlight.

'Yes.'

'There's a waiting list for this model. It's an expensive car,' Pankaj said. 'It must look out of place in Utol where there are only auto-rickshaws and cycles.'

'I'll see you there,' Sanjog said, walking towards his car.

Pankaj and Chupplejeep got into their faded blue Maruti.

'Whenever I see a Skoda I want to change my car,' Chupplejeep said.

'But sir, you've had this car for a long time. It must hold so many memories. Didn't you catch that serial killer with this car?'

Chupplejeep smiled, remembering his most famous case. Pankaj was right, the car did hold memories for him. He gripped the steering wheel a little tighter.

'And when was the last time it broke down? You don't want a car like that fellow's, sir, utter high maintenance. You never know what dead-end places we'll have to visit when investigating a crime. The car has to be fully functioning, always. And you know how jealous these villagers can be. They'll say, "*Arrey*, look at that big-shot detective showing off in his car, instead of solving crimes." You don't want them to say that do you, sir?'

'Pankaj, you're making a lot of sense.' After some thought Chupplejeep added, 'Christabel would like a more comfortable car though.'

'This much I agree. Cars like that are more comfortable for women,' Pankaj said, shaking his head. 'Children also,' he bravely added.

Chupplejeep pretended not to hear.

~

At the counter of the shake shop, they ordered two mango drinks. 'The café's quiet,' Chupplejeep said. He walked towards a small table, sheltered from the sun by coconut trees and thick shrubs. Pankaj was still at the counter – the boy was a dreamer. He sighed and checked his watch. It was still early for kids to be here. They would still be in school.

Pankaj and Sanjog joined him a minute later.

'To drive a car like that you must be earning big money?' Chupplejeep said, as Sanjog sat down.

'I do okay.'

'And what exactly do you do?'

'Antiques.'

'Come on, Sanjog. Police Officer Pankaj and I are not stupid. Rumour has it you're the village loan shark and your wife so much as admitted it to my officer here.'

Sanjog was silent.

Pankaj opened his mouth to speak, but Chupplejeep cautioned him with his eyes.

'No such thing,' Sanjog said eventually. 'My wife lives in a dream world. I deal in antiques. I used to do some money lending. I don't anymore.'

'So you're telling two officers of the law that you're not what everyone else says you are?' Chupplejeep asked. He narrowed his eyes at his suspect before turning to Pankaj. 'Tell me Pankaj, what does it say in the *Good Practice Policing Handbook*? Is it worse to lie to an officer or worse to be a loan shark?'

Pankaj opened his mouth, but his voice caught. He rubbed his chin. He knew the handbook off by heart, yet he didn't know anything about this.

Chupplejeep suppressed a grin, then he turned back to Sanjog. 'I know what you are, Sanjog, so you may as well admit it.'

'I don't know what you mean.'

'The house you came out of. That fellow owes you money. You were at his house threatening him.'

'Lies,' Sanjog said, looking away.

'It's true. I know it, and you know it. Never forget that I know your business. And don't call me a liar when you know I'm telling the truth.'

Chupplejeep wondered how a loan shark would stay in business without being able to pay off the cops. From what Pankaj had said, his predecessor Detective Prashant was in Sanjog's pocket. There would be no exchange of *baksheesh* here for him to turn a blind eye. But being an incorruptible cop had its price. He was still suffering the after-effects of the Panaji incident where he had refused to take a bribe from a key suspect in a murder investigation, who also happened to be a government official. They were the worst – every one of them thought that they were above the law.

The Inspector General at the time had swiftly made the whole case 'go away.' But not long after, he transferred Chupplejeep to Little Larara as a detective instead of giving him the promotion he deserved. After that he had lost his faith in the justice system, but just as he was contemplating a career change, the Inspector General was booted out of the force for reasons unknown and a new one had been appointed. Inspector General Gosht had been brought in from Chennai after tackling crooked cops over there. Chupplejeep had approached Gosht to explain his position, but the Inspector General ignored him. 'Solve some cases and I'll consider your position. Corruption starts in the villages. You keep the villages clean and in time we'll see whether you are fit for a transfer or promotion,' the Inspector General had said. Chupplejeep had been dumbfounded by this comment. In his experience it was the cities that were corrupt, not the villages.

Chupplejeep wondered if Gosht was fobbing him off. Apart from the Panaji case, he had a record that would put the Inspector General's to shame. Nevertheless, he avoided confrontation with his superiors and was a strong believer that everything in this life happened for the best. He was proved right when a week after moving to Larara, he met Christabel. Over the past few months he had realised that things with Christabel were serious so he could no longer just transfer to another city. She had made it quite clear she wasn't moving.

Chupplejeep wasn't one for avoiding hard work though, and he felt he owed it to himself to prove his worth to the Inspector General. If he no longer wanted to move from Larara then at least he could work for a promotion and everyone knew that in this line of work, you were only as good as the result of your last case. From now on there would be no shady business going on in Larara. But just how shady was it, being a loan shark?

All villages needed a lender. Where would the villagers get any money to make substantial purchases without one? There were few banks in Goa that would lend to the lower-paid echelons of society. Those on the bottom rung of the caste system or those who made a modest living would never get a legitimate loan.

Villagers relied on people like Sanjog. Everyone in India knew this. Even Pankaj's father had borrowed from a local loan shark when their fridge at home broke beyond repair and once or twice Chupplejeep himself had been tempted. Maybe even his beloved Nana used a local loan shark, he reasoned. An image of a red and white cycle wrapped in newspaper came into his mind. How could Nana have afforded a bike when she could barely afford shoes? Of course Nana had used a loan shark.

The loan shark, he decided, was a necessity for everyday life. His hands were tied. Even if he wanted to arrest this fellow Sanjog for illegally lending money, he couldn't. Yes, it was against the law, but there had to be loan sharks for the villages to work. Chupplejeep looked at Pankaj who, as usual, looked lost in thought. The boy would realise soon that you couldn't always live by good practice.

'Don't worry, I'm not going to do anything about your little enterprise,' he said.

Pankaj let out a small gasp.

'But don't get me wrong,' Chupplejeep said. 'If I ever hear you are threatening your clients, I will come down on you like a ton of bricks. I know the villagers need you.

159

I won't take away their lifeline, but at the same time I won't let you hurt or bully them.'

Pankaj smiled.

'What d'you want to know?' Sanjog asked.

'I take it from your lack of response that we have an understanding.'

Sanjog shook his head from side to side in the typical Indian style of agreement.

'Good. Now let's get down to why we need to speak to you. Did you know that Sandeep Shah had your name written on a piece of paper in his bedroom?'

'Two mango, one chikoo. Please collect.' Chupplejeep heard over the tanoy. He raised his hand in front of him and twisted it. 'What's this?' he asked Pankaj.

'Sir, this is what they are doing now – Mumbai style. You collect your own drinks.'

Chupplejeep looked at Sanjog. 'Really?'

'This is the way Goa is heading,' Sanjog said.

'I've never heard such nonsense. No wonder this place is empty.'

Pankaj shrugged. 'Kids don't mind. They think it's trendy.'

'They call it modernisation,' Sanjog said, 'but really they are only getting rid of people's jobs. Why do that in India? Here labour is cheap and people are looking for odd jobs. It probably cost them more to get that loudspeaker than to send someone out with our drinks.'

Chupplejeep couldn't help but agree with Sanjog.

'I'll get them, sir,' Pankaj said, rising to his feet and walking towards the servery.

'Back to my question, Sanjog,' Chupplejeep said. 'How did your name come to be on a piece of paper in Sandeep Shah's bedroom?'

Pankaj returned carrying the three shakes. Sanjog seemed to relax after taking a sip of his chikoo drink. 'Detective, are you certain you won't arrest me for money lending? I heard about the Panaji incident.'

Who hadn't heard about the Panaji incident? 'We had an agreement. I won't go back on my word, provided you play by the rules.'

'You want payment?'

Chupplejeep pursed his lips. 'You can ask any of the thieves or *goondas* you know – Detective Chupplejeep does not take bribes.'

'Very clever, Detective. This will make scoundrels even more scared. You won't have any problem in Larara.' Sanjog smiled, taking another sip of his shake. 'That incident in Panaji then, what they say is true?'

'Just answer my question.'

'Simple. Someone must have given him my name on the paper,' Sanjog said. He put the straw of his drink in his mouth.

'Don't be smart.'

Sanjog raised his hand. He looked at the detective. 'Okay, I'm getting there. He borrowed money from me because he owed some money to someone else. Why he had my name on a chit, I don't know. I'm not a mind reader.'

161

'To who?' Pankaj asked, wiping mango froth from his upper lip.

'You didn't hear this from me.' Sanjog looked around the deserted café. 'Gonsalves.'

Pankaj let out a low whistle. 'He's one big *goonda*.'

'I agree. He's not the person you should be owing money to,' Sanjog said.

'How much did he owe?'

'He told me seven thousand rupees.'

'*Wooo*,' Pankaj said, 'big sum. Do you normally lend such large amounts?'

'Four thousand is normally my limit in the villages.'

'You made an exception?'

'Sandeep had been a good customer. But he had not been in the village long and he was borrowing more and more. I was concerned for him. Some of my clients become like family.'

'So he borrowed money often?'

'Three or four times a month.'

'Did he pay you back?' Chupplejeep asked.

Sanjog's face soured. 'Usually yes. This time, no.'

'Why did he need so much money? He wasn't sending it back home,' Pankaj said.

'The villages suffer from two main vices: alcohol addiction and gambling. Sandeep was a driver so drinking was not a good habit to have — although it has been known.'

'So the man was a gambler?'

Sanjog shook his head from side to side in agreement. 'He came from Kukurul. It's a much bigger

162

village than Utol. Time in small villages passes slowly. He needed some time pass.'

'Oh, I think our Mr Shah found plenty of time pass,' Chupplejeep said, thinking of Lavita and Utsa. 'When did you lend him this money?'

'A month ago.'

'He didn't pay any of it back.'

'No.'

'Hmm, I see. Isn't that odd? Or do you give such long payment terms?'

'I told you he usually paid. I knew him. He asked for another week. I didn't think it would hurt. Then the bugger ends up dead under a coconut tree, much like this one,' Sanjog said, pointing to one just outside in the café garden.

All three of them looked up. There were a couple of tender coconuts, ripe for plucking.

'I thought he was like family?' Pankaj asked. 'Yet, you're not showing much remorse?'

'I didn't kill him if that is what you are thinking.' Sanjog moved his gaze from the top of the coconut tree back to Pankaj.

'When did you last see him?' Chupplejeep asked.

'Must be the week before his death. The money was due. I had given him a full month. That's when he asked for an extension of time to pay.'

'Did you go to his lodgings?'

'I've never been there. He, *tho*, came to the house. Ask my Kamana?'

Pankaj blushed.

163

'The fact he owes you money gives you motive for murder. Will you just write off the seven thousand rupees?' Chupplejeep asked.

'Where is the motive? The debt is still there. It is up to his family to pay.'

'They are in mourning,' Chupplejeep said, giving Sanjog a firm look.

'Maybe I'll write this one off then,' he said sheepishly.

'Good idea. Seven thousand is not much to someone like you. I'll know if you don't keep your word. Now please tell me your whereabouts on the tenth November.'

Sanjog looked away from Chupplejeep and Pankaj. He took the last sip of his chikoo shake. 'I've a terrible memory. I usually have to write everything down.'

'Didn't your wife speak to you? I thought you would have had enough time to think. Come on, we need to know.'

'Detective, she mentioned it, but I didn't think that I would be classed as a suspect. Really, my mind is a blank. You see, she lost her diary.'

'Okay, so no alibi. I advise you to have a good think and tell me if you remember your whereabouts, because right now you're looking like the number one suspect. You have motive and opportunity. Your wife was away, na?'

'I must have been at home alone, watching television, perhaps. On the ninth I went to a wedding. I was there from sundown till when the sun came up

164

again. Excellent wedding. You know Kaur's daughter? He gave a proper wedding for her. You know what these Sikh weddings are like, too much alcohol. Yes, I must have not been feeling so good the next day. It was in Margao. It was a long way to travel back that night.'

'Well, don't leave town any time soon,' Chupplejeep said. He stood up and Pankaj did the same. 'Come on Pankaj, lets get the bill.'

'I already paid, sir. I had to, when I collected the drinks.'

Chupplejeep put his hand to his head and tutted. Goa was becoming too modern for its own good.

Chapter Twenty

'Gonsalves's story matches Sanjog's and despite his thuggish appearance, I think he's telling the truth,' Chupplejeep said. He heaved himself into the faded blue Maruti. 'The last time Gonsalves saw Sandeep was late in October when he visited him at his home and cleared his debts. The total was six thousand rupees.'

'So Sandeep lied to Sanjog about how much he owed?' Pankaj said.

'He either wanted some extra money for gambling or perhaps our loan shark lied.'

'Why?'

'To extort the money from Gita Shah and her parents. Unless he thought Sandeep came from a well-off family. Remember it isn't only the seven thousand rupees that is owed, it's the interest as well. Loan sharks take solid interest. Think about how much thirty per cent interest on seven thousand rupees would be? That's how these sharks work. How else do you think they make their money?'

Pankaj tried to do the math, but arithmetic was not his strong point. He was better off waiting till he had a calculator. 'You think Gonsalves is innocent?'

'He and his thugs have alibis. Luckily for him it was his fiftieth birthday. They were all celebrating in Morjim – far away from the scene of the crime. I checked with the owner of the bar where they were celebrating. They had hired the establishment for the full night and didn't leave till gone six in the morning. The owner said they could barely walk. They drank the bar dry.'

'I can believe that, sir.'

'Sanjog is still a suspect though,' Chupplejeep said.

'Sandeep Shah owed Sanjog seven thousand bucks. Maybe he found out Sandeep only needed six thousand and got angry. After all, he was doing him a favour by lending him so much money. I bet Sanjog went to threaten him. He lured Sandeep out of his room and *phatack*, he couldn't control his anger and hit him on his head. Or perhaps he hit him because Sandeep wasn't paying back the money he owed.'

'Don't run away with your thoughts, Pankaj.'

'It could have happened that way, sir. From what I hear in the village, Sanjog doesn't have any *goondas* working for him. He operates alone so he can keep all the money he makes. You see a man who operates with no helper means business. Who would want to go around making threats when you could pay someone to do it on your behalf? He's a very greedy fellow and greed leads to violence. See how he lied to us when we saw him coming out of that house.'

'Life is full of characters like Sanjog. The older you get, the more you realise this. Even Poirot said men always tell such silly lies.'

Chupplejeep started the car. 'I was speaking to one of the police force down in Sangolda. Sanjog started his loan shark business there. From what this fellow was saying, Sanjog doesn't use thugs for a reason. Apparently he used a thug once, a long while back, when he was just starting out. This thug accompanied him to this house of a poor fisherman who had borrowed money for a new fishing net. Before they entered the house, Sanjog said to his only employee, "If he doesn't pay you make him. I want everyone to know I'm not someone who they can mess with."'

Pankaj leaned in to listen to the story.

'They entered the house and Sanjog was shocked to see the state in which this poor fisherman lived. The old man was looking after his sick mother and child. Apparently, the fisherman begged Sanjog to spare him and give him another week to pay back the debt. He explained that his wife had run off just that week with a local cook leaving him to look after his family by himself. Sanjog had opened his mouth to say something but the words would not come, he was too disturbed to say anything. You see, Sanjog came from money – his father was wealthy so he never really saw how these villagers lived. This was the first time he had seen such squalor.

'The thug employed by Sanjog was heartless though. He didn't care. He knew he would only get paid if his boss got paid. So, towering over the fisherman, he snapped the man's little finger. The fisherman started wailing, the daughter and the fisherman's mother started crying too. Sanjog stood there in shock, still saying nothing. The thug broke the fisherman's second finger – more wailing, more crying.

'Finally, Sanjog spoke and told the thug to leave, ensuring he would pay him in any event. When the sobbing stopped, he told the fisherman to forget the debt. That say he walked out of Sangolda and moved to Utol. From then on he vowed never to employ any thugs ever again.'

'Shut up, sir!' Pankaj said, his mouth gaping. 'If that were true, nobody would pay up.'

'On the contrary, villagers are good people. They heard the story and they made sure they paid back what they owed. That poor fisherman thought the thug was going to kill him. He must have been singing Sanjog's praises for years. Villagers borrow from Sanjog because they know he will not harm them and ultimately they pay him back. They don't want to get a reputation for not paying and they know sooner or later they'll need money again for something or the other. They don't want to go to a shady character like Gonsalves.'

'I'm not convinced.'

Chupplejeep looked at Pankaj and back at the road. He smiled. 'Exactly, Pankaj. This is just a tale told to me by some old policeman from Sangolda. It's not fact. It's just speculation. We need proper evidence.'

'Sanjog's holding on to some anger,' Pankaj said, remembering a recent talk show on emotions. He had hoped it would have helped him with Shwetika but the show made no mention of loving someone from afar. It was all about letting go of anger. 'It's odd for a loan shark to be so considerate. If Sanjog is a quiet soul, he may have been storing up his fury. I think that possibly all this rage came out the night he went to see Sandeep. If we need hard evidence, what about the trace evidence and fingerprints from the crime scene?'

'Several fingerprints were lifted, but Kulkarni's team have matched them all to the Laljis, Lavita and Utsa. They all had reason to be there. No suspicious fingerprints were found. Soon, I should get the analysis from the hair that was found on the body as well as the other hairs found in his room. But Lavita and Utsa have both confessed to being in his room so that rules them out as having been somewhere they shouldn't.'

'The hair on the body would provide evidence though.'

'But it won't prove much in court, Pankaj. It could have been picked up by Sandeep whilst he was in his room.'

'Sir, if you don't mind me saying. This case is going nowhere.'

'I have a lead.'

'You do?'

'The Goa Dairy man you spoke to in Joe's Taverna has identified the man he saw on the night of the murder.'

'How? He didn't know who it was.'

'He happened to see a photo in the *Larara Express* showing the same man who was lurking around the village in the early hours of the morning, the day Sandeep Shah's body was found.'

'A tall man?'

Chupplejeep nodded. He pulled out the article from his shirt pocket and handed it to Pankaj.

Pankaj studied the picture. It showed three generations; a mother, father, daughter and baby. The caption read: *Extended Family of Sandeep Shah.*

Chapter Twenty-one

'So you really think Neeraj Dhaliwal did it?' Pankaj asked as they parked up some distance away from the Dhaliwals' house.

'There are several people who could have done it, Pankaj.'

'I know. The list is long, sir. Firstly, there is Bala with no alibi – not only ragged at school by Sandeep Shah, but he is further humiliated when the driver ignores him. To add insult to injury his rival is now a driver, which according to our baker is an elevated position in society. The final straw for this poor chap is that Sandeep is also dating the love of his life. Several motives there, plus the stain on his shirt when we interviewed him. To me it looked very much like blood. I wish we could have taken it straight to Kulkarni for testing. We should have asked him for it. He was adamant it was grease.'

'Kulkarni said that the blood splatter was minimal. That was a large stain on his shirt. Also would you wear the same shirt you murdered someone in if you knew there were police sniffing about?'

'Blood had oozed out of Sandeep's head. We saw it. And minimal blood is still blood. Also when blood is absorbed by cloth it looks bigger. He could have picked it up from when the body fell. And as to why he was wearing the same shirt, maybe he put it on by mistake. Maybe he has two shirts like that and he thought it was the clean one. And then there was the stone figurine of his mother's that was missing. All the models had round heads and are solid stone. I bet that stone could make some damage.'

'Then there is Lavita and Utsa. They were in some kind of love triangle.'

'More like a love hexagon, sir.'

'Oh yes, your friend Sailesh is also a suspect.'

'Sir, I didn't mean – ' Pankaj started.

Chupplejeep interrupted as he swerved the car, avoiding a goat in the road. 'Passion is a big motive for murder. Sailesh loves Utsa and he knew Sandeep was trying it on. Maybe he knew Utsa liked the driver also. You have to admit there is motive there also.'

'But sir, was the crime really one of passion? I studied in class that passionate crime is often frenzied. This was one fatal blow to the head. Not a hundred stab wounds.'

'Murders are never textbook, Pankaj. But money could also be a motive in this case.'

'We've ruled out Gonsalves but Sanjog had money as a motive, plus he has no alibi. Sandeep owed Sanjog a lot of money.'

'And then of course there is this house,' Chupplejeep said, looking at the whitewashed house in front of him.

The one-eyed cat padded over to the Maruti and mewled.

'The father-in-law Neeraj, and the wife of the deceased, Gita Shah. From what Lavita said, if it's true, we have reason to suspect that Gita Shah was having relations with her husband's friend. Another suspect to add to our list.'

'Karma, sir.'

Chupplejeep tilted his head and looked at Pankaj.

'Not that he died, sir. Sandeep was sleeping around. It's karma that his wife was doing the same.'

Chupplejeep pulled his key out of the ignition. 'Come on Pankaj, let's pay them a visit.'

~

Paavai Dhaliwal and a welcoming smell of simmering guava jam greeted them at the door.

'Come in, please make yourselves comfortable,' Paavai said with a smile. 'Can I get you any drinks?'

'Water's just fine for us.'

'I'll bring you some *kul kuls*. I bought them fresh this morning from Miranda's.'

Detective Chupplejeep's eyes lit up at the thought of the deep-fried dough. 'We need to speak with your husband.'

Paavai frowned. 'Yes, you called my neighbours youse. Neeraj is just in the bathroom making himself ready,' she said as she disappeared into the kitchen.

Chupplejeep and Pankaj waited silently in the sitting room. They heard a loud clanking sound coming from the kitchen and peered in that direction.

'Oh you're here already,' Neeraj said from the hallway.

Chupplejeep and Pankaj turned back to face him.

Neeraj fiddled with the buttons on his *kurta* as he made his way over to the sitting room. He sat next to Chupplejeep, slipped off his *chappals* and put his feet up. Chupplejeep noticed that his eyes were focused on Paavai who had returned to the room with a tray of drinks and an earthenware bowl full of snacks. He waited till he was offered and then immediately took a handful of the golden brown treats.

'Can I ask where you were on the tenth November, in the evening? The night of the tenth November to be exact,' Pankaj asked.

'Of course. I have thought about that evening many times. My poor daughter has lost her soul mate.' Paavai made a sad face and wiped her eyes with her peacock blue *dupata*.

'So madam, where were you?' Pankaj pressed.

'At my sister's in Diwar, near Old Goa. She has a youse there. We are very close, my sister and I.'

'You go there often?'

'Sometimes I go Saturday and I stay till Sunday, sometimes on weekdays too. If I go for the day, I try to be home before sunset to make my Neeraj his dinner. On weekends like the tenth I came yome the next morning.' Paavai put her hand on husband's knee.

Neeraj smiled. 'She looks after me well.'

'And can you give us your sister's address?'

'Of course, Detective,' Paavai said. Then she raised an eyebrow. 'Surely we are not suspects, no? We are family.'

Chupplejeep smiled. 'Just standard questions we have to ask everyone. It's a process of elimination.'

'I wouldn't want you to worry my sister.'

'We'll explain when we speak to her.'

Paavai narrowed her eyes at her husband and removed her hand from his leg. 'If I had a telephone I could have explained myself.'

'And, sir, were you with your wife that evening?' Pankaj asked.

Chupplejeep noticed Neeraj glance at his wife.

Paavai answered. 'I normally visit my sister alone. Neeraj doesn't like to make the trip. It's a long way from Kukurul to Diwar just to listen to two women gossiping. Neeraj would have been at yome alone.'

'Were you, sir?' Chupplejeep asked. 'Were you alone at home?'

Again, Neeraj looked at his wife.

'Tell them, na? You were at yome alone,' Paavai said, her smile fading.

'Yes, yes. Of course I was,' Neeraj said, with some hesitation. 'I was at home.'

'Are you sure?' Chupplejeep probed. 'You don't seem very sure.'

'I'm sure, Detective. I remember what I was doing the day…' Neeraj trailed off mid-sentence. He looked towards the ceiling fan and back down again to meet Chupplejeep's eyes. '…I can't believe he's dead. My only son-in-law.'

'We're sorry for your loss, sir, madam,' Pankaj said.

Paavai nodded.

'Can anyone vouch for you being at home? Were you alone all night?' Chupplejeep asked.

'Well, first I was babysitting,' Neeraj said.

Paavai laughed. 'Look at him. Babysitting, never. He does not know the first thing about babysitting. He means our daughter and Ashu were here.'

Neeraj was silent.

'Is that so?' Pankaj asked. 'Can we check with your daughter?'

'Of course,' Paavai interjected, 'she'll tell you, no problem. Gita will be yome from work soon.'

'Hm-hmm,' Neeraj cleared his throat. His eyes flicked again towards the ceiling fan. 'Well, not exactly.'

Paavai's smile disappeared.

'Gita went out. I was babysitting.'

Paavai shook her head. 'He doesn't know what he is saying. He really doesn't know how to babysit. He never looked after Gita when she was a child, wouldn't know what to do with a baby. And where would our Gita go? Tell me?' Paavai let out a nervous giggle.

Detective Chupplejeep looked at Neeraj and back at Paavai. 'You know it maybe better if we interview your husband alone. Would you mind?' Chupplejeep asked.

Paavai's face contorted. 'Neeraj has nothing to hide. There is nothing he can't say in front of me.'

'Gita has friends, Paavai. She has to have a life also. She can't just be looking after Ashu and working.'

Paavai tutted. 'Which of her friends did she go to see?'

'Who knows? She's young. She has friends.'

Paavai turned to her husband. 'I know she has friends. Don't speak to me in front of these officers like I am not letting her go out with her friends.' Paavai turned back to Chupplejeep and Pankaj and smiled. 'I just wanted to know which of her friends she was seeing. That is all.'

'Does she leave you with the baby often?' Pankaj asked.

'Some evenings.' Neeraj mumbled.

'Oh I see. She does, does she?' Paavai retorted.

Chupplejeep sighed. 'Tell me, did you know that your son-in-law was a gambler?'

Neeraj was silent.

Paavai eyed her husband then she turned back to Chupplejeep. 'No, that I know is not true. My husband used to dabble with games. You know how men are sometimes, Detective. He was friends with Sandeep. He would have never let our daughter marry a gambler.'

Neeraj slipped his feet back to the floor and into his *chappals*. He avoided the glare of his wife.

'You stupid fellow!' Paavai shouted at her husband.

Neeraj winced.

'Madam,' Chupplejeep said, rising to his feet. 'I think we should finish this interview alone with your husband.'

Paavai's shoulders dropped. She sighed loudly, stood up and gave her husband a look, which made Chupplejeep sit back down. Paavai stood next to her husband as if she was waiting for him to defend her right to be there.

Neeraj carried on looking at the floor.

'Madam, it'll be quicker this way,' Pankaj said.

'Hmpf.' Paavai adjusted her sari blouse and shuffled over to the kitchen, mumbling something inaudible.

The three men watched her until she was out of sight.

'So Mr Dhaliwal,' Pankaj started.

'Please call me Neeraj.'

Chupplejeep twisted one end of his moustache. So Sandeep and Neeraj were both gamblers, casting even more suspicion on Neeraj. 'Did Sandeep owe you money?'

'If you're trying to find a motive, you'll find none. I didn't harm that man. Yes I knew that like me, he was a gambler. I regret introducing him to my family.' Neeraj looked towards the kitchen. 'My wife will never forgive me, but I did not murder Sandeep. I couldn't. He is…was my daughter's husband.'

'But you didn't answer the question. Did he owe you money?'

179

Neeraj looked ashamedly at the floor. 'He paid off my debts once and I returned the favour before he left for Utol.'

'How much and when?'

'Some time back. Maybe two years ago he had paid four thousand rupees I had owed before he married Gita. Just before he left for Utol, I cleared his debts to some *goondas* from Belgaum for less than half that amount.'

'You're getting this down, Pankaj?' Chupplejeep asked.

'Yes, sir.'

'So your daughter was out, and you were looking after the baby. Until what time was that?'

'My daughter arrived home at around midnight, I think.'

'And then?'

'Ashu was sleeping.'

'What time is the baby normally put to bed?'

'Seven-thirty,' Neeraj said. He fiddled with his kurta.

'And do you ever leave Ashu alone and go out when the baby is asleep?'

Neeraj looked at the detective with wide eyes. 'Never.'

The one-eyed cat jumped up and nestled itself on Neeraj's lap. He scratched the pet behind its ear.

'I'm not a fool, Detective. I would not leave a helpless baby by itself.'

'And did your daughter see you when she came back at midnight?'

'She did.'

'Do you know who Gita was with?'

Neeraj shrugged.

'You sat and talked to your daughter when she returned?' Chupplejeep asked.

'No. I said hello and then we both went to our own rooms to sleep.' Neeraj hesitated. 'Have you ever looked after a baby?'

Chupplejeep shook his head. No, he didn't have a baby to look after and he didn't want to be reminded about such things.

'Looking after a child is very tiring,' Neeraj said.

'So you just went straight to bed and you were there all night till the eleventh November?'

Neeraj nodded.

'That's odd, don't you think, Pankaj?' Chupplejeep said.

'Very odd, sir.'

'*Che*, why is that?' Neeraj asked. His eyes darted upwards and then towards the kitchen.

'Because we have an eyewitness who places you in the village of Utol around the time of Sandeep Shah's death.'

'That's impossible. Kukurul and Utol are at least one hour away from each other. What a hassle that would be.'

'But there was enough time to go there and come back in the dead of night without raising suspicion.'

'Who said they saw me there?'

'This is a murder investigation. We cannot disclose who has told us this information.'

'Listen, Detective, clearly I'm a suspect.' Neeraj whispered the last word glancing towards the kitchen. 'There might be a death in this house tonight after what you said to my wife. She'll kill me after finding out that I knew Sandeep was a gambler when I introduced him into our home. But she'll make mincemeat of me if she thinks I did the boy any harm.'

'You shouldn't joke about murder when you have just lost your son-in-law in suspicious circumstances,' Chupplejeep said.

Neeraj bowed his head and mumbled an apology.

'If someone reports seeing a stranger in their village the same night of a murder, we have to follow up the lead. We wouldn't be doing our jobs if we didn't.'

'They are all drunks in that village,' Neeraj said.

'Ah, so you know the village well?'

'No, I know no one else in that village, apart from my late son-in-law.'

'That's interesting because I spoke to the Da Costas' *dhobi* yesterday and he told me something different. He told me you knew about Sandeep and his flirtations in the village. I don't know how I would feel if I found out my son-in-law was cheating on my daughter,' Chupplejeep said, even though he had no daughter to speak off. 'Did you keep this from your wife as well?'

Neeraj rubbed his forehead with the palm of his hand.

'You can tell us why you were in Utol that night now, or I can call you into the station tomorrow for questioning. You're not planning on going anywhere, are you?'

Neeraj looked towards the kitchen. There was a thin film of sweat on his brow. 'I wasn't in Utol that day,' he said, scratching his nose. 'Call me to the station if you must.' Then he rose to his feet and asked them to leave.

CHAPTER TWENTY-TWO

'*Chya*,' Ramesh said, sucking on his *beedi*.

Sailesh put his lips to a bottle of Kingfisher, avoiding his father's stare. How could he have let this happen? Why didn't someone tell him that his father had been moved to a construction project next to the cross? He knew it was game over for him because if his father knew, it wouldn't be long till his mother also knew. Then the drama would really start.

Raja's words rang in his ears. 'What will you do when you are taking the *pheras*, vows, around the ceremonial fire? You can't pretend to your family then! Grow up Sailesh. Just tell them.' Raja had been right. Sailesh knew he had to tell his father the truth if he wanted to live out his dreams, not those of his parents.

He looked at his father whose expression was blank. Once again he silently cursed himself for making out with Utsa in their usual spot. It was a stupid place to make out. There had been several other young couples there, sitting on bikes or hiding in cars, because unmarried Goans in Larara usually had no other place to go.

Utsa had been the one to spot his father, staring down at them from the first floor of a half-built house. She had made a quick exit, jumping off his bike and running towards her village. He had been left to face his father on his own. But he couldn't blame her. It was bad enough when your father gave you a telling-off, let alone someone else's.

'What is this?' Ramesh had asked Sailesh as several cars and bikes started their engines and sped off. 'Is this what I want to see whilst I am at work?' Father and son matched each other in height and build, but Sailesh wanted the ground to open up and swallow him. Ramesh had tutted and shaken his head. His parents had the disappointed look down to a tee. Sailesh had crossed his arms and looked back at his father, bracing himself for the tirade of abuse he was sure would follow.

Silence.

Eventually, when tiny beads of sweat had started to form on his forehead and he had begun to bite his nails, Ramesh asked, 'You like this girl? Or are you just having fun?'

Sailesh had unfolded his arms. All the other couples had left. A lone granny was walking with some flowers to the cross. Looking away from the old lady, he studied the red dust particles on his bike instead of looking back at his father. Was it a trick question? He bit his lip as he weighed up his answers. If he said yes, there would be a whole host of other questions – an inquisition as to how he met her, what caste she was, what her parents did. And then when they found out she was a servant, his pop would tell his mom and then there would be fireworks – solid fireworks. He could hear his mother's wailing in his ears already. They might even send him to his *kakaa's* house in Mangalore. Sailesh shuddered. Mangalore was the back of beyond and he had no intentions of leaving Utsa or Goa.

If he told his father he was serious about Utsa and his mother found out, then no doubt, she would closely examine Utsa's reputation. And if that happened, the whole Sandeep Shah business would come out. He couldn't afford for that to happen. Why had he not met Utsa before she met that rascal? He pushed the thought of the dead man to the back of his mind. Thinking about Sandeep Shah wasn't going to help him answer his father's question.

On the other hand, if he said he didn't like Utsa and was just fooling around, he would just be stalling from telling his parents the truth. In which case they may think he was giving himself a bad reputation and try and marry him off. And he had to tell them some day because he had decided that he wanted to marry her.

'Come on son, spit it out. You like her or not?'

'I don't know.'

'I see, son. Then I think we need to have a talk. You wait here. I'm going to tell the contractor I have a family emergency then I am taking you for a drink.'

Now sitting in Pinto's, with yellow paint on the walls and a faded Lipton Iced Tea sign painted behind the bar, Sailesh tried to pre-empt what his father was going to say. Ramesh raised his hand to catch the waiter's attention and ordered another two Kingfishers.

'So, who is she?' Ramesh asked, lighting a *beedi*.

'Utsa.'

'Oh, so it's true,' Ramesh said, blowing cigarette smoke towards the open door. 'Your mother has already told me about her.'

Sailesh raised his shoulders and sunk his head. He started pulling at the label of the beer bottle. He was stupid to have thought his mother wouldn't have known already. She was such a gossipmonger. It made sense now why she was so adamant to tell him about the shame Lipi's son had brought on his parents.

'Your mother, she thought it was a passing thing. Now she's going to have a heart attack, for sure. For sure, she is going to have one.'

'How does she know?'

'*Chya,* I hate these gossiping folk. More often than not it's all bloody hearsay.' Ramesh took a sip of his beer and another pull on his *beedi*. 'I overheard your mother mention it to her sister on the phone the other day,' he said as he blew out smoke. 'She's worried. Confidently your mother said you were having some fling. That is the only reason why my ears pricked up. It's not often your mother tells her sister about her son's girlfriend. I thought there must be a problem with this girl. Then I overhear your mother say that this girl is a *daasi*. I was sure this was false.' Ramesh shook his head and stubbed out his roll-up. 'When I saw you today, I needed to find out who it was. I was hoping it wasn't Utsa so I could tell your mother to stop listening to idle gossip. I didn't expect you to be with *that* girl.'

Sailesh clenched his teeth as he heard his father refer to Utsa as a *daasi*, servant. It was a dirty word. He took another swig of beer. Gossips were bloody everywhere. You couldn't do anything in Goa without some pokey-nose finding out. 'You'll tell Mom?'

'I don't like keeping things from your mother.' Ramesh lit another *beedi*. 'But at the same time, you children always want to rebel. And I don't want to be the one who pushes you further into her arms.'

'Her name's Utsa,' Sailesh found himself saying.

Ramesh shook his head. 'See, son, you must forget this girl. She'll only bring you pain. I'm telling you for your own good. This girl's mother must be super-pleased that her daughter has met someone in a better class, someone with his own business, even.'

Sailesh studied the tablecloth.

'Look at me, son.'

He lifted his head towards his father.

'You must not forget that you are an eligible bachelor. You could have your pick of girls.'

'People talk too much in the villages.'

'Your mother was thinking that this girl's *mai* must be the one spreading the rumours about you. Telling all her friends that her daughter has bagged a good prize.'

'So now you too are gossiping?'

'Son, I am only repeating what your mother is telling me. I have to listen to my wife, no?'

'Utsa's mother isn't happy about it,' Sailesh said, looking at the brown beer bottle. He knew from speaking to Utsa that her mother had only found out about them this morning. It had been the reason why he had picked her up from the circle and taken her to the cross. He was trying to make her feel better. Utsa had no choice, she had to tell her mother because she had been harassing her about the Sandeep Shah situation. Sailesh gripped his beer bottle tighter, remembering the faint mark on Utsa's cheek where her mother had shown her anger

'So her mother knows,' Ramesh said, stubbing out his cigarette. 'This must be serious, son. Once a servant girl meets someone, she's expected to marry. They only have their reputations going for them so they have to close the deal fast. I don't want to hurt you, son, but from what I hear this Utsa had been going with that driver.'

Sailesh shifted in his chair.

'You know which driver I am talking about? The dead one found in Utol.'

Sailesh was silent.

Ramesh eyed his son. 'You're not involved with any of that are you?' Then in the same breath he answered for him, 'No. Of course not.' He swallowed the remainder of his beer and wiped his mouth with his handkerchief. 'But still you're involved with a maid. This has to stop.'

Sailesh knew what his father was about to say. He was going to threaten him with his uncle's house. He couldn't manage without Utsa, she meant the world to him. He had once said to her, that he would do anything for her and he had already proved that he would. If it meant standing up to his parents for her, then so be it. Speaking to his parents about her should have been far easier than what he had already done, but somehow it wasn't. He carried on peeling the label off his beer bottle.

'Don't look so dejected,' Ramesh said rubbing his forehead. 'In India, three out of four youngsters experience forbidden love. Forbidden love is a double-edged sword. You forbid it and it makes you want that person even more. When you love someone your family hates…no, hate is too strong a word. When you love someone your family dislikes then you feel even more bound to your love. It's you and your lover against the world. You feel like Dona Paula and Gaspar Dias, no?

'Dona Paula?' Sailesh asked. Dona Paula was a place on a hill near Panaji. What was his father talking about? Gaspar Dias was a tennis club.

'You don't know the legend? *Chya.*' Ramesh leaned in towards his son. 'No wonder you have landed up this way. Madam – or Dona, as the Portuguese say – Paula was in love with Gaspar Dias. Their parents forbade their love, so they tied themselves together and jumped off the jetty in the place we now call Dona Paula. They said they'd rather die together than live separately. Like Romeo and Juliet. But, son, life is not like these legends. You and Utsa are not Gaspar Dias and Dona Paula. That is all *naatak*, nonsense. You'll not tie yourselves together and jump off a jetty. Trust me. You'll probably run off, get married and live in a hut somewhere. If your families don't get on or accept whom you marry, what will happen after one year, two years? Tell me? Who will help look after your babies? Who will you tell your problems to? You'll have nobody. Your friends will be busy with their own lives. They won't have time for you and you'll have estranged yourselves from your family. Then you will resent marrying this girl. See, Sailesh, I am telling you for your own good.'

'But Pop,' Sailesh said, straightening in his chair. He slumped back down again. It was no use trying to plead with his father. 'You wouldn't understand. Mom was your true love.'

His father's face softened. 'Son, there are many things you don't know about me. Like I said, three out of four Indians face this problem.'

'You too were in love with someone you shouldn't have been?'

'I didn't say that,' Ramesh said.

'You married straight after college. And you studied in Ahmedabad when your parents lived in Mumbai. Oh…now I see, I see it clearly. They sent you away, didn't they? Nana and Papa sent you away because you were seeing someone you shouldn't have.'

'Your mother was the only woman for me. She still is.'

Sailesh noticed a brief flicker of something in his father's eyes. Was it empathy? Nostalgia for a past lover?

'Son, there is a lot to think about before you go falling in love. You'll realise this as you get older.'

191

He smiled. His father had been a young man too and he had been in love. He must have known what it was like. 'Please Pop, don't start with this "when you get older" crap. In the West, people marry who they want and their parents accept it.'

'*Haan*, so now we are getting somewhere. You're thinking of marrying this girl?'

'I was just saying.'

'You're not in the West, sonny boy.'

'I don't know how I feel about her.'

'I can see how you feel, son. All this talk of love. If a boy of your age says he doesn't know how he feels for a girl, let me tell you it's something more than nothing. Men are too quick to say when they don't like a girl. Remember, I'm your father, I know you more than you think. Because that is my job! Regardless of the words coming out of your mouth I can see how you feel.'

Ramesh stood up and walked over to the bar to settle the bill.

~

Was there really any harm in his son marrying a Shudra? thought Ramesh as he drummed his fingers on the counter. Sailesh was making good money. He could support a wife if that's what he wanted.

The bartender interrupted his thoughts. 'Your change, sir.' He took the money and slid ten rupees back across the bar. A guilty feeling came over him, but he shook it away. He had done what his wife had asked and there was nothing more he could do.

CHAPTER TWENTY-THREE

Lavita stuck out her lower lip and folded her arms across her chest.

'Go change,' Mrs Lalji ordered, 'then peel those carrots if you are too precious to gut the chicken.'

Lavita would be glad to get out of the emerald-green satin number her aunty had shoehorned her into.

'Such a lovely colour,' Bala's mother had said, praising her aunty's good taste.

Of course, every Indian mother who wanted to marry off their useless son or daughter knew exactly what to say to win over the other family.

'It sets off your eyes,' Bala's mother had continued, grabbing Lavita by the chin and squeezing it. Mrs Mukherjee turned Lavita's face both sides so she could get a good look at her prospective daughter-in-law.

My eyes are the same colour as my skin: brown. There's no setting off of any eye colour here, Lavita had wanted to say but she held her tongue while her aunty wallowed in the compliments.

Now, Lavita hovered around the carrots whilst Granny and Aunty discussed the proposal.

'Such fair skin,' Mrs Lalji said. 'You heard Mrs Mukherjee, *beta*? She said you had such fair skin. What a lovely compliment?'

Lavita dragged her body to her bedroom with hunched shoulders and a scowl, but secretly she was happy. Fair skin was indeed a good compliment to receive. She picked up her face cream. It was new, with a promise to lighten skin colour. It only cost ten rupees more than her usual brand. The compliment had been proof that the cream was worth the extra money.

Lavita let her mind drift to Bala. He wasn't her type at all, but if she really thought about it, she could see some potential there. He adored her and she doubted that he would ever cheat on her, the way that Sandeep had. This way, she could always have the upper hand in their relationship. Also, he was a kind fellow, not just to his friends and family but to anyone he met. He was just that type. This included his mother and that was a good sign. If he treated his mother well he wouldn't treat her badly. That, Sonali said, was better than travelling abroad.

~

'You're too soft on that girl,' Granny Monji said, glancing over in the direction of Lavita's room.

The door was open. Good, Granny Monji thought, her niece would be listening. 'She'll have to learn to clean meat when she's married,' Granny continued, turning her attention back to the dead bird. 'You and Baba have spoiled that girl. No gutting meat, no going out to work, sleeping on a bed and now Star TV. That girl will think she's a *Brahmin*. See how Utsa works every day, she even sleeps on a tatami mat!'

'Lavita would be doing all that, if Baba's produce wasn't making so much money.'

Granny Monji shrugged.

'The Mukherjee mother seems nice,' Mrs Lalji said, changing the topic back to her niece's proposal. 'But I don't know, Mummy. Maybe Lavita is right. Is it all too soon?'

'Too soon? No, my child. You're lucky it's not too late.'

'Why?'

'Lavita is her mother's child. You never believed me before, I told you that your sister had been seeing a local driver before she died. She was getting ready to leave her husband before the fire. The fire only happened because of the bad luck she brought upon their house with her shameful behaviour. At least now with Sandeep out of the scene, we have been saved from another disaster like that.'

'Good luck, bad luck, it's all luck with you. Not this again, please.'

'We can learn from the past, na?'

'Leave the past in the past.' Mrs Lalji strained her neck to look in the direction of Lavita's bedroom. 'I don't want Lavita listening to such tall tales about her mother.'

Granny Monji shook her head. 'You haven't heard what they are saying in the village then?'

Mrs Lalji concentrated on picking grit and husks from the rice.

'Ah, so you have heard. That niece of yours has already got a reputation because of the driver. If we don't act fast she'll be damaged goods and we can't let that happen. Who wants a girl like that as a wife?'

'Maa, I wouldn't be surprised if you started those rumours yourself,' Baba said, walking into the room. Both women turned to look at him. He had changed out of his formal trousers into his comfortable shorts and singlet.

Granny Monji raised her hand to her mouth and focused on her son-in-law with her smaller eye. 'How can you say such a thing to your Maa?' She quickly turned to her daughter. 'See how your husband is treating me.' Granny Monji stuck her hand inside the carcass of the chicken and pulled out its bloody innards whilst waiting for the apology that she was sure would follow.

Mrs Lalji made a face at her husband.

'Maa, I didn't mean it,' Baba said, hovering around his wife.

'Don't lie. I can tell when you're lying.' Granny Monji wiped an invisible tear with the back of her hand.

'Oh come on, Mummy. He means it.'

Granny Monji cocked her head to one side. She looked at her son-in-law and frowned.

'What I'm saying is that we have to look carefully at the Mukherjees before we allow them to marry into our family,' Baba said.

'You can talk, Baba. Not once have I heard you tell your niece off for fooling around with that driver. It's a good job he died when he did.'

Baba picked a stone out of the rice and shrugged his shoulders.

'He is too embarrassed to talk to his niece about things like that,' Mrs Lalji said.

'Yes, because it is his wife's job,' Granny Monji said, rinsing the chicken under the tap. 'Your sister would have wanted this marriage for her daughter. I know my daughter would have wanted this.'

'Bala Mukherjee is still a suspect,' Baba added. 'And Lavita is still young.'

'That Sandeep has bought nothing but bad luck to Utol,' Granny said.

'Yes,' Mrs Lalji agreed. 'How will I find another lodger? Who will want to stay in a room where someone has died? Murdered even.'

'He didn't die in the room. He died outside,' Granny Monji said. 'If you want extra cash, send the girl out to work. Toughen her up a little.'

Baba asked what nobody was thinking. 'What about Lavita's opinion? What does she say?'

'She'll be fine. A match takes time to get used to,' Granny said confidently. 'I remember when my daughter first met you.'

'Oh really,' Baba said, rolling his eyes.

'Yes, Mummy, we all know that story,' Mrs Lalji said, as her mother opened her mouth to regale the tale. 'How many times do you want to repeat it?'

'We make a good living so we're not in a rush to marry off our only niece. We have to think of Bala's motives. Some men don't marry for love.' Baba winked at his wife. 'You women carry on chatting. It's six already and it's been a long day. I'm going to sit on the veranda and read the newspaper before the mosquitoes make an appearance.' Baba took the newspaper from the kitchen table and walked out.

'He's a *pau wallah*,' Granny Monji shouted after him, 'he makes more money than you!' She turned back to her daughter. 'Before this Sandeep Shah business, you were all set to propose the marriage to Lavita. Why are you worried now?'

Mrs Lalji stopped sieving the rice. She stood up and sat at the table, 'I was not sure, remember, I was considering Sandeep – '

'*Chup,* quiet,' Granny Monji said. 'Never speak like that again. You cannot go around telling people you were going to set your niece up with a married man.'

'But Mummy, I was only telling you.'

'Don't tell me. I don't want to know,'

'Mummy, about Sandeep, there are rumours spreading...'

'Yes, about your niece and – '

'No, Mummy, about Bala and Sandeep.'

Granny Monji washed her hands. 'They were not involved, were they? Really, if you tell me that then I'll have heard everything.'

'No, Mummy. Not involved, romantically.'

Granny Monji breathed a sigh of relief. If Bala was gay, she would have to do some serious thinking before she encouraged Lavita to marry him. Marrying a fellow who liked other fellows was a big burden to carry. Her sister had found herself trapped in that same position and had been depressed her whole life.

'Bala told me in deepest confidence two days before Sandeep's body was found dead that a man would bring shame on our house. I think Bala was going to do something about it.'

Granny smiled. She had overhead this conversation herself. 'So what? What Bala said was true. Sandeep would have brought shame on our house had he not been stopped.'

'Don't you see, Mummy? He told the police he didn't know who Sandeep was when the body was found. Now, I hear rumours that Bala knew Sandeep since school.'

'You didn't question him?'

'I wasn't thinking at the time. I suppose, I was in shock.'

'You didn't tell the police he said that?'

'I didn't want to add to the masala. Also I didn't want to incriminate myself.'

'Why would that implicate you? You don't have any motive to get rid of a driver.'

'It seems everyone knew Sandeep was making a fool of Lavita. They would say that I wanted to protect her name.'

'This is Utol, not some back-end Bihari village. We don't go around honour killing.'

'Murder also didn't happen in this village, but now it has. Bala knew Sandeep Shah well. Sandeep had ragged him in school. That is the latest rumour going around,' Mrs Lalji said. 'Before the police questioned him, no one knew. The police must have prised that information out of him.'

'That's their job.'

'But don't you find it strange that he denied ever knowing Sandeep? And now that the man is dead, Bala is marrying the woman he's been in love with ever since he was young. Everyone knows how much he loves Lavita, he doesn't make it a secret. If being bullied by Sandeep Shah wasn't a motive then maybe love was. Can I let a monster marry our Lavita?'

'Shhh,' Granny Monji said placing her finger on her lips. She walked over to the kitchen table, pulled out a chair and sat next to her daughter. 'Lavita will hear you. You want her to think that Bala is a murderer? We don't know if he has killed anyone. She'll have a good excuse not to marry him if you let her think that.'

Mrs Lalji put her head in her hands. 'I don't know what to do.'

'I'll tell you what we're going to do. We are going to encourage Lavita to accept his proposal.'

Mrs Lalji frowned.

'Don't look at me like that, child. What I'm saying will make sense. We'll get the priest to pick a wedding date, one that is good for a happy marriage and we'll continue with the plans. By the time the date for the wedding arrives, the police will have caught the crook who murdered the driver.'

'Wouldn't that ruin Lavita's reputation further if she were engaged to a murderer?'

Granny Monji ignored her daughter. 'That television your husband bought is rotting your mind. Stop watching *C.I.D.* and all that! I'm telling you that Bala Mukherjee is not a murderer. When has your mother ever been wrong?' she said with conviction. 'Bala is short. I doubt if he could even lift a cricket bat above his head. And the fellow is soft. He doesn't have the guts to murder anyone. Once I saw him avoid treading on a line of ants. Anyone who cares for ants isn't capable of murder. I'm sure of this. And in all years I've never been wrong.'

'Maybe you're right,' Mrs Lalji said, going back to the rice. 'I don't see Bala as a murderer either. This whole affair is so confusing.'

'Don't worry, *beta*. Don't worry.' Granny Monji watched her daughter silently sieve the remaining rice. She let her mind drift to the future, a future where she would be eating hot bread and having her grandson-in-law spoil her with new pickles and sweets. That's why Mrs Mukherjee was so plump, she thought. A baker's family knew how to eat. 'Maybe we'll have a monsoon wedding,' Granny Monji said. 'A nice monsoon wedding.'

Chapter Twenty-four

Lavita had had enough of listening to Granny and Aunty's conversation. By the time Granny threatened to tell the story of her aunt and uncle's first meeting, she closed the door and made her plan.

Whilst Granny Monji was planning Lavita's monsoon wedding, Lavita had jumped out of her window and slipped past the tallest coconut tree in the village. She had walked around the back of the garden and through the gates into the land behind the house. Lavita shuddered just remembering Sandeep's lifeless corpse in their back garden. She walked around Utsa's house to her friend's window and threw a small stone at it.

Utsa appeared with a grin. 'Come in,' she shouted.

'Quiet!' Lavita whispered. 'I don't want to have to make polite conversation with your mother. Where is she?'

'In the pantry. Here, jump over the balcony.'

She did as her friend suggested and silently slid into Utsa's room. The room was bare apart from two tatami sleeping mats on the floor; one for Utsa and one for her younger sister.

'Go,' Utsa ordered her sister, pointing her finger at the door.

'But where?' her sister asked.

'I don't care. Tell Mamma you'll help her with dinner.' Utsa gave the child a menacing stare until her sister had disappeared out of their room. 'So lucky you don't have any siblings, *yaar*,' she said to Lavita.

'Why are you looking so happy?'

'I can tell you now that my mother has found out.'

'Found out what?'

'I'm in love.'

'With who?'

'Sailesh Krinz.'

Lavita took a step back. 'The auto-man?'

'Yes.'

'Does he know?'

'Funny. We've been going out for some time. But today we were very foolish,' Utsa said with a coy smile. 'We were at the cross and his father caught us.'

'Very impressive, Utsa,' Lavita said with a grin.

'Shut up, I'm not like that. I love him. We love each other.'

'You love him or his money?' Lavita asked with a stab of jealousy.

'Don't be like that.'

'You got over Sandeep pretty quickly, given he was making eyes at you. See, he only had eyes for me,' Lavita said, trying to console herself. But she didn't feel any better for saying it. She had to admit it – Sandeep was a bastard. He had a wife and child and had been trying to make a move on her best friend. There was no way he was planning to run away with her. She had been foolish. Now, she was jealous of what Utsa had.

Utsa had been smart, keeping her relationship with Sailesh quiet. The girl had also managed to keep whatever she had with Sandeep underground as well. Lavita knew she had been thoughtless. She never told anyone she was dating the driver, but she was careless when they met because secretly she had wanted other girls to find out to make them jealous. But it had backfired. Instead, she had become a local laughing stock and now she was soiled goods. Only yesterday two boys had whistled at her. What shame! Thank goodness no one had been in the vicinity to witness it. Since yesterday she had been worried to go for walks with Granny. She imagined some boy whistling at her in front of her grandmother. That would be the end for her. They would marry her off to Bala the same day.

But perhaps Bala was the best solution for her. Utsa had found love; she could also find love with Bala. He still showed her respect, and she had to carefully consider that. Today, when she met him he had avoided the topic of Sandeep altogether. Yes, Bala was a good friend, but a good husband? She wasn't sure.

'You had a date today, didn't you? Meeting the Mukherjees. Forgotten Sandeep so quickly?' Utsa asked.

Lavita pouted.

'Sorry. That came out all wrong. I know what family can be like.'

'I suppose you jumped over the wall the night he died just to talk?'

'How did…?'

'You know Granny, she has eyes in the back of her head. She saw you. I heard her talking.'

'How does she see with that white film over her eyes?' Utsa asked, shaking her head.

'She sees everything.' Lavita walked over to her friend and hugged her. All this rivalry had driven a wedge between them, but now that Sandeep Shah was no longer in their lives they could go back to the way things were.

'I jumped over the wall just to talk,' Utsa said. 'Sorry, I lied before. I didn't want to see him that day, but I had to tell him to stop harassing me at work. I realised I was in love with Sailesh and I told him so.'

Lavita released her friend. 'And you went into his room that night, after I saw him.'

'I didn't know, Lavita, that you were in love with him. For me it was a bit of harmless flirting. Sailesh and me had just started to date. But we fell in love fast. When he found out about Sandeep – '

'He found out?'

'There was nothing to find out really. I couldn't help it if the driver was making eyes at me.' Utsa walked to her bed and sat down on the mat.

Lavita looked at her friend, her mouth ajar. 'You didn't discourage him, though.'

'Don't look at me like that. I've never had so much attention in my life. You can't blame me for enjoying it.'

'Double *Bhaji*.'

'It was foolish. I love Sailesh. He said he would do anything for me, and he did.'

'What did he do?'

'I wish now that I never met Sandeep.'

'So Sailesh knew that you and Sandeep were an item and he wanted to put an end to it?'

'No. Never!' she exclaimed.

'I hope you told the police this. Your boyfriend had a motive to kill Sandeep.'

'What? Have you gone crazy? Who would kill someone over some flirting?' Utsa scratched her neck. 'The police know that I spoke to Sandeep that night. That I jumped over the wall. Your meddling granny must have told them too.'

Lavita shrugged. 'Did the police take a hair sample from you?' she asked as she sat on a cushion next to Utsa.

'Yes.' Both girls looked at each other. Utsa bit her lip. 'What do you think they're going to do with them?'

'They must have found some evidence. They want to check our hair samples for DNA,' Lavita said. She had read something recently in the newspapers about this.

'What's DNA?'

'Never mind,' Lavita said, chewing on a fingernail. She wasn't quite sure herself how DNA worked but she knew it could help identify criminals.

'I'm the last known person to see him alive. What if I left one of my hairs there? My hair is always falling. Can they convict me of murder based on that alone? They may take me in for questioning again. They may want to speak to my mother. If there are too many questions, people will start talking. What if Sailesh's mother hears?' Utsa stood up and started pacing the room.

'I don't know,' Lavita said. Her hairs would be all over Sandeep's room too. 'The police know that we were both seeing Sandeep. We have reason to have been in his room, I guess. Stop pacing!' she shouted at her friend. It was making her feel nervous.

Utsa did as she was told and attempted a smile. 'I hope you're right. I wonder if they are taking samples of men's hair also? Perhaps not, if it was a long hair they found. Did they say?'

'No. They didn't say.'

Utsa began to pace again. 'Suppose hair from another person is found at the scene, hair which doesn't belong there, will that person be blamed?'

Lavita looked up at her friend. Was Utsa being her usual slow self, asking stupid questions? Or did she know something she was not sharing? It was time to find out the truth from her friend. 'Utsa, earlier, when you mentioned that Sailesh said he would do anything for you and that he already had, what did you mean?'

Chapter Twenty-five

'There is something Neeraj is not telling us,' Chupplejeep said to Pankaj as he shut the gate of the Dhaliwals' house behind them.

'All gambling men are suspicious,' Pankaj said.

'Have you never played the lotto, Pankaj?'

'Yes, sir, I've played.'

'And you've never visited one of those casino boats at Panaji jetty?'

'With Sailesh.'

'There's an entrance fee that you get back in chips, no?'

'Yes, sir.'

'You played on the roulette machine?'

'It was good fun,' Pankaj said with a grin.

'So, you too cannot be trusted,' Chupplejeep said.

Pankaj stopped in his tracks. He looked at his boss with his mouth open.

'Oh, sir,' he said with a smile. 'I see what you're saying.'

Chupplejeep laughed. He ruffled Pankaj's hair. 'Never mind. You're right, Pankaj, Neeraj is suspicious and the gambling is another lead to follow.'

'Neeraj looks after their grandchild often, yet his wife doesn't know. You'd think that would earn him some points with Paavai. Why would he keep that from her?'

'Pankaj, there are some things you don't know about women,' Chupplejeep said, thinking about Christabel. 'They have their own ideas about what earns you points or not.'

Chupplejeep closed his eyes, remembering an incident with Christabel not so long ago. He had bought her a large box of her favourite butterscotch chocolates. She ate the entire box in one sitting. This should have earned him enough points to cancel their planned dinner so he could watch the football at Joachim's. Joachim had a large television and Tata Sky. But only one hour after the chocolates had been digested, just as he was about to broach the subject of the game, he heard a scream from Christabel's bedroom. He ran to her, hoping that it wasn't a gecko she was shouting about. He could not face having to get rid of one of those creepy reptiles. He was relieved when he realised there were no house lizards in sight, but it was not all good news.

Christabel was shouting at him. How was he to know that she had put on two kilos since dating him? She was standing on the scales, wearing a peach colour dress but the zip was only half way up. Chupplejeep had to stand there for a full fifteen minutes whilst she accused him of fattening her up.

211

'You're doing this purposefully!' she shouted. 'I know your games. You want me to be fat so if I leave you I won't be able to attract any other men. This is your plan, is it not?'

Chupplejeep had stood in the doorway, his brow furrowed, wondering if all women had such twisted thoughts about life and love. But it did a strange thing to him. Instead of being angry, it made him love her even more. Christabel was beautiful when she was angry. And her angry moods never lasted for long. This thought alone had made him smile, and then he had to hear her screaming for another fifteen minutes about how insensitive he was.

The detective sighed and opened his eyes. Looking at Pankaj he said, 'It's best not to try to understand women. You'll soon realise that.'

Pankaj blushed. 'I hope so,' he said under his breath.

Chupplejeep shook his head. He had forgotten about Pankaj's unrequited love for Shwetika. 'Look, if you're thinking of Shwetika, you're better off being single for the time being. Once you start going steady with her it'll be game over. You'll be stuck like me – never saying the right thing. In fact, never knowing what to say! Women, I tell you! Really, their thought process is very different to ours.'

Pankaj shrugged. 'But it must be nice to have someone, right?'

Chupplejeep smiled. 'Right.'

The sun had set whilst they were interviewing Neeraj. Now it was dark outside and Chupplejeep and

Pankaj could barely see one another as they slowly walked to the car. Street lighting was minimal in Kukurul.

The gate they had just closed behind them creaked and they both spun around.

'Hello?' Pankaj said, looking towards the house.

They could see the light in the front room of the Dhaliwals' house was on. But that was all they could see.

Pankaj put his hand on his baton.

They could hear footsteps. A silhouette of a man started to approach them.

Pankaj unbuttoned the clasp holding his baton in place.

A squeal came from behind them.

Chupplejeep turned back towards the car as a pig ran towards him, nearly knocking him off his feet.

'Bloody…' Chupplejeep started.

'Detective?' came a barely audible whisper.

'Neeraj?' Chupplejeep said as he turned again and Neeraj's features became visible.

'Shhh,' Neeraj whispered, as he looked back at the house. 'I don't want my wife to know I'm talking to you.'

Chupplejeep nodded. Paavai didn't seem the type of wife to give her husband two minutes alone. She would know where he was and either come looking for him or be waiting inside ready to give him the third degree when he got back.

'She thinks I've gone to toilet,' Neeraj said as if reading Chupplejeep's mind.

'What is it you want to tell us?'

'It's about that night. The night Sandeep died.'

Chupplejeep pointed towards his car. They all walked towards it and Chupplejeep motioned for them to get inside. He realised he was going to miss dinner with Christabel again. He imagined her sitting alone at the dinner table thinking horrible thoughts about him. It made him sad, but there was nothing he could do. The case had to be solved. 'This better be good,' he said to Neeraj Dhaliwal. 'This better be very good.'

~

Neeraj filled in Chupplejeep and Pankaj on his association with Sandeep. How he had introduced him to the family and how he had let the marriage between the crook and his daughter take place. His hands were trembling as he spoke.

'That's a good story. You could sell that to Bollywood,' Chupplejeep said. 'But I want to know why you were in Utol in the early hours of November eleventh.'

'I told you, Detective, I wasn't – '

'I know what you told me. But I've been a detective for many years and I can see that you're lying. You're not a seasoned liar, that much I can tell. Inside the house you kept looking up and touching your nose. When people lie they look up for God because they know they are doing a bad thing. They also touch their noses because they are scared it will grow like Pinocchio. Seasoned liars

214

are worse – they look directly at you. The more you lie, the more you'll seem suspicious. Can you not see that?'

Neeraj was silent.

'Okay. Please leave this vehicle. I'll be back tomorrow morning with a warrant for your arrest.' Chupplejeep leaned across Neeraj to open the passenger door. 'Go back to your wife. I'm sure she'll have more questions for you when we come back tomorrow.'

Pankaj fiddled with his notepad and pen in the back of the car. What was Chupplejeep playing at? He was certain that if Neeraj were the culprit, he would do a bunk in the night. They may never be able to catch him.

'Wait…' Neeraj said.

Pankaj remembered to breathe.

'Okay.'

A silence followed. Pankaj opened his mouth to talk but then closed it again. Chupplejeep's advice rang in his ears. 'If a suspect begins to talk and then keeps quiet, don't say anything,' Chupplejeep had said. 'Silence is golden for a reason. Nervous suspects can't bear silence. They have to fill the void with words. If you allow silence for a long enough time, they crack.'

Pankaj started to click the push button of his ballpoint pen in and out, in and out.

Chupplejeep turned around and gave him a stern look.

The silence was obvious now. Even Pankaj could see Chupplejeep's nose begin to twitch. Just when thought that Neeraj wasn't going to speak, he spoke again. 'You were right. I was in Utol that night.'

'Now we're getting somewhere,' Chupplejeep said.

'I was the one who'd brought Sandeep into our lives. I had to do something about it. It started like this: Paavai had complained that he wasn't sending enough money home for Gita and Ashu. I told my wife not to worry.'

'You said you would speak to your son-in-law?'

'I never spoke to Paavai about Sandeep's gambling, but I was suspicious that he had broken his promise to me and had started gambling again. It explained why he was not sending any money home. Paavai didn't ask me outright if Sandeep was a gambling man and I didn't tell her. That way we were both not lying to each other. But I was sure she had her suspicions and I assumed she knew.'

Chupplejeep nodded. 'Marriages can be extremely complicated.'

'Did you go to Utol to speak to him about it, that night?' asked Pankaj.

'Once a gambler, always a gambler. I heard mumblings that Sandeep was losing. The people who knew found it funny because he had taken money off all of them in the past.'

'Before we go any further, I want to clear up something,' Chupplejeep interrupted. 'Did Sandeep Shah owe money to anyone in your group?'

'Not that I know of.'

'I want their names. All the gamblers in your group.'

Neeraj put his hand to his mouth. 'You cannot suspect those gambling fellows. We just play for pastime.

216

I don't think any one in that circle would stoop so low as to kill. And anyway they didn't have to – Sandeep left.'

'That is not the point,' Pankaj said.

'Don't worry, I'll be discreet. Their wives and neighbours won't find out anything,' Chupplejeep reassured him.

Neeraj reluctantly provided the names and addresses of the other gamblers that had played with his son-in-law whilst Pankaj scribbled them in his notepad.

'*Aacha*, so back to your story,' Chupplejeep said when Neeraj had finished. 'You were angry that he was no longer sending money?'

'Sandeep was family. I had to think of my daughter and their child. I don't make so much money that I can support them financially, forever. I was going to try and convince Sandeep to stop gambling – seek help, and of course try to convince him to start sending money home. The boy has no family of his own so I had to take it upon myself to guide him.'

'I think it was more than that. I think that you knew about his reputation with women. You knew if your daughter found out it would ruin her and you felt guilty. Why? Because you had introduced this man into your daughter's life, you wanted him to pay for his sins.'

'Never.'

'Why would you visit at one o'clock in the morning then? Why not visit in the day?' Pankaj asked.

'It was because he was up to no good, isn't that so?' Chupplejeep asked.

Neeraj hesitated. 'No.'

'No? Please don't lie anymore. I'm coming back tomorrow to arrest you.'

Neeraj rubbed his forehead with the tips of his fingers.

'Tell us what happened.'

Neeraj turned to face Pankaj. Then he turned back to Chupplejeep. 'You're correct,' he said.

'You killed Sandeep Shah?' Chupplejeep asked.

'No! You're right that I went to see him about his cheating on my daughter as well as the money issue. You see a couple of days before I went to visit my son-in-law, I asked around to see if what the *dhobi* said was true. What the *dhobi* told me about Sandeep's flirtations in Utol angered me.' Neeraj wrung his hands and narrowed his eyes. 'I had such anger in my heart. I wanted to…I wanted to…just…'

'Just what, Neeraj?' Chupplejeep leaned in towards the suspect.

'Just…I don't know, hurt him I suppose.'

'You admit that you wanted to cause harm to Sandeep Shah? The same man who is now dead.'

'I never killed him,' Neeraj said, holding his hands up in protest. 'I went to the village that night with the intention of hurting him. That's why I went so late. How could he do that to my daughter? They had a child together.'

'You spoke to him and things got out of hand. You couldn't control your anger. You hit him on his head.'

'Never.'

'You didn't mean to kill him. You just wanted to teach him a lesson.'

Neeraj shook his head.

'First you tell us that you were never in Utol – that was a lie. What's to say that this too is not a lie?'

'I'm telling the truth!' Neeraj said, pinching the skin on his neck. 'Mother promise.'

'You're not a child. Mother promise is not going to get you off the hook.' Chupplejeep hit his own forehead with his palm. '*Aye Saiba*! I'll have to take you in for questioning. Pankaj, make a note to get a search and arrest warrant for tomorrow.'

'Let me at least tell you what happened,' Neeraj pleaded, clasping his hands together and shaking them at the detective.

Chupplejeep nodded for him to continue.

'I left for Utol as soon as Gita came home. I crept out of the house after they went to sleep.'

'Another lie you told us earlier then.'

'I hitched a lift to Utol. If I had taken the scooter, some neighbour would have seen and told Paavai, even at that time at night. They see everything, these neighbours. But the light is not good so they would never have seen me leave the house on foot. I walked to the main road and hitched. I got dropped off at the top of the hill near the Da Costa house. It was simple, really. I walked down the side of the house unnoticed. I started walking towards the Laljis where I knew he was staying. As I was walking, I tripped and almost sprained my ankle.'

219

Neeraj looked back towards his house. All the lights were on now. 'My wife will wonder what I'm doing in the bathroom for so long. She must have banged on the door and realised I wasn't inside. She must know that I'm outside talking to you.'

'You sprained your ankle, and then?'

'I'll have to explain everything to her.'

'Carry on with your story.'

'It was a rock that I tripped on, a nice smooth rock. I picked it up. I was going to throw it far. After all, I had fallen on the bloody thing.'

'But then you thought it may come in handy for your meeting with Sandeep. Tell me, did he know you were coming?'

'I never told him.'

'A surprise attack!' said Chupplejeep. 'You hid the rock in your pocket or behind your back. Concealed by the darkness of the night and knocked on his door. You were filled with rage, after all, he had cheated on your daughter and brought shame on your family. Even the *dhobi wallah* was talking about it. You were worried everyone would know. This was the man you invited into your home. You introduced him to your own child and then allowed this monster to marry her.'

'You were driven to it,' Pankaj chipped in.

Neeraj was silent.

'You waited till he came outside and then hit him with the rock. When he fell, you panicked. Suddenly you were aware of your actions, of what they would mean.

You knew the police wouldn't spare you. So you hitched a lift back here and crept in to the house before sunrise.'

'That isn't what happened,' Neeraj protested. 'Where did your witness see me? Ask him that. I never even made it to the Lalji house.'

'Oh, we will,' Pankaj said even though he already had. What Neeraj was saying could have been true – the Goa Dairy man saw him near the church.

'You're right. I considered threatening him with the stone. You already know my reasons. But then I passed the church and it made me stop dead in my tracks.'

'Don't tell me all of a sudden you grew a conscience.'
'It's true.'

'You're not even Catholic.'

'I'm not Catholic, but God is everywhere, na? Something happened to me outside that church. I couldn't go through with my plan.'

'Where's this rock?'

'I threw it out on my way back. It's somewhere between Utol and Kukurul, in a ditch.'

Pankaj rolled his eyes. They would never find it. It wasn't even worth trying.

'At the church it was as if my legs couldn't move. I knew then some higher force was at work. The gods were telling me it was the wrong thing to do and there and then I promised God that I would not harm Sandeep Shah. I turned around followed the path to the top of the hill and hitched a ride back home.'

'That's how it happened?' Chupplejeep turned to Pankaj. 'You got all that?'

'Yes, sir.'

'Can you identify the two people who gave you lifts to and from Kukurul?'

'Both were mumbaikers passing through.'

'So we'll never find them to verify your story,' Pankaj said. 'Very convenient.'

'Don't leave this village any time soon,' Chupplejeep pointed to the car door.

Neeraj opened it and got out of the vehicle. Chupplejeep leaned over and pulled the door shut behind him.

Neeraj peered back down through the window. 'God took the life of Sandeep. He didn't want me to bloody my hands.'

'Sure,' Chupplejeep said before winding up the window, 'go tell that to your wife.'

Neeraj knocked on the glass. 'Detective, if you had a daughter you would know how much it hurts when the whole village knows her husband's business and you can see the pain in her eyes.'

Chupplejeep shook his head.

Pankaj climbed into the front seat. 'You think he's telling the truth?'

A ringing sound coming from Chupplejeep's breast pocket stopped him from responding. 'Christu, sorry,' he said, answering his phone.

'Don't you Christu sorry me,' Pankaj heard through the telephone.

Chupplejeep looked out of his window away from Pankaj. 'Christu, sorry. It's a murder. I have to work all hours till it's solved.'

Pankaj looked out into the blackness of Kukurul, trying to make himself invisible.

'Christu…of course…yes darling…next time I will definitely call…' Chupplejeep hung up and put his phone back in his pocket.

Pankaj turned to his boss and gave him a comforting smile.

Chupplejeep's phone rang again. 'Christu darling, I said…oh sorry Kulkarni…bit late for you. Yes of course. No nuclear DNA.' Chupplejeep looked at Pankaj and gestured that he did not know what the forensic was talking about. 'Chemical analysis…I see…interesting. Thank you for letting me know.' He hung up for the second time.

'It'll be good getting home for some late dinner, sir. It's been a long and tiring day,'

'We're not going home yet, Pankaj. We've someone else to see.'

'What do you mean?' His stomach made a loud noise.

'The hair sample results have come through.'

'So soon? Kulkarni never works so quickly.'

'We have a match.'

'Who is it?'

'Perhaps the thing Neeraj saw in his daughter's eyes was not pain but anger.'

'Sir?'

223

'Pankaj, tell me, if the whole village was laughing at you because of what your husband was doing behind your back, how angry would you be?'

CHAPTER TWENTY-SIX

'Gita! She certainly had motive. People in her village knew her husband was cheating on her. But is she a killer?' Pankaj asked.

'Never underestimate a woman's wrath,' Chupplejeep said.

'If Lavita is to be believed, Gita also had a lover.'

'Kulkarni said that the hair sample she provided is a perfect match.'

'He's got tests wrong before.'

'He said he ran the tests twice. She was the victim's wife though. It's quite possible that she had visited him when he was staying at the Laljis.'

'When we took her to the morgue, Gita said she had never been to Utol, but I bet it was her. I can feel it in my bones.'

'Listening to your gut is an essential skill. And believe me, you become in tune with it when you're a detective. But don't actively try and pin a crime on someone until you have examined all the evidence and have proof. I can understand her hairs being in the room. Maybe they transferred with him from their home at some point.'

'It's her, sir. It *is* her. I'm sure of it.'

Chupplejeep shook his head. 'You said it yourself, killings driven by passion are often more horrific than this. Usually there are multiple injuries. This was one clean hit. There was no passion involved. It looks to me as if it was pre-meditated. Clean and simple.'

'Yes, sir,' Pankaj said. 'But for her hair to be found on his naked body, I find that odd. There are slim chances that it would have transferred unless she had been in contact with him recently.'

'Maybe, Pankaj. Maybe,' Chupplejeep said. They pulled up to the Bata shop.

When the detectives entered the store, Gita Shah was dusting around the shoes.

'She looks quite content. Not like a woman grieving for her husband,' Pankaj whispered.

Gita's eyes scanned the store as Pankaj and Chupplejeep approached her. 'You're here to see me? Have you found out who killed him?'

'We would like to ask you a few questions, Mrs Shah. We haven't arrested anyone yet.'

'About my husband?'

Chupplejeep nodded. 'Where were you the night of Sandeep's death?'

'Oh, so you think I might be involved. You're wasting your time, Detective. I was at the shop on the Saturday night.'

'But the shop closes at what? Eight?'

'I'm here for half an hour more. It's my job to clean. Not sell shoes.'

'Tell me, do they pay you to clean the shop all day?'

'Only in the evening. I come at seven. I leave at around eight-thirty, sometimes nine. Sometimes, I come in the afternoons to clean. Occasionally, I come to clean in the mornings.'

'So basically you work shifts. Where did you go after your shift?'

'Home.'

'Your father said you were out with friends. According to him you didn't get back till midnight.'

Gita hesitated. She lifted a pair of shoes and wiped the shelf with a damp cloth. 'Oh yes, I forgot. I went out with friends first.'

'I think if someone close to me died I would remember exactly what I was doing that day,' Pankaj said.

Gita stared at him. 'My mind is confused. I keep mixing up days and dates. I'm a mess.' She looked away and then sat down on the padded bench. She put the dusting rag next to her and wiped her eyes with her blue tunic.

'Can I have the names and addresses of the friends you were with?'

'Of course,' she mumbled under her breath.

'Can you tell me their names now?' Chupplejeep asked.

'Vasudev,' she muttered.

'Sorry. I didn't catch that.'

227

'Vasudev Bhandari,' Gita said a little louder this time. She bit the fingernail of her index finger.

'And?' Chupplejeep asked as he wrote the name in his notepad.

'That's it.'

'Just one gentleman?' Chupplejeep and Pankaj shared a look.

'Yes.'

'That's hardly a group of friends that your father mentioned and that you alluded to just now. This Vasudev Bhandari wouldn't by chance be the same person you are having an affair with?'

Gita looked up at the detective, then she looked down at the floor.

'There's no use denying it.'

She held her hand to her mouth. 'How did you know?' she asked quietly.

'It's our job to know,' Chupplejeep said. He silently congratulated himself for taking Gita by surprise and trusting what Lavita had said. At least they wouldn't have to go through the drama of more lies before they arrived at this truth. In being a detective, there were always ten lies for every truth.

'Natasha must have told someone,' she whispered. 'Or perhaps someone has seen us together.'

'Who is this Vasudev? We'll have to interview him.'

'The knife sharpener in our village,' she said. She twisted the grey dusting cloth in her hands.

'You met when he came over to sharpen the kitchen knives? I know your mother likes to cook,' Chupplejeep said. He remembered the smell of the guava jam simmering on the stove when he went to interview her parents.

'She likes to cook. But no, I didn't meet him that way.' She looked away and shifted on the bench.

'Then how did you meet?'

'I met him, first, at our wedding. Vasudev was Sandeep's best friend.'

~

'A best friend doesn't do that,' Pankaj said with a frown. He briefly let his mind drift to Shwetika. If Sailesh ever made eyes at Shwetty, he would be horrified. This was not the correct behaviour for a wife and a best friend.

Pankaj examined the woman before him. His boss was right. He had to scrutinise the facts before pinpointing the blame with such conviction. Gita Shah was short, much too short to be able to effectively hit Sandeep over his head, unless he was kneeling. And he wasn't, because Kulkarni said there was no bruising or imprints of husks on his knees. Perhaps this Vasudev was tall and strong. If so, it would make sense that he was the one to take a rounded object to Sandeep's head. One whack and it was over for his lover's husband. It would also explain why there was no evidence of a struggle. After all, Vasudev and Sandeep were best friends. They could have been having a friendly chat when Sandeep was struck as if out of nowhere, but that would not explain Gita's hair found on Sandeep's body. 'Wait,' Pankaj mumbled to himself. Perhaps Gita and Vasudev visited Sandeep together. Vasudev hid whilst Gita lured him outside. A husband would comfortably speak to his wife naked and then when they were chatting outside, Vasudev had pounced. 'Yes,' Pankaj said.

'Yes, what?' Chupplejeep asked.

Pankaj looked at his boss and back at Gita. 'Nothing, sir.'

Chupplejeep sighed. 'How long were you having an affair with your husband's friend?'

'You don't have to put it like that,' Gita said. She put one hand on her hip. 'We started seeing each other just recently.'

'Can you define recently for us?'

'Six months.'

'You were not happily married?' Pankaj asked.

'Sandeep was a womaniser. I didn't know that until after Ashu was born. I found out he was seeing some peasant girls soon after Ashu came.' Gita scrunched her nose as if she had smelled something bad.

Pankaj smiled. Gita Shah thought she was in a higher class than a servant girl. He couldn't help but think of Sailesh's situation. He too was in love with someone one rung lower than him on the caste ladder. But Pankaj was certain that Meenakshi would do more than just turn her nose up when she found out. He was certain he would be able to hear her screams in Porvorim.

'I was tired of his gambling also,' Gita said. 'He was never there for me. It was always other girls and cards.'

'Were you planning to leave him?'

Gita was silent.

'You're in love with Vasudev. I can imagine what it was like for you. Your husband never around, too busy losing money and chasing other girls. The whole village knew what he was getting up to. Vasudev showed you affection. Anyone would understand what you were going through,' Chupplejeep tried.

Pankaj shook his head. Gita remained silent.

'Where were you till twelve that night?' Pankaj asked.

'We were at his place.'

'I see,' Pankaj said, still shaking his head.

'You never went to Utol that evening?'

'I went home at twelve. Ask my father – he saw me come home. Am I a suspect?' Gita asked, blinking hard.

'We found your hair on your husband's body. Can you explain that?'

'You know cops have been known to plant evidence before now.' She narrowed her eyes at Chupplejeep.

'They have, Mrs Shah. It can be a common problem in the smaller states of India.'

'Even the big cities,' Pankaj added.

'But let me assure you, Mrs Shah, such corruption does not happen on my watch.'

'I never went to visit my husband in Utol. I don't know how my hair landed up on his body.'

'My problem, Mrs Shah, is that you have motive and opportunity. Plus there is physical evidence in the form of your hair that tells me that you were at the scene of the crime.'

'I told you I was at home that evening and with Vasudev before. There is no way I was in Utol. Where was the chance?'

'Did anyone see you two together that evening?' Pankaj asked.

'No,' Gita said. 'We try to avoid people. If people see us together, they talk.'

'Sorry to say, but they are already talking.'

Gita scowled.

'You could have returned home and then left again. Your bedroom window faces the front of the house, does it not? A window you can easily climb out of.'

'But I did not leave the house again.'

Chupplejeep flicked through his notes. 'I'm curious as to why your husband was naked in the garden. I find it odd that he met someone without any clothes on. Tell me, was your husband always covering up his body or was he, I don't know, how shall I put this? I suppose what I am trying to ask is – was he comfortable with his body? Did he walk around the house naked?'

'He wouldn't walk around naked in broad daylight, Detective. He had some pride. But yes,' Gita said quietly, 'he always slept naked and sometimes I …' She blushed.

'Carry on.'

'Sometimes, I had to tell him to wear a *lengha* or a towel when he went to pee in the night. He was not shy, I suppose.'

'*Aacha*, thank you.'

Gita crossed her arms over her chest.

'Is there any reason you can think of as to why your hair would be on your husband? Did he visit you recently?'

'No.'

'You sent him anything?' Pankaj asked, remembering the green mangoes in Sandeep's room.

'No,' Gita said.

'Sure?'

'Oh hang on, yes. I did send him something.' Gita smiled.

Chupplejeep twisted the end of the right side of his moustache.

'I sent him pickle. A friend of mine was passing Utol. I asked him to drop it off at the Laljis'. My hair falls easily. Perhaps a hair or two fell in the newspaper I wrapped the jar of pickle in.'

'What kind of pickle?'

'*Brinjal.* His favourite.'

'You send a man you no longer love his favourite pickle?' Chupplejeep asked. 'I find that odd.'

'I never said I stopped loving him. We have a child together.'

Chupplejeep nodded. 'Please stick around for the next couple of days.' He turned to leave and motioned for Pankaj to follow him.

Pankaj followed his boss and pulled the glass door shut behind them.

'I get the feeling she's telling the truth about the pickle,' Chupplejeep said. 'It was aubergine pickle that we found.'

'Unless she saw it when she was there.'

Chupplejeep raised an eyebrow. 'All the items from Sandeep Shah's room were bagged?'

'Yes, sir.'

'Even the food stuffs?'

'Not the curry, sir, that went straight to the lab, but the pickle – that was bagged.'

'Phone Kulkarni and ask him to run a toxicology report on it and prints. Ask them to check if Gita's prints were on the jar. Lets see if she really sent it. I don't think they'll find anything but I want to be sure. It is easier to kill someone who has been drugged.'

'Sir, they didn't find any poisons in Sandeep's body.'

Chupplejeep looked at Pankaj. 'Just ask them to test the pickle, Pankaj. Just ask them.'

Chapter Twenty-seven

There was something bothering Detective Chupplejeep as he arrived at Little Larara police station. He could see Pankaj standing outside the station with the hose, watering the red hibiscus. Without catching his attention, he slipped inside the building. He liked it when the office was empty. The ceiling fan churned the air slowly making a soothing click-click sound. It gave rhythm to his thinking.

A loud gurgle came from his stomach. He rubbed his round belly and knew what was to blame. He was still suffering from indigestion caused by the spicy prawn *balchao* he had eaten late last night.

Christabel was up to something. Yesterday, even though he had missed dinner with his girlfriend, she had kept a plate of *balchao* ready for him when he returned to his empty house. She had also made a crème caramel. He couldn't have asked for anything more. It was a beautiful end to a miserable day. And this morning he noticed she had pruned the pink bougainvillea, which was growing wildly at the front of his house. He smiled. Whom did Christabel think she was trying to fool with her Goan delicacies, after all he was a detective. But this is what set his Christu apart from the others. She was bloody persistent and determined to get her way.

But it wasn't thoughts of Christabel worrying the detective; it was something else, something about the Sandeep Shah case. Chupplejeep picked up the autopsy report on his desk and started to read it.

'Sir, you're in,' Pankaj said. He wiped his feet on the mat by the door.

Chupplejeep looked up.

'*Chai*, sir?' Pankaj asked as he walked over to the kitchenette.

Chupplejeep looked at his watch. 'Tea would be nice. I couldn't sleep. I wanted to check over the autopsy report one more time.' Chupplejeep turned the page in the flimsy red folder. The colour of the folder reminded him of death, mostly it reminded him of unnatural death. A shiver ran down his spine. 'Here it is!' Chupplejeep exclaimed excitedly.

'Sir?' Pankaj said, walking into the room.

'I knew there was something we were missing. The bruise.'

'What bruise?'

'Near Sandeep Shah's right eye. There was a bruise when we first saw the body.'

Pankaj tried to remember the lifeless corpse. Just thinking about it gave him the shivers. He could feel his breakfast of *channa masala* rising in his throat. 'No sir, I don't remember.'

'Useless. Get used to looking carefully at dead bodies. Perhaps you should spend a day with Kulkarni. That will toughen you up.'

Pankaj shrugged and walked back to the kettle.

'See here,' Chupplejeep said pointing to the report. 'Kulkarni says that the marking was a bruise. I completely forgot about it. It says here that a blow to the face must have been delivered perhaps a week prior to death.'

Pankaj walked back into the room carrying two cups of tea. 'Sandeep must have had a fight.'

Chupplejeep shook the report. 'The bruise is good. But we have to figure out how Sandeep got this bruise.'

'I'm sure once we do that, sir, we'll find the culprit.'

Chupplejeep shook his head. 'Every suspect in this case has given me the runaround. First Neeraj says that he wasn't in the village then he says he was. Utsa said she never saw him that evening. Then all of a sudden, when confronted, she admits not only seeing him, but to being in his room also. Bala too, he's another bloody liar. He claims he didn't know the victim and then all of a sudden the victim turns out to be his childhood bully. Even Sandeep's wife had motive. Poirot said in one of his cases that it is easy to utter lies as truth. He was correct, Pankaj, as always the Belgian detective was correct.'

'That wife though, Gita Shah, saying she was sleeping in her bed after twelve the night of the murder, my foot!' Pankaj added.

'The only people we can dismiss are Lavita and Gonsalves,' Chupplejeep said.

'Really sir? You're dismissing Lavita Lalji?'

'She was in love with him. You saw her that day. Her heart was broken.'

'But she found the body. She was the first to see him dead. You said you must look at the evidence and not just trust your gut.'

'There is no evidence to point the finger at her. What motive did she have?'

Pankaj scratched his chin.

'Sandeep's best friend, Vasudev, was sleeping with Sandeep's wife. We've not interviewed him yet. Perhaps he has some bruises on his body too. We should visit him soon,' Chupplejeep said.

'The bruise could have been from one of several people. Gamblers have many enemies. And they deal with slippery fellows like Gonsalves and Sanjog.'

'Gonsalves has an alibi. A watertight one.'

'Sanjog is still in the running.'

'And the other gamblers in Sandeep's gambling circle in Mapusa and Utol?'

'We have the names from the Mapusa group from Neeraj. But finding the names of the Utol gang, where would I start?'

'Start in Mapusa. Visit all the five names on Neeraj's list. See if anything is suspicious about them. Then ask Sanjog if he knows the Utol group.'

'Yes sir, I'll get on it right away.'

'You're also forgetting one other suspect that we need to interview again.'

'Who, sir?'

238

'Your friend Sailesh, he too had motive. Sailesh knew that Sandeep was pestering Utsa. Your friend had motive and opportunity. Utsa may have dramatized the whole Sandeep situation to Sailesh. I can see someone like Utsa doing just that.'

'Why would she do that?' Pankaj asked.

'Some women like their partners to feel jealous. It makes them feel like they're in demand.'

'You should start a "dear aunty" column,' Pankaj said with a grin.

Chupplejeep ignored Pankaj, because what he said was a little too close to home. He had read this piece of information about jealousy in one of Christabel's glossy monthly magazines. Lately, she had a habit of leaving them lying around the house. He was sure she was trying to hint at something, but he still hadn't worked out what it was and he was too afraid to ask.

'I know he's your friend and all, but Sailesh wanted Sandeep to stay away from his girl and, surprise surprise, he doesn't have an alibi for the night Sandeep died.'

'I just don't think…'

'Don't think,' Chupplejeep said furrowing his brow. 'Perhaps you shouldn't speak to him again until this case is solved. You said that Sailesh knew about Sandeep, that she had told him about their flirtations. Sailesh must have been in a bad mood after she told him. She probably told him that this driver, Sandeep, was making promises to her. Her plan must have backfired. A little jealousy is fun, too much creates rage. You yourself said that Sailesh was angry when Utsa told him. That he

239

dropped her at the Utol circle straight away and left. He could have held on to that anger until the day Sandeep Shah died. When did Utsa tell Sailesh about Sandeep?'

'A couple of weeks back, he said. But I know Sailesh. He wouldn't have been able to hold on for a week without confrontation. He's like that, sir. He'd have gone to see Sandeep immediately.'

'Maybe he did. And that's why Sandeep had the bruise.'

'No one we interviewed has mentioned seeing any newcomers in the village over the last couple of weeks, apart from Neeraj,' Pankaj said. 'Sailesh has one of those bikes that make a big sound. Someone would have heard it in the village for sure.'

'He may have parked his bike far away from the village and walked.'

'Let me speak to him, sir.'

'You've just told me that it is in your friend's nature to fly off in a rage without being able to control himself and I've just shown you that he can be cunning enough to park his bike somewhere else and walk into Utol as to not alert anyone to his presence.'

'Sir, you are putting words into my mouth. Let me speak to him.'

Chupplejeep smiled at his protégé. 'You'll make a good detective, Pankaj. But no matter what grade you are, whether you are detective or inspector general even, if ever your friends or family are involved in a case it is best to stay well away.'

'I would never jeopardise this case, sir.'

'You wouldn't on purpose,' Chupplejeep said, 'but you might do so without knowing.'

CHAPTER TWENTY-EIGHT

'Sailesh Krinz?'

'Yes,' the boy responded.

'My name's Detective Chupplejeep.'

'I know who you are. You're Pankaj's boss.'

'I've a few questions for you.'

'Where is he?' Sailesh wiped the grease of his hand with a wet rag and stared at Chupplejeep.

'Pankaj isn't coming. I've asked him not to speak with you again in relation to this case.'

'I'm a suspect then,' he mumbled as he peered under a car bonnet.

'What's the problem?'

'Battery.' He stepped back and looked at the detective.

Chupplejeep nodded as if he understood, but the truth was he wasn't remotely interested in the mechanics of cars. He was just glad that they saved him from walking long distances and taking the bus.

'Do you think you are a truthful person or a liar?' Chupplejeep asked.

'What is this?' Sailesh took a step back. 'I've been set up by the cops before.'

'Just answer the question.'

'I tell the truth,' he said, disappearing under the bonnet again.

'Is that a lie?'

'You're worse than my mother, Detective.' He wiped his hands on his overalls before picking up a pair of pliers.

'When was the last time you told a lie?'

Sailesh laughed.

'Once I had a suspect who lied throughout the case. He was a very good liar. He almost had us fooled, but in the end we got him. Lies always catch up with the people who tell them.'

'You should be a teacher.' Sailesh paused. 'Yesterday, I told a lie.'

'A big lie or what they call a white lie?'

He shifted on his feet and looked around the garage. 'Come inside, to my office,' he said. Sailesh started walking towards the back of the auto-shop. 'Pankaj speaks highly of you and he's very difficult to please. I suppose you must be legit if Bhendaa works for you.'

Chupplejeep suppressed a smile. It was a regular and acceptable pastime to criticise one's boss, so hearing this was a bonus.

'I hear you don't take a second salary? You know, one from the government, the other – *baksheesh*.'

'Ha! I have to admit the wages are low, but I'm not in the force just for the money. I want Goa to be a better place.'

'Three years ago a cop pulled me over for a minor traffic offence. I mean who the hell cares if you give way or not? This is India not the UK. What does a stop sign in India mean, when indicating right means you want someone to overtake you?'

'Well, some cops like to play the rules by the book.'

'By the book, my ass, by the book. He pulled a bag of marijuana from his pocket and asked me what I was doing with it. Can you believe it? It cost me three hundred bucks to avoid jail.'

Chupplejeep shrugged. 'I see.' It didn't surprise him. This type of behaviour had been a regular money-maker for power-hungry cops for some time now. But the practice was dying down, or so he kept telling himself.

He followed Sailesh into a pokey room at the back of the garage. It had a glass window, which looked out onto the workshop and contained only four pieces of furniture: a cheap wooden desk with two mismatched chairs and a coat stand with dirty, old boxing gloves hanging off it. The whole room was painted a garish yellow. Chupplejeep felt as if he was standing inside a jackfruit.

'You want to know what my last lie was, it was to my mom.'

'Your mother?'

'She doesn't approve of my girlfriend.'

'Utsa?'

'Apparently a servant girl is too low a class for me. People will talk, our family will be shamed. I am sure, Detective, you have heard this a thousand times. Everyone in India suffers from the disease of superiority, in a country where there is an ever-increasing divide between the rich and the poor. Let me tell you the rich were once poor – somewhere in their ancestry. Everybody has a history. Sometimes you have to be bad to realise what good is. They just can't see it. In every relationship someone is not the right caste, class, religion or their family has a bad name.'

'Of course,' Chupplejeep said nodding in agreement.

Sailesh dropped his shoulders. 'Yesterday, I told my mom I had broken it off with Utsa because she threatened to set her sari alight on the stove.'

'Would she have done?'

He shrugged. 'Nah. Mom's a very good actress. Bollywood is missing out. But you can never be sure.'

'You love Utsa?'

He hesitated. 'Going out with a girl like Utsa is a full commitment. I know what'll happen. My father will offer Utsa money to stay away from me. She won't take it. I'll tell my parents I still want to be with her. My mother will starve herself for a day or two, threaten me with her health. My aunts will call to ask me why I'm bringing shame on the family. My brothers will tell me I'm putting my mother into an early grave and that I'm selfish. But eventually they'll come around, one by one. All in all, in five years time I'll be accepted back into the family as will Utsa. It will be five years of pain, for what?'

Chupplejeep was silent.

'Their pride.'

'You're willing to go through all this, for her?'

'At least my family will eventually accept her.' Sailesh walked around the desk.

'You must love her enough to do anything for her.'

'I now see where your question was headed. I walked straight into your trap, didn't I?' He smiled. 'You got me!' he said, as he took his seat behind the large desk. He motioned for the detective to sit down.

Chupplejeep sat down. 'You didn't tell Pankaj the whole truth about Sandeep.'

'What d'you mean?' Sailesh picked up a ballpoint pen from a glass on his desk and started drawing rectangular boxes on the wooden table.

Chupplejeep watched him draw for a moment. 'That's why I've asked him not to speak to you about this. You thought you could pull the wool over the eyes of my officer and because he's your friend you though he would believe you.'

'He's in trouble?' Sailesh looked at the detective, but Chupplejeep ignored the question.

'You admit trying to deceive him?'

Sailesh started to colour in the boxes. 'It was complicated to discuss. That's all.'

'I spoke to Utsa.'

Sailesh shifted in his chair.

Detective Chupplejeep noticed Sailesh pressing hard onto the pen in his hand. 'You'll ruin that table.'

'It's ruined already.'

'What I want to know is why you went back to attack Sandeep a second time?'

Sailesh looked up, startled.

Chupplejeep smiled. 'Tell me your version of events.'

'I never attacked Sandeep a first time or a second time. What are you saying? I haven't done anything wrong. You cops always get it wrong.'

He could see that he had rattled Sailesh's cage so he pressed on with his theory. 'You visited Sandeep Shah on the Monday after dropping your girlfriend home, immediately after Utsa told you he was making advances. This was a week before Sandeep's body was found. You visited him at his home and gave him a pasting. You warned him to stay away. But he didn't, did he? So you went back the following Saturday night to finish him off. He still had the bruise when his body was found.'

'What the hell?' Sailesh said holding the pen in his fist. 'You cops are all the same. Making up lies to get an arrest. Lazy, the lot of you. I thought you were different, but no, Pankaj is misguided.'

'That Monday evening after your rendezvous you were angry, you dropped your girlfriend at the Utol circle and rode off. But you didn't go home, did you?'

Sailesh fiddled with the pen.

'You're hot-headed. You couldn't hold on to your anger. You waited fifteen minutes till you knew your girlfriend would be safely back at home and then you rode to the Da Costas', parked your bike behind the betel tree outside their house and walked down to the outhouse in the Laljis' garden.' Chupplejeep paused.

247

There was nothing better than revealing to the perpetrator that you knew their actions step by step. He had stopped at Utol on his way to see Sailesh. A neighbour had said they had seen a bike matching the description of Sailesh's, parked outside the Da Costas' the Monday before Sandeep's body was found, which backed up his theory.

'You snuck into the Laljis' garden,' Chupplejeep continued. 'Their gate is never locked and it's well oiled so they would not have heard it creak. I noticed that when we went to inspect the scene. Even if they did hear the gate they would not pay much attention to it. After all, their lodger was free to have guests. You saw the opportunity when Sandeep Shah was in his room.'

Sailesh shrugged.

'Your anger at this man spoiling the name of your good lady was enough to send you over the edge. That Monday you spoke to him, told him to stay away from Utsa, didn't you? But he laughed at you, said he would see whomever he wanted. So you hit him hard with your fist, a hooked punch with your left hand. You're left-handed, na?' Chupplejeep said, motioning to the pen in Sailesh's hand.

Sailesh immediately dropped the pen.

'You see it was evident that out of my list of suspects the person who caused the bruise to Mr Shah's face was left-handed, because the bruise was near Sandeep's right eye. And you're a good aim. Let me guess, you box.' Chupplejeep looked up at the boxing gloves that were hanging on the coat stand in the office.

248

Sailesh bowed his head. 'Okay, okay. I hit the man. He was a no-good womaniser.'

'And at the end of the week when he carried on with his womanising, you went back to teach him a lesson. I know you didn't mean it. Your anger consumed you. One thing led to another, and when you hit him, *phatack*, he fell. You got scared and you ran. Many people turn to boxing as a way of channelling their anger. Really they shouldn't. You need respect for any sport. Have you seen the Thai boxing? It's art more than sport.'

'It wasn't like that.'

'Then tell me how it was?'

'That Monday evening I visited him. You're right, he laughed at me. He said he'd have Utsa if he wanted. I got angry and so I hit him. I tell you I didn't regret it at the time. I told Utsa I would sort him out. She liked that I said I would do anything for her and one punch to the face was enough. I proved my love for her.'

'You regret it now?'

Sailesh nodded.

'You regret that you hit him or that I found out because the poor man is now dead?'

'After I dropped Utsa at the circle, I called one of my friends on my mobile. This friend of mine is local. He knows everything, and if he doesn't know he can find out. He told me this Sandeep was married. After I hit Sandeep I threatened him with this knowledge. I said if he tried anything more with Utsa I would tell everyone about his wife. I even threatened to tell his wife and her family.'

249

'And did you?'

'I had no reason to. Later I spoke to Utsa. I didn't tell her what I'd done, but I assumed she figured it out because she kept calling me her hero. But she said she too would speak to him and tell him to leave her alone once and for all. I believed her. I thought she would tell him at work and cut all contact with him. I told her that other than if she had to speak to him at work, not to go near him. I didn't realise she had been to see him the night before he died, until she told me just the other day.'

'Did Utsa know about his wife?'

'No. I never told her that I was asking around about him. Some chicks don't like that.'

Chupplejeep sighed. Unknowingly, Sailesh had corroborated Utsa's story as well. 'Okay, so what you're saying is that you hit the man, but never went back to the village after that Monday. You didn't go back to finish him off, so to speak?'

'Never.'

'You lied to a police officer once before, what's to say that you are not lying again?'

'I'm not. You have to believe me. I wouldn't kill a man, ask Pankaj.'

'Be reachable at all times. And I mean at all times. If I find out you have left Goa...' Chupplejeep stood up to leave, swaying as he did so. The bright yellow walls were making him feel nauseated.

CHAPTER TWENTY-NINE

Arthur Chupplejeep decided to take a detour on his way home, just so that he could stop at Mr Baker's. He wanted to surprise Christabel by buying some lunch and taking it to her house. Over the last week he had barely managed to fit in lunch at home, let alone an afternoon siesta, but today he was determined that he would. It wasn't as if he was some big-shot homicide detective in the city anymore. He was a detective in Little Larara – an all round village detective.

He needed to switch off. The case was going nowhere fast. The trace evidence examined had brought nothing new to light. It had been over a week already and they had made no real progress. Sailesh and Neeraj seemed to have been telling the truth and Lavita had no real motive given that she didn't know about Sandeep's wife. But Bala, Sanjog and Vasudev – not to mention Gita Shah, even though she was a little too short to hit her husband on his head – were all still suspects.

Chupplejeep's thoughts drifted to Inspector General Gosht. What would the Inspector General think of him if he failed to solve this simple crime? It was the only crime of some importance that had happened in Little Larara in the last year. If he couldn't solve it, he wouldn't be able to prove himself and he could forget about a promotion.

Chupplejeep twisted the ends of his moustache as the thought of his fast-approaching birthday crossed his mind. Recently policing had become very ageist. The new Inspector General was always talking about *young* Detective Gupta and *young* Detective Fernandes. Could they fire him for being too old or too straight-laced? In Goa, anything was possible. He shuddered. He couldn't imagine what he would do if he wasn't doing detective work.

Chupplejeep leaned towards his steering wheel and hit his forehead with the palm of his hand. 'Stop thinking,' he scolded himself loudly. Thinking was getting him nowhere. For the next three hours he would try not to think. Pankaj would call him if there was anything urgent. For now he would forget about his fortieth, his career and Sandeep Shah, and he would make the drive into town to get his girlfriend the chicken patties and potato chops she loved.

Chupplejeep pulled up outside the bakery and got out of his car. He stood outside the baker's along with everybody else. 'Bloody hell!' he swore when he saw the gathering outside the bakery. A nun stared at him. He quickly raised his hand and mouthed an apology as best he could whilst nodding his head in an apologetic manner. The nun continued to stare. Were nuns allowed

252

to give such evil looks? Were they not supposed to instantly forgive?

What did he know, as one of the mammas in the orphanage said to him when he was leaving, 'Motherless, fatherless, religionless. Good luck Arthur, you'll need it.' Just the memory of that awful place brought a lump to his throat. If it wasn't for Nana taking him in at twelve, giving him an education and letting him watch the Belgian detective, Poirot, Chupplejeep was sure he wouldn't be where he was today. He had Nana to thank for everything, and of course Poirot.

"Ext!' Chupplejeep heard from the inside of Mr Baker. He heard a woman scream her order in Konkani, advertising to the rest of the queue that Mr Baker had fresh prawn rissoles today. His mouth began to water, he would buy some to snack on for the journey to Christabel's house. He imagined the pushing and shoving at the front of the crowd – hungry customers trying to grab Mr Baker's attention by throwing their twenty Rupee notes at him. Poor Gandhiji, he would never have expected to have his face printed on money only to be shoved between fisherwomen's breasts and eventually handed out in return for patties.

Someone pushed Chupplejeep from behind.

Chupplejeep pushed back. The unspoken rule in India was that queuing was for idiots. If it was one thing Indians couldn't do, it was to queue. Even with a population of over one billion, nobody felt they should have to wait for anything. The British should have at least left that trait behind when they went, he thought.

The gathering outside was moving. Soon it would be his chance to stick his elbows out and push his way to the front. If Mr Baker saw him, though, he would serve him first. Not because he was a cop, but because Christabel's auntie's cousin's wife was a friend and so they were almost like family. Chupplejeep moved with the mass of people. He looked through the window of the hardware store as he followed the crowd. He needed some new zinc wire to hang a picture that Christabel had given him. She had recently accused him of not liking it – which was true. The picture of the bullock and cart was lopsided, but her cousin had painted it so what choice did he have, but to hang it. The things he had to do for love. He strained his eyes to the back of the shop. If he could get the vendor's attention, he could call him out and buy the wire without leaving his place.

The shopkeeper was busy with a customer. Chupplejeep looked around him, asking someone to get his order was not an option. He put his hands to the glass of the shop window to reduce the reflection from the midday sun and looked inside the store. This time, instead of catching the shopkeeper's attention, something else caught his eye.

Bala was standing in the hardware shop holding a large stone object. The light reflected off the polished stone.

Chupplejeep watched as the shopkeeper took back the object, held it up to his thick lenses and ran his finger around the top. The detective knew he had no choice but to leave his position in the so-called queue and intervene on the scene in the hardware store. What the vendor was holding could have easily been the weapon Bala used to smash into poor Sandeep Shah's head. After all, this fatal piece of evidence, the murder weapon, had not yet been recovered.

Chupplejeep cast his mind back to when he and Pankaj visited the baker's house, just a few days ago. There had been several ugly looking ornaments that littered the kitchen and sitting room. Pankaj had mentioned it at the time because a thick settling of baker's flour and dust had settled around a missing figure. Could this be the item that Bala was collecting from the shop? Had it broken as it hit Sandeep's head, which was why Bala had brought it in for mending?

Chupplejeep watched the volume of people in front of him shrink, his feet glued to the spot as he eyed his suspect. He could hear grumbling from customers behind him; lots of teeth-sucking, *aye saibas* and tutting. He either had to shift up or leave. The decision was easy. He couldn't carry on like he hadn't seen anything just for a handful of fried snacks. Lunch, his long anticipated afternoon siesta and Christabel would just have to wait. Chupplejeep took one last look around him before releasing himself from the throng of people. Once again his conscience had won.

'Sir,' Chupplejeep said, walking into the shop. He tightened his stomach muscles as he walked so that the people in the shop wouldn't hear his growling stomach.

'Officer?' Bala said, taking a step back.

'Detective,' Chupplejeep corrected him.

'*Thik hai*, Detective, sorry,' Bala said bowing his head.

'Never mind. Tell me what's that there?'

'Oh this, sir? My mother's ornament.'

'The one missing from your house?' Chupplejeep asked, taking the ornament from the shopkeeper and examining it.

'Looks like nev' the shopkeeper said with a grin. 'Ve gave it a polish just like the customer asked.'

Chupplejeep shook his head with disappointment.

The shopkeeper smiled. Leaning forward, his thick-rimmed glasses rose up with his cheeks.

Chupplejeep peered over the counter. He noticed the man was standing on a plastic crate so that the counter was waist-high. Otherwise, Chupplejeep imagined, the vendor would be too small for his own shop.

The vendor strained his neck to see the ornament that Chupplejeep was now holding. When he did this, he reminded him of a tortoise.

'The figure vas chipped. You see marble is soft, Detectiwe. If it hits something hard, it can chip.' The shopkeeper switched on a bright light above the counter.

'Is that so?' Chupplejeep said. He looked at the object again. This time with the reflection of the light he could see that it wasn't just a chip. It was a big crack. The statue was particularly horrible. It was a yellowy brown colour with dark brown streaks. It had an equally ugly face carved into it. Chupplejeep wasn't sure if it was supposed to be a human face or that of a gargoyle. The features were mixed. Maybe it was half and half.

'I can tell you all sorts of things about marble,' the tortoise said.

'Okay, very good,' Chupplejeep interrupted, sensing a geography lecture. He turned to Bala. 'Can I ask when you brought this item to the shop?'

Bala stuttered. 'I-I can't remember.' He stood with his mouth open, scratching his head.

'Here, here,' the tortoise said, taking out a book almost as big as him. He opened the book and started running his fingers along the handwritten entries. His face was almost pressed up to the page. With the size of his lenses, Chupplejeep wondered how this chap still couldn't see properly. 'Found it!' the man said with triumph. He grinned at the detective again.

'Go on, then. Tell me, when did he deliver this item to you?'

'Sir, the elewanth Nowember.'

'You're open on a Sunday?'

''Es, Detectiwe. Sunday is my best day. Ewerybody needs something after attending mass. I cater specifically to the Catholics on Sunday.'

'Give us one moment, sir,' Chupplejeep said to the shopkeeper.

'I can't leawe my shop unattended.'

'I am a detective, na?'

'Okay, okay.' The tortoise pulled his neck back, and walked off the shop floor through a beaded curtain. As soon as he was out of earshot, Chupplejeep turned to Bala. His stomach growled.

Bala looked at the detective's protruding belly.

Chupplejeep clenched his stomach muscles again. 'Bala, you must be very efficient if you had time the day Sandeep Shah was found dead to deliver this item to this shop. You were the one who reported the crime. Your cycle had a flat. Yet you still managed to come all the way into town to drop this ornament off. It must have been important for you to do that, no?'

'I…'

'Were you waiting outside the Laljis' for Lavita to scream or did you not intend for Lavita to find the body? Or was that your plan – frighten her so much that she turns to you? Is it true that you have asked for her hand in marriage?'

'I…'

'From what I hear, they are considering it. You think Lavita would have even considered your proposal if she was still running around with Sandeep?'

Bala narrowed his eyes. 'Don't…don't talk about her like that.'

'Does it make you angry?'

Bala was quiet.

'Did Sandeep say something about Lavita? Is that why you attacked him?'

'I never did any of these things you're accusing me of. I told you my mother saw a rat snake and in the commotion broke the statue.' Bala shook his head vigorously. 'I never did anything like what you are saying.'

258

Chupplejeep lifted up the ugly ornament and ran his finger over the crack. 'We'll see,' he said walking out of the shop.

'Detective, my mother's statue.'

Chupplejeep shook his head as he looked at the ugly creature. 'Police evidence, I'm afraid.' As Chupplejeep left the store, he noticed that there was no longer a crowd outside Mr Baker's. The smell of prawn rissoles filled his nostrils, but he had lost his appetite.

CHAPTER THIRTY

Pankaj held the marble figure, now concealed in a plastic evidence bag, up to the light. 'He's done a very good job of the crack, sir. Which shop was this?'

Chupplejeep sucked his teeth. 'Why? You have some items to take to him? Put the ugly thing down. I don't want you dropping it. I have to give it to Kulkarni to examine against the indentation on Shah's head. He may be able to tell us if it was the weapon used.'

'It'll be a breakthrough, sir, if we find the murder weapon. Do you think we should start searching Bala's house?'

'We need warrants to do that. You know how long it'll take. The Chief Justice is not keen on officially searching in the villages. First, we need to shorten our list of suspects before we go to him for a warrant.' Chupplejeep put his hands behind his head and his feet on his desk.

'Is something troubling you, sir?' Pankaj asked as he waited for the slow internet connection to open a page on how to get rid of cockroaches. Recently, more and more of the damned things were finding their way into their office. 'Krazy Lines,' he said under his breath, remembering an advert he had seen years ago. He would buy the chalk and use it in the office to stop the little creatures from getting in. He shuddered as a cockroach scuttled right past his feet. 'They are getting very confident, these little buggers.'

'Who?'

'Nothing, sir'

Chupplejeep sighed. 'The whole murder case is bothering me, Pankaj,' he said, dropping his feet to the floor and sitting upright. 'Something is not right. Everyone seems to have a motive, but I am not sure if they have enough motive to kill.'

'Sir, I'm not sure I know what you mean. Motive is motive.'

'As a detective you learn to read people. That's a very important skill. Can I let you in on a secret?'

'Surely, sir. But you also said that you shouldn't only trust your gut. You said you must also look at the evidence.'

'Don't tell me what I already said, *baba*. I know what I said. Listen, when you become a detective you sharpen certain skills. You learn to read people. You have an instinct that you combine with the evidence and facts to catch the culprit. It's always a combination of the two. Normally, I can do this, but with this case – nothing. So far, no one I've interviewed seems like a killer.' Chupplejeep rubbed his forehead. 'Am I losing my instinct as a detective? Or is there something else about this case that I'm just not seeing?'

Pankaj was silent. He had never before heard his boss question himself. Normally he was so full of confidence. If his boss lost confidence at this point, the case may never be solved. Many murders suffered the same fate in India, but Pankaj had no intention to become part of this statistic. He wanted a one hundred per cent success rate, otherwise he was certain he wouldn't be able to sleep at night. One couldn't sleep, when there were murderers on the loose. No, this attitude his boss had acquired was not going to work. If Chupplejeep gave up now, Pankaj's dream would be only that, a dream.

'What's bothering you, sir?'

'My fortieth birthday, lack of confidence, the fact I've forcibly been retired to the villages,' Chupplejeep said under his breath.

'Sir? I didn't catch that.'

'Oh nothing. Tell me, why did you want to work in Larara, Pankaj? I've seen your application. You chose to work here after graduation. You had top marks in your year, you could have gone to one of the bigger districts.'

'Larara is my home. I wanted to be based here,' Pankaj said. 'The villages have charm, sir. You'll see that one day.'

'Of course I see that,' Chupplejeep said, biting his lip and thinking of Christabel. He paused before continuing. 'Shwetika had nothing to do with it?'

Pankaj blushed. 'No, sir. Not at all.'

Chupplejeep grinned. 'If you say so. So tell me how's it going with Shwetty?'

'I saw her the other day at the *gado,* buying a watermelon juice.'

'And?'

'This time, sir, I was going to ask her out, I swear.'

'What happened?'

'By the time I plucked up the courage, her friends had joined her. There were three girls. I couldn't ask her out in front of them.'

Chupplejeep laughed. 'I'll be married by the time you ask that girl out.'

'Sir?' Pankaj asked with a smile.

'Oh shut up! Forget it, forget it, nothing doing. It was a figure of speech. Back to the case,' Chupplejeep said. 'I just don't know what we're going to do with the Sandeep Shah case.'

After a moment's hesitation, Pankaj spoke, his eyebrows knitted together. 'Sir, we cannot give up now. What will the Inspector General think? You have the answer, sir. I know it. Like that detective on television, sir, he said that the truth is out there. You are a great cop, sir. You caught that serial killer. When I was in Police Training School it made big headlines. I wanted to be just like you. I nearly fell off my chair when the Inspector General announced that you were replacing Prashant here. I thought why would a big-shot detective come to a small village but then I heard about the...'

'Yes, lets not talk about the Panaji incident.'

'Sir, if you don't mind me saying, we cannot fail on our first big case together. We cannot give up.'

'Drama queen, who said anything about giving up? I said there's something I'm not seeing, something obvious. And Poirot never said that "the truth is out there". I think you are quoting something from *The X-Files*.'

'Oh.'

'You leave the Poirot quotes to me.'

Pankaj shook his head from side to side in agreement.

'Tell me, how did your day go yesterday?'

'I interviewed all five of the Mapusa gamblers.' Pankaj smiled with pride.

'That was quick. Were you thorough?'

Pankaj pursed his lips before he spoke. 'Of course I was thorough, sir. You can see my notes.' He took his black notepad out from his breast pocket and held it out to the detective.

Chupplejeep waved it away. 'Alibis?'

'No motives, sir. Each one gave their version of Sandeep Shah. They liked the guy. He won some and he lost some. He lost more than he won towards the end. Generally, he took them to the tavernas for a drink afterwards and even gave the labourers in the group contacts, within the construction industry, so they could find work. He was generally liked.'

'A husband can love his wife. Still he kills her.'

'They didn't love him, sir, they liked him,' Pankaj said hesitantly.

Chupplejeep smiled.

'Also, they all had alibis which I'm checking out.'

'All?'

'They were at some card event in Margao.'

'Convenient, but good. And the Utol crew?'

'I have a list of names, sir, put together from Sanjog and a few locals. I'll visit them today.'

'Do that. But my instinct tells me there is nothing there. If something was suspicious, another name would have cropped up by now.'

'I was thinking the same, sir.'

'Still, check them out.'

'Of course.' Pankaj lifted his foot and brought it down on a cockroach. 'Bastards,' he said.

'It still worries me that no one I've met so far seems like a cold-blooded murderer.'

'You say that all the suspects you've met don't have that murderous instinct, sir. But there is still one suspect that you have not yet interviewed.'

Chupplejeep rested his chin in his hand. 'Somebody always knows something. You're right, Pankaj. Let's go pay him a visit. And bring that stone figure,' Chupplejeep said as he stood up. 'We can drop it by at Kulkarni's lab on the way.'

~

Pankaj shook his head as he entered Kulkarni's lab. It was nothing like the labs they showed on *Crime Scene Investigation*. It was more like the *CSI* cleaning cupboard. You could barely move inside it. On the counter there were a couple of microscopes and a few chemicals. It wasn't an efficient lab, or so Pankaj thought. And he was certain samples could easily be contaminated. It didn't surprise him that it took their department ten times longer to solve any case than Mumbai. It was a good job that in Goa they had ten times fewer crimes.

Pankaj knew that in order for the lab to be more efficient, and for everything to be labelled correctly, Kulkarni needed a trained assistant. But the budget cuts had meant that any sort of training costs were hard to meet. They had been told no training and no testing. Any serious testing such as DNA could be sent to the labs in Mumbai. This meant more delays and quite an added cost if you thought about the travel involved and the fact that the samples could be interfered with along the way.

If the forensic pathologist sent samples out of the lab, there were countless people whom criminals could bribe along the way, such as flight crew and baggage handlers. All criminals knew at least one flight attendant or pilot on all the major airlines. Sometimes it was better to figure it out in-house than send it off to another city for testing.

Pankaj looked around. He knew it was pointless dwelling on the inadequacies of their crime lab. It was clear from Inspector General Gosht that the Greater Larara crime lab would not be getting any funding for better equipment. 'You need the equipment – you take it to Bombay!' the Inspector General barked the last time Chupplejeep had broached the subject. They had to make do with what they had. And who really knew what their crime lab looked like? It was never open to the public. So unless someone broke in, nobody would know what a state it was in. Pankaj was sure that to rest of Goa, they looked pretty efficient and that small sliver of comfort would just have to do for now.

Kulkarni examined the marble object. 'It certainly looks like this is a plausible instrument to make such a mark on the victim.' He passed Pankaj and Chupplejeep a photo of the clean wound on Shah's head. Kulkarni lifted the lid on a large, rectangular black plastic box. He peered inside it and then put his hand in. Eventually he fished out a metal instrument.

'What's that?' Pankaj asked, wrinkling his nose. The crime lab had a faint smell of disinfectant that made him queasy.

'It's a measuring device, eh,' Kulkarni said as he held the two metal prongs up against the stone figure. 'This figure is ugly, is it not?'

'Very,' both Chupplejeep and Pankaj said.

'I've never seen such an ugly thing,' Pankaj confirmed.

'These are collectibles though. They can be expensive. You say the *pau wallah's* mother collects them?'

'Yes.'

'These *pau wallahs* must make good money, eh.'

Chupplejeep and Pankaj nodded. It seemed everyone was making good money these days, except the police.

'Would you say he was making better money than a driver?' Pankaj asked, remembering his conversation with Chupplejeep.

'Of course,' Kulkarni said dismissively.

'You see, Pankaj, it's all perception. Bala, like you, thought Sandeep was better than him even though his job pays less.'

'But in Bala's case, money was not the only issue. Who gets paid more is irrelevant because Bala was still jealous of the driver, because he had Lavita's attention.'

Chupplejeep nodded.

'The happy couple, Bala and Lavita, are not getting married though,' Kulkarni said. He let out a chuckle.

Chupplejeep looked at the medical examiner. 'You know this, how?'

'Sister's friend.'

'*Aacha*, so Bala's plan is not going as planned.'

'No, Bala's plan is not working and this object is not the murder weapon. See.' Kulkarni pointed to the picture of Sandeep's head and then to the statue. 'It couldn't be this item, although it's a good match. The head of this ugly figure is too round. The victim was hit with something more conical, something not so smooth. You see the texture patterns on the scalp?'

'Before, you said the instrument was smooth. Now, you are saying slightly textured. What could make this marking?'

'No, boss. I said smooth and I mean smooth, eh. The item could have been wrapped in a cloth to make the marking. See, the pattern is only just visible. It wasn't something *very* textured.'

Chupplejeep squinted as he looked at the photo again. 'You're sure it isn't just some dirt on camera lens?'

Kulkarni was silent.

He looked away from the photo. What kind of scientific term was 'very textured' supposed to be, anyway?

Chupplejeep strained his eyes looking at the photo once more, but he could not see what the pathologist was talking about. 'Are you sure?' he asked. It wouldn't be the first time that Kulkarni had got something like this wrong. But then what did he expect from a man working inside a broom cupboard with insufficient lighting? They were never going to win any awards for detective work in Larara.

'One hundred per cent sure,' Kulkarni said. 'This is not the murder weapon. I'll run it for any fingerprints, or bloodstaining. Although it looks like it has been cleaned up pretty good. Also, even though it's marble and the break is pretty clean, I would have expected to see some stone fragments in the skull or around the body. All we found in the coconut husks surrounding the body were coconut husks.'

'And the *brinjal* pickle, did you manage to test it?'

''Es. Positive and negative.'

'Don't speak in riddles, please.

'Fingerprints found on the bottle were Sandeep's and Gita's. No toxins in the pickle though. Nothing but what you would expect to find in a pickle. Aubergine, vinegar and so on.'

'Fine. Call me if anything suspicious is found on the statue then,' Chupplejeep said before motioning to Pankaj to follow him out of the crime lab.

'I was sure that that was our bloody murder weapon,' Chupplejeep said, hitting the top of his blue Maruti.

'But sir, you said you didn't think Bala was hiding anything?'

'What did I say about facts, Pankaj?'

'Yes sir, I remember.'

'Okay,' Chupplejeep said, getting into the passenger seat. He was in no mood for driving. His suspect list was a joke. 'Let's see what Gita's boyfriend has to say.'

CHAPTER THIRTY-ONE

'Are you sure this is the address?' Chupplejeep asked.

'Yes, sir,' Pankaj said, reading from his notepad. 'Behind the Andheri Sweet Mart, opposite the guest house.'

'But which house? There are three.'

'Lemon Villa – the yellow one,' Pankaj said, pointing towards the middle house.

'Looks more like Ramshackle Villa!' Chupplejeep said, laughing at his own joke. The detective turned off the engine and hoisted himself out of the car. 'They should start giving roads names and houses numbers. Finding houses would be a lot simpler if that was the case.'

Lemon Villa was a modest bungalow but certainly not a villa like Pankaj had imagined. He noticed, as they walked up the path to the house, that the flowers and shrubs were mostly dead and the white goat tethered to a large tree in the garden had eaten everything around him. Just to the right of the house was a big round stone; Pankaj assumed it was where Vasudev did his knife sharpening. How nice for Vasudev to be able to sit and watch the comings and goings of the guest house whilst he did his work outside in the fresh air.

For a second, Pankaj felt a pang of jealousy. Being a knife sharpener was a simple job; no dead bodies to smell or look at, no dealing with criminals. But sharpening other people's kitchenware couldn't be the most exciting of jobs. 'Idle mind equals idle hands,' his father's voice rang in his head. No wonder Vasudev had started an affair with his best friend's wife. Pankaj decided police work was the best thing for him. He was rarely *bekaar,* idle.

He felt a tap on his head as they reached the front of the villa.

'Get your head out of the clouds,' Chupplejeep said.

'Sorry, sir. I was thinking.

'Thinking of interrogation questions, I hope?' Chupplejeep knocked on the knife sharpener's door.

'Actually, sir – ' Pankaj started.

Chupplejeep cut him off. 'That's his scooter?'

'Gita said that he rode a Hero Honda – black colour.'

The door opened to reveal a small woman, almost half Chupplejeep's height. She wore glasses and a plain white sari. If Pankaj had been standing any farther away he would have thought the woman was a school child because she was so petite, but up close he could see the lines on her face; lines you could only get by having lived a full life.

'We're here to see Vasudev Bhandari,' Chupplejeep said.

The woman nodded in silence but made no attempt to move aside or invite them inside.

'Can we see him?' Pankaj asked.

Again the lady nodded but made no further sound or movement.

'Sir, maybe she can't speak, or maybe she doesn't understand. You want me to shout?' Pankaj opened his mouth in readiness.

Chupplejeep held his hand out to stop him. 'Maybe she's scared. If you shout you'll frighten her even more.'

'Very good, sir. I didn't think of that.'

Chupplejeep bent his knees to make himself level with the woman. He asked her again if they could see Vasudev.

This time she tilted her head, but still she made no noise.

Before Chupplejeep could say anything further, a man appeared from behind the mute woman in the white sari. Chupplejeep straightened up.

Pankaj took a step back. Vasudev was not what he imagined the knife sharpener to look like. They were usually such spindly men who looked like they were in need of a decent meal, but this fellow looked like he had eaten a whole cow.

Vasudev flexed his muscles under his tight-fitting blue tee-shirt. He was at least six foot tall, tall enough to whack Sandeep Shah on the top of his head.

'*Kaun*?' Vasudev asked. He looked down his nose at the policemen.

Chupplejeep cleared his throat. 'Vasudev Bhandari?'

'Yes.'

'We're from Little Larara Police Station investigating the death of Mr Sandeep Shah. Can we ask you some questions?'

Vasudev turned and motioned for Pankaj and Chupplejeep to follow him into his house. However, the small lady had not moved.

'Erm…excuse me, Mr Bhandari. This lady is in our way.'

Vasudev walked slowly back to the front door. He crouched down next to the woman and said something barely audible in Konkani. The woman hung her head, like a child who had just been scolded. She walked off. 'Don't mind my mother, Detective,' Vasudev said. 'She's a little mad.'

Pankaj wondered how such a small woman had given birth. She was tiny. Maybe she had shrunk over the years. Only recently, he had read an interesting article in the *Larara Express* about how people shortened as they got older. Since then, he had been monitoring his own parents for shrinkage, but he hadn't noticed any change as yet.

Pankaj and Chupplejeep introduced themselves as they sat around the Vasudev's small kitchen table. Pankaj stared at the knife sharpener. He certainly didn't look like a knife sharpener, he looked more like a body builder.

~

'You go to the gym?' Chupplejeep asked as if reading Pankaj's thoughts. It was men like Vasudev who gave men like Arthur a tough time with women. No wonder Christabel was continually trying to put him on a diet when there were specimens like Vasudev out there.

'Yeah, I like to keep fit. Can't handle not going to the gym.'

Chupplejeep shook his head in disappointment. 'You were a friend to Sandeep?'

'Oh yes, good friends. I was best man at his wedding.'

'Good friends?' Pankaj asked. He leaned towards their suspect.

'Yes.'

'Even though you were sleeping with Sandeep's wife, you class yourself as a *good* friend?'

'A soft drink, officers?' Vasudev said, rising to his feet.

Chupplejeep noticed how tall Vasudev was. He could knock them both out if he wanted to. He declined a drink. 'We want to make this interview short,' Chupplejeep said. He looked around the kitchen. It was a well-used space. No wonder Vasudev was the size he was. 'As you can imagine we're extremely busy right now. We've a murder investigation under way.'

'Of course,' Vasudev said as he walked towards the kitchen window, which he peered out of. 'I know what you must be thinking, but what to do? I had no choice.'

Pankaj shifted in his chair. He opened his mouth to say something but Chupplejeep raised his hand to silence his officer.

'I loved Gita the moment our eyes met,' Vasudev said a moment later. 'Unfortunately it was at their wedding.'

Pankaj and Chupplejeep were silent.

'Sandeep was a very good friend, but he had no respect for women.' Vasudev turned to face them. 'Surely, officers, you must know that by now.'

Chupplejeep raised his hand to his eyes to reduce the glare from behind Vasudev.

'Sandeep slept around. His wife was lonely. It didn't take me long to persuade her to start seeing me. I knew she had feelings for me. Soon we started going steady.'

Pankaj narrowed his eyes at Vasudev. 'Going steady is for teenagers. You were going out with a married woman!'

Vasudev shrugged. 'When you fall in love, you cannot decide who this special someone is going to be. If she is married, then what?'

Pankaj briefly thought about Shwetika. Colour rose to his cheeks.

Chupplejeep nodded. He remembered his first meeting with Christabel. At the time he had innocently gone to the market with no intention of meeting a woman. Not so soon, after his break up with Atika. He had merely been passing his time one morning, smelling the end of a mango to check its ripeness, when Christabel walked up to the vendor and demanded twelve of his best Mankurads. The detective couldn't help but look at the lady making such demands. Once he did, he knew that if she would have him, he would spend the rest of his life with her. Perhaps it was love at first sight, but then he didn't believe in such things.

He had been lucky Christabel wasn't married when he had met her. What would he have done if she were? Nothing. Christabel would never have allowed it. She was a solid Catholic. She wouldn't even have looked at him, had she been married. Chupplejeep fiddled with his moustache. He had been lucky indeed, but this was just another reason to consider marriage. If he and Christabel were not married then Christabel could easily meet another man. She was often at the market buying fresh produce.

'I would never do such a thing,' Pankaj said, waking Chupplejeep out of his daydream.

'If you love Gita,' Chupplejeep said to Vasudev, pushing the thoughts of marriage to the back of his mind, 'would you have killed for her?'

Vasudev laughed. 'Officer, have you gone mad like my mother? Nothing doing. I couldn't kill anyone.'

Chupplejeep eyed Vasudev suspiciously. He was certainly tall enough to hit Sandeep Shah with a blunt instrument from above. A knife sharpener would probably have access to different types of instruments. And there was no doubt that Sandeep would have left the outhouse to see his friend, even if he was naked. Some men didn't mind talking to close friends without clothes on and Gita had said that her husband was not shy of his body. It made perfect sense. Vasudev also had good motive – he was in love with Sandeep's wife and perhaps Gita was too scared to leave her husband. The easy way out was murder. With one blow to the head, Sandeep was dead and Vasudev and Gita's problems were solved.

Yes, Chupplejeep thought, Vasudev had it all worked out, all he needed was the opportunity. Where was Vasudev the night of the murder? If Gita was telling the truth, then she had been with him for the first part of the evening. But Gita could have sneaked out later that night, met Vasudev and both of them could have ended her husband's life. Or Vasudev could have gone to visit Sandeep alone. Maybe Gita didn't want to see her boyfriend murdering her husband in cold blood.

'Sandeep was killed with a blunt object – Gita told me. Don't you think I would have used a knife?'

'No. I wouldn't expect you to use a knife. That would really make it obvious, no?'

'Okay, I see what you're saying,' Vasudev said, scratching his head.

Chupplejeep sighed. Was Vasudev intelligent enough to kill Sandeep Shah and cover his tracks? Unless the plan was Gita's and Vasudev was just the muscle.

'So please tell us your exact whereabouts on the evening of November tenth and the early hours of November eleventh.'

Vasudev took his seat at the kitchen table. He crossed his right ankle over his left knee and removed his *chappal*. 'You want *paan*?'

'No thank you,' Pankaj said. Chupplejeep shook his head also.

'You mind if I have *paan*? I find it relaxing.'

'Please go ahead. Talk to us whilst you make it,' Chupplejeep said, realising the importance of letting the fidgety types keep their hands busy whilst they confessed to things.

Vasudev stood up and retrieved a large, round, metal tiffin. He sat back down again and opened it to reveal all the ingredients he needed. He took a fresh betel leaf from the kitchen table and started filling it with items from his tin.

'I picked Gita up at Bata after work, and brought her straight here. Must have been nine when I collected her. I dropped her back to her house at eleven-thirty. Maybe twelve,' Vasudev said as he filled the betel leaf with *chuna*, *supari* and powdered tobacco.

~

'Did anyone see you with Gita?' Pankaj asked, turning his nose up at the *paan*. Chewing *paan* was a disgusting habit. He wondered if Vasudev used the *katha* and quick lime that some used to give it a red colouring. He assumed he didn't – Vasudev's teeth were white.

Vasudev added some more powder and folded the edges of the leaf inwards to make a little parcel. He held the leaf up to his mouth and pursed his lips. 'My mother may have seen us when I went to drop Gita home, but

279

she can't vouch for us. She doesn't really talk. Sometimes she does, but mostly she just talks to herself.'

'We could try questioning her,' Pankaj said.

'She's been saying more recently,' Vasudev said, 'But it's difficult getting her to talk. She doesn't like people, especially new people. And by new people I mean people she didn't know when my father was alive.'

'Why doesn't she talk?' Chupplejeep asked.

'My father died three years ago, she stopped talking then. They married young – did everything together. With the shock of his death, she stopped talking.'

Chupplejeep understood how heartbroken his mother must have been, but to go into a madness? He didn't understand that. He decided to keep those thoughts to himself. 'Has she seen a doctor?' he asked genuinely concerned for the welfare of not just Vasudev's mother, but Vasudev himself.

'We've seen a doctor. They can't do anything, but a lady from that Daisy Chain charity comes to help out most days.'

'*Aacha*, it's good you have some help.'

Vasudev popped his neat package of *paan* into his mouth. 'When Gita moves here, she's going to care for my mother. I won't make her work in that Bata shop like her husband used to make her do.'

'Her husband was your friend,' Chupplejeep reminded him.

'I know,' Vasudev said, chewing on the filled leaf. He sucked back and swallowed the spittle that was escaping from the corner of his mouth. 'But he didn't treat his wife right.'

'Perhaps Gita would prefer to work at Bata, than to stay at home all day caring for someone,' Pankaj said.

Vasudev shrugged.

'Tell me then, you dropped Gita back to her house and just returned home. No stops along the way?' Chupplejeep said.

'Nothing. I returned here,' Vasudev said. He pushed the half-chewed *paan* into the corner of his mouth with his tongue.

'Did anyone see you?'

'No.'

'Not even your mother?'

Vasudev shifted in his seat. 'Nobody saw me. I went straight to bed.'

There was a noise behind Chupplejeep. He turned to face the entrance of the kitchen.

Vasudev's mother was standing in the doorway.

Chapter Thirty-two

Chupplejeep considered standing up, but then realised that being seated was a better position at which to talk to Vasudev's mother.

'I saw him return that night after he dropped his woman back to her village,' she said in a small voice.

There was a clatter behind Chupplejeep. He turned back to Vasudev whose mouth was ajar.

Chupplejeep took a deep breath and then turned his chair to face the woman giving her his full attention. 'Ah, you speak!' he said with a smile.

Mrs Bhandari didn't respond.

'What time did your son leave to pick her up and what time did he drop her that evening?'

'He was out at the gym. He didn't come home after the gym so I can't tell you what time he left. He brought her back at nine-thirty. They fooled around in his bedroom,' the small woman said. 'Then when they had done their business he returned her.'

Vasudev stared at his mother. The half-chewed *paan* fell from his mouth onto the table.

'Do you remember the time at which your son returned?' Chupplejeep asked, glancing back at Vasudev and then turning towards Mrs Bhandari. He wondered if she had been listening to what her son had been saying all this time.

'Around midnight, maybe half-twelve.'

'He went straight to bed?'

'No,' she said, looking at her son and then looking away.

'Mamma don't,' Vasudev said. He stood up, the metal chair screeched against the stone floor and fell with a loud clatter.

Chupplejeep noticed that Vasudev had turned red and he had anger in his eyes.

He placed his hand on his baton to check it was still there.

The small woman looked at her son and raised her hand, '*Bas*,' she said.

'Mamma, why?' Vasudev pleaded.

Chupplejeep realised that it wasn't anger in Vasudev's eyes. It was shame. He now seemed smaller than he first appeared. What power a mother can have over her son, regardless of his size.

'You haven't spoken to me in years. Why now? Why to these people?'

'Because son, they need to know. You want to be thought of as a murderer? For what? You've looked after me for three years now. You think I don't know that. I've been foolish and in my own world, talking to your dead father.' A tear ran down her cheek. 'I'm turning

283

into a crazy woman. Let me at least do this one thing for you before I really go mad.'

'Mamma, you are not mad,' Vasudev said. He walked over to his mother and hugged her.

'It's time to lift the curse, son.'

What curse? Chupplejeep wanted to ask, but this was a weird enough situation to begin with. He didn't want any further revelations of their family history. He wanted answers about Vasudev's whereabouts.

'What curse?' Pankaj asked.

Chupplejeep sighed.

'When my husband died, his sister cursed me. She said it was my fault he died because I was a cold woman, and after years of her brother trying to love me, his heart gave up and died.'

'My father had a heart attack,' Vasudev explained. He popped the *paan* back in his mouth and chewed with new vigour.

'I vowed not to talk because of the tragedy I caused. It was difficult for me at first, but after a while, I got used to it. I started talking to my husband and occasionally my son. I allowed myself to do that.'

'She said that?' Pankaj asked, 'What a woman.'

'She didn't mean it,' Vasudev said. 'Auntyji was angry at my father's death. She needed someone to blame.' He turned to Pankaj. 'Papa's sister is old, very old.'

Chupplejeep nodded. This may have been a life-changing moment for Mrs Bhandari and her son, but it was not going to solve the murder of Sandeep Shah. 'So

284

Mrs Bhandari, tell me what did your son do when he returned home that evening?'

Vasudev picked up his chair and sat back down. He looked to the floor as his mother walked over and stood behind him. She put an arm on his shoulder. 'I messed the bed,' she said so quietly, Chupplejeep had to strain his ears to hear. 'He cleaned it, gave me new bedding and scrubbed the old ones clean. It took him at least a couple of hours. Then I heard him go to his bedroom to sleep.'

Chupplejeep and Pankaj were silent. Chupplejeep hoped Pankaj wouldn't ask why, but he didn't have to.

'I have faecal incontinence,' Mrs Bhandari said. 'You can check with the nurses that visit.'

Pankaj's eyes widened. Chupplejeep nodded his understanding, hoping she wouldn't elaborate any further on the matter.

'I went to bed after that,' Vasudev said. The spark had truly disappeared from his voice.

'When did you next see Gita Shah?'

'We see each other nearly everyday, Detective,' Vasudev said. His mother had now seated herself at the table.

Mrs Bhandari was silent. It didn't look like she would speak again. Perhaps finding her voice had tired her.

'So you saw Gita the day Sandeep's body was found.'

'Yes. After you had been to visit her family, she told me then about the death.'

'How did she seem to you?'

'How do you think? She was upset – wanted to break off her relationship with me. She felt guilty, you see.'

'But you talked her out of it?'

Vasudev nodded. 'It helped that rumours were flying around about village girls her husband was fooling around with.'

Chupplejeep stood up. Pankaj did the same, putting his notepad back in his breast pocket. 'I think we have what we need,' Chupplejeep said.

'Let me show you out,' Vasudev said, walking them to the door.

As they stood in the entrance of Lemon Villa, Pankaj pointed to the large stone. 'Is that the what you use to sharpen knives?'

'We don't live in the dark ages anymore,' Vasudev said with a smile. 'That's my knife sharpener over there.' He pointed to a bright yellow metal contraption by the side of the house that looked like it had half a bicycle attached to it. Vasudev bent down and picked up a stick. He walked over to the machine and started peddling. A metal disc started rotating and he held the stick in front of it. 'See, imagine this stick is the knife.'

'Oh I see,' Pankaj said.

'They call me the knife sharpener, but I'm giving it up because the trade is dying. Some people in the big houses have metal contraptions at home to sharpen their own knives.'

'But surely that is more work for them,' Pankaj said. He had seen these products in the store and wondered if people actually bought them. 'If I bought one for my mother, she would complain that I'm giving her more work to do!'

'I have just started my own little gym in Mapusa,' Vasudev said. 'Just some weights now, but as soon as I get more customers I'm going to buy a machine – maybe a running machine. I'll build it up slowly. Perhaps, Detective,' Vasudev said, his eyes resting on Chupplejeep's round belly, 'you can come by. For free of course.'

'Very good,' Chupplejeep said, unsmiling. He turned and walked down the path. The last thing they needed was another gym in Mapusa, encouraging people to slim down. And anyway, why did people need machines to run when they could run outside for free?

CHAPTER THIRTY-THREE

'Go and fetch Sanjog. Let's see if he has bothered to think of an alibi,' Chupplejeep said to Pankaj. 'I need a minute to think. There's something in this case that we're missing. I just can't put my finger on it.' Chupplejeep made his way through the hotel lobby towards the pool.

Pankaj looked through the glass window of the coffee shop and took a deep breath. Sanjog was dining with his wife, Kamana. The woman made him feel uneasy. She was always winking at him and playing with the end of her plait. Was she what his friend, Raja, referred to as a man-eater? Quite possibly. Pankaj was sure a woman like Kamana could eat him for breakfast.

Kamana sat facing her husband, but she looked more interested in the syrupy *gulab jamuns* in her bowl than what her husband was telling her. Pankaj glanced over to his boss. He had seated himself on a recliner in-between the pool and the beach and seemed to be deep in thought.

~

Chupplejeep made himself comfortable on the lounger and motioned for a waiter, who was clearing a nearby table, to come over.

They had interviewed all their suspects. Many had motives, some had motive and opportunity, but none of them seemed like the murderous type. Their disputes with the victim were just part of village life; one fellow had a better place in society than the other, this one in love with that one, and that one in love with someone else.

Chupplejeep considered Bala. Right now he was still in the running for being the number one suspect. After all, he had lied when he was first questioned and to top it off he was a suspicious-looking fellow with his wide-set eyes and his lack of alibi. Bala had been successful in deceiving the whole village by pretending he didn't know Sandeep or that Sandeep was living with the Laljis. He was also in love with Lavita. But killing off Lavita's lover did not guarantee that the girl would marry him. Was Bala intelligent enough to see this? Or was love really blind?

Chupplejeep twisted the right end of his moustache. He thought of the women involved in the case. It was rare in Goa for a woman to be a murderess, but in recent times many women across India had started to commit these horrible crimes. They had moved from behind the stove into the great arena of murder. It was almost understandable for men to kill – so many men didn't have a heart. But women, they were supposed to be caring by nature. Wasn't it their instinct to look after and nurture things? Utsa, Gita and Lavita all had the motive to murder this lothario. There was no doubt about that.

Lavita was meek, though, and she genuinely loved Sandeep. Chupplejeep had recently examined the circumstances in which her parents died in the village of Soco. The file notes put her miles away from the scene of the crime. And there were two credible witnesses who had seen her taking the buffalo to graze, so there was no suspicion there. The Laljis and Granny Monji were in Utol at the time. Granny Monji had gone into detail in her statement about the bad luck she had warned her daughter of before the accident, but none of them had a motive or opportunity to kill.

Utsa and Gita were the type of women you wouldn't want to cross – with a steely determination in their eyes. They were living exactly how they wanted, as if they were in America or something. These two women were not going to be held back by their sex. Gita was merrily having an affair with Vasudev and Utsa was casually flirting with Sandeep when she knew her best friend was after him!

These were modern women and Chupplejeep knew he had to think of them as equally suspicious. Modern women didn't accept their husband or lover's infidelity lightly. And crimes of passion were common in the villages. But with one blow to the head, was this really a murder fuelled with passion? If it was, they had done a good job to conceal this. Perhaps these women were more cunning than he had thought.

Passionate people often made mistakes; they left clues – they messed up. Chupplejeep shook his head. These thoughts were all well and good, but if he was honest with himself and considered all the evidence carefully, then this didn't seem like a crime driven by passion. And if this was the case it instantly ruled out half his suspects, but one of them was the culprit.

Sailesh and Vasudev also fell into this category of lovelorn suspects; one a jealous lover and the other desperate to be with the victim's wife. Chupplejeep visualised the crack and the small depression made in the skull of Sandeep Shah. Sailesh couldn't verify his whereabouts that night, he was just watching television at home, but Vasudev had an alibi. It wasn't watertight, after all his odd little mother was his only witness, but in both cases their stories were a darn sight better than Neeraj Dhaliwal's.

It was obvious that Neeraj wanted revenge for what Sandeep had done to his daughter. Little did he know that his daughter was having her own fun. Again, in this instance, if Neeraj had committed the crime it would be a crime fuelled by love – love for his daughter. But for some reason Chupplejeep was finding it difficult to accept this, because one blow to the head was not impassioned. It was cold and pre-meditated.

The only person with no emotional ties to Sandeep was Sanjog. Owing money to a loan shark was a dangerous way to live. But even Chupplejeep had to admit that Sanjog was more like a *pomfret* than a shark. Sanjog didn't have an alibi though. What was worrying was that he didn't seem to be bothered to think of one. Any sane person would think about where they had been. They wouldn't just say they forgot, when they were under the suspicion of murder. Was this a man who was so cold-blooded that he just didn't care? Or was he stupid enough to think that an alibi meant nothing these days?

Chupplejeep watched the waves crash against the shore. Whoever had committed this crime had to pay for what they had done. It was a simple crime and there were a limited number of suspects. There was no doubt that someone wanted Sandeep Shah dead. Had he overlooked the true culprit? Or a vital piece of evidence? He put his head in his hands. Failing to solve this simple village crime would be a disastrous start for him at the station and it would definitely mean a black mark on his near-perfect record.

Even when evidence was conveniently misplaced and suspects suddenly disappeared across borders, Chupplejeep had brought, in total, seventy-four criminals to justice. 'Perhaps you should retire,' he could hear the Inspector General say. And of course there would be comments from the other detectives at Greater Larara Police Station. He could almost hear the taunts of young Detective Gupta and young Detective Fernandes. 'Too good to take bribes, too old and useless to solve crimes!' he sighed. 'The simplest cases are the hardest to solve.'

Chupplejeep lifted his head out of his hands and looked up to the sky. 'Nana, can you hear me?' he whispered, 'Give me a clue. Who committed this crime?'

Even now that she was gone, he hoped Nana was still looking after him. Then he looked down towards the unhurried waiter slowly making his way over to him before looking back up again. Something caught his eye. He noticed that nets had been tied carefully under the tender coconuts that hung precariously over the swimming pool of this five-star hotel.

'Sir?' the waiter asked, holding a pen poised over his notepad.

'Ah, one *nimbu pani*, salty,' Chupplejeep said, looking back down.

'Anything else, sir?'

He thought about asking for a plate of French fries but held back as he felt his belt dig into the soft round of his stomach. He shook his head. The waiter dawdled off in the direction of the pool bar, leaving Chupplejeep to reflect on his fat belly. Had Vasudev been hinting at him to lose weight when he mentioned his gym the other day? There was no denying that a detective had to be fit. And since leaving Panaji he had let his fitness levels slip. Imagine if he was in a position of having to chase someone. Maybe he would take Vasudev up on his offer.

'Sir, your drink,' the waiter said, handing the glass and the bill to the detective from a silver tray he was carrying.

'What? One hundred and twenty rupees for a lime juice and water?'

The waiter nodded.

'Is this really the price?'

'This is a five-star, sir.'

'Five-star with five-star prices.' He took a sip of the drink. 'Tastes the same like the local taverna. In fact it's a little too salty. At Joe's it costs me less than thirty rupees. No discount for locals?'

The waiter was silent.

'Here,' Chupplejeep said sitting up in his recliner, taking out his wallet and handing the money to the waiter.

The boy took the money and waited.

Charging over a hundred rupees for a soft drink! The waiter wasn't going to get a tip for his slow service as well. He lay back down with his drink in hand and in his mind played out how the murder of Sandeep Shah could have happened.

He hoped that Sanjog would provide an alibi today. He looked up again. The net under the ripe fruit bothered him. It was not a normal sight to see in such a tranquil setting. It destroyed the beauty of the natural coconut tree. Did tourists really want their photographs of palm trees ruined with ugly netting? What was this world coming to? He picked up a baby green coconut that had missed the net and had fallen next to his lounger. It fit neatly in the palm of his hand. He rolled it around with his fingers like a Chinese Baoding ball whilst he sorted out his thoughts.

Eventually, he looked over to the waiter who was now cleaning around the pool area. Chupplejeep called over to him. 'Tell me, why are those nets under the coconut tree?'

'To prevent falling coconuts,' the waiter said.

'I can see that, but I have never seen nets like this put up anywhere in Goa.'

'Three months ago a coconut fell missing a foreigner lady by this much,' the waiter said, holding his thumb and first finger just a fraction apart. 'Lady made a fuss, shouting and screaming like a fisherwoman. Saying if she was injured she would sue, that her husband was some big-shot lawyer. After that, boss said "enough". It was too risky to expose delicate foreigners to falling coconuts. He ordered the nets to be tied around the trees.'

'But how often do coconuts fall?'

'Not very often sir.'

'So really is there need for the nets?'

'"Just in case, just in case," boss says, "With tourists, comes lawsuits."'

Chupplejeep smiled. 'I see.' He pulled out twenty rupees from his top pocket and indicated for the waiter to take it.

'Sir, Mr Sanjog Viraj.' Chupplejeep heard Pankaj's voice from behind him.

'Detective, I see you've discovered one of the finest spots in Goa,' Sanjog said. 'I come here often with my wife at this time, just to watch the sunset. Nothing is as beautiful as an Indian sunset. Although don't tell that to my wife!' Sanjog smiled and extended his hand to the detective.

'Please, please, take a seat.' Chupplejeep signalled to the waiter to move the other loungers closer. 'You're right. It's a beautiful sunset,' Chupplejeep said, looking at the setting sun for the first time. 'But you have to pay for the privilege. Even a lime juice water is more than a detective's salary can provide.' Chupplejeep gave the loan shark a knowing smile as sat upright on the edge of the recliner. 'You must be a rich man, Sanjog, to be having dinner here.'

Sanjog was silent. He sat next to the detective on the next lounger.

'Tell me, you're still without an alibi for November tenth? The night of Sandeep Shah's murder.'

'Do you expect me to make one up?'

'Of course not. I just wanted to be sure you had thought about it. Did your wife check her diary?'

'Strangely, it's gone missing.'

'Missing?'

'Yes, another crime for you to solve, Detective.'

'Don't act smart. Let me remind you that you are one of our main suspects in the murder of Sandeep Shah.'

Sanjog shook his head. 'I didn't touch the man. I don't need an alibi.'

'Don't be ignorant, Mr Viraj. Your time is running out. We're close to concluding this case. I've received some vital evidence that'll pinpoint the murderer. Without an alibi it could be their word against yours. The witness is an upstanding citizen, not someone who makes his or her money illegally. They're more likely to be believed.'

'I see, Detective,' Sanjog said wiping his brow with a handkerchief. 'Then you don't need to interview me, if you already know.' He stood up to leave.

'We'll be seeing you shortly,' Chupplejeep said as Sanjog dug his hands into his pockets and walked away.

Pankaj sat down and waited till Sanjog was out of sight before he spoke. 'But sir, which witness are you talking about? I told you, I interviewed those other gamblers. There was nothing of interest, nothing that pointed us to Sanjog. If anything it exonerated him. Many had owed large sums of money to the loan shark. Like you said, sir, he's a pussycat. No mention of broken kneecaps, not even vicious threats.'

Chupplejeep smiled as he relaxed back on the recliner and looked up at the coconut tree.

CHAPTER THIRTY-FOUR

Chupplejeep finished the last of his *bolinhas* and *chai* and wiped his mouth with a paper napkin. The jewellery store across the road appeared to have sprung up overnight. Something was willing the detective to go inside. Just yesterday he had another confrontation with Christabel.

'Why are you doing this to me?' she had asked with a pained expression after he had swallowed his last mouthful of okra and rice. She hadn't mentioned what she was referring to but it didn't take a scientist to figure out what it was. It was the dreaded word that was starting to plague his life – marriage.

Chupplejeep had opened his mouth to say something, but the words did not come. How could he tell the woman he loved that he was scared of commitment? Shunned as a child at birth, he didn't know what it was to make a real commitment or to have a family of his own. The orphanage had been hell. Thank goodness he had been saved from that place by Nana. Nana had been his only form of stability. What would she have said on the topic of marriage? She would have said that he had to be true to himself. And if he wanted to remain single then that was his choice.

But did he want to stay single? He couldn't imagine a life without Christabel. Just looking at her face made his heart melt. She brought a smile to his lips no matter what kind of mood he was in. And how did he repay this woman he claimed to love and who always cheered up his day? By refusing to talk about marriage. He was hurting her. How long would she stick around whilst he pondered over his decision?

'Of course, Arthur,' Christabel had said to his gormless response. 'Keep silent like you normally do.' And with that she had stood up and left. No offer of sweet *bebinca* and no intention to stay longer. Chupplejeep could see that if he didn't play this carefully, he would lose her fast.

He stared at the window of the jewellers. Perhaps this jewellery store opposite was a sign. It wouldn't hurt to just look. He paid for his tea and biscuits and walked over to Gopal and Sons across the road.

'Sir, can I show you something?' the shop attendant asked.

'Oh no, just looking.'

'Rings are a very good choice. They are circular that means they are eternal. A gift for your wife perhaps?'

'How much would this ring cost?' Chupplejeep asked, looking at a gold ring with a red stone.

A man dressed in a white kurta appeared from behind the curtain and walked behind the counter to where Chupplejeep stood. The shop owner lifted his eyeglass loupe. 'We do good deals for officials. What is your good lady's ring size?'

'Huh?' Chupplejeep said. He had not even thought of Christabel's ring size. Now that the shopkeeper had asked, he felt foolish for not having thought of it himself. This had been a terrible idea.

'Never mind,' said the shopkeeper. 'You can tell me if your lady friend is small or big and we can decide. Then you can always get the ring widened or made smaller.'

'I think I'll come back.'

'Perhaps a bracelet?' the shop assistant said. 'Or a necklace?'

Chupplejeep shook his head. He had interviewed hundreds of criminals without so much as breaking out in a sweat and yet this innocent jeweller was making him hot under the collar.

'Here, take my card. I am the proprietor here,' Mr Gopal said, pressing his business card into Chupplejeep's hand. 'Perhaps if she already wears rings you could bring one in to me and I can tell you her size from that.'

Chupplejeep nodded at the idea and pocketed the card. He thanked the vendor and turned to leave. But as he opened the shop door, Mrs Lalji and Lavita walked in.

'Oh, Detective,' Mrs Lalji said. 'What are you doing here?'

Chupplejeep was silent. The jewellery store had been a bad idea. What had he been thinking?

'Our Lavita is getting married,' Mrs Lalji said, saving Chupplejeep from answering her question.

'Anyone I know?' The name Bala was on the tip of his tongue.

'You know Bala Mukherjee, the *pau wallah*? That is whom Lavita is to marry.'

'A good match.'

Mrs Lalji cleared her throat. 'You know you can't enter a good family like that empty-handed. We must buy our Lavita some jewellery to take with her. And of course she'll need some sets for the wedding. It will be a small ceremony but she must have some jewellery. You know at first I was worried,' Mrs Lalji said as her voice lowered to a whisper. 'I was worried about this scandal of murder. I know that Bala had been questioned. I didn't want my Lavita caught up in all of that.'

'And then?' Chupplejeep asked. He leaned in to hear Mrs Lalji better. 'What changed?'

Mrs Lalji looked around. The shop assistant and Mr Gopal were busy with another customer. 'My mother made me see sense, Detective. Bala Mukherjee is not a murderer and I think he is the best match for Lavita. She is getting older and is not even working. We spoiled her, Detective. It is her duty now to get married.'

Lavita looked down at the floor.

'I see.' Chupplejeep put his hand through his hair. Kulkarni's rumour had been incorrect. Thinking of Kulkarni's gossip made him wonder when he would get back to him with the tests from Bala's statue. 'When was your engagement finalised?'

'Only yesterday,' Lavita said with a smile.

'*Aacha*, this is very interesting.'

301

'Interesting? Why? Detective, you can't still think that our Bala is a suspect.'

Lavita's eyes widened.

'I didn't say that – ' Chupplejeep started to say.

'Detective, surely – '

Chupplejeep looked at his watch. 'Really, is that the time,' he said, interrupting Mrs Lalji. 'I must be going.'

The shop assistant immediately looked up, scurried to the front of the store and opened the door for him. 'Please visit us again,' the assistant said.

Chupplejeep smiled as he started towards the door. Then, suddenly, he turned around. 'Oh, Mrs Lalji, I had a question I wanted to ask you. Something that is bothering me.'

'Yes, Detective, what is it?'

'Did you ever see Sandeep Shah out in the garden at night? Sleepwalking perhaps or something like that?'

Mrs Lalji bit her lower lip.

'Lavita, did you ever see anything like that?' Chupplejeep asked.

Both Lavita and Mrs Lalji were silent.

'Not to worry, but if you remember, let me know.'

'Actually,' Mrs Lalji started as Chupplejeep was halfway out of the door. She put her fingers to her lips. 'A few times when I had got up to pee in the night, Sandeep was also doing the same. I noticed once or twice he never made it to the toilet. He would just pee on the bushes. Granny saw him too – she claimed he did it every morning at exactly two o'clock. She was angry he was pissing on the shrubs especially after the hibiscus

302

died. That was Granny's favourite plant. She said she would give him a warning.'

'A warning?'

'Oh, not like that, Detective. She was suspicious of Sandeep – said he was bringing bad luck on the house…' Mrs Lalji trailed off. She looked at her niece and then turned back to Chupplejeep. 'Because of his wandering eye,' she whispered. 'You know how it is. Granny has never really gotten over the death of my sister. Blames all that on bad luck. Thinks she can smell it! Granny is too superstitious. She won't wash her hair on certain days. She even tried to put *kajal* on Lavita's forehead to make her look ugly to ward off evil eye, but Lavita was having none of that. These young girls, they want to look their best, Detective,' Mrs Lalji said with a laugh.

'I see. Thank you, Mrs Lalji,' Chupplejeep said. And with that he walked out of the shop.

~

'Oh hell,' Neeraj said, grinding his hands into his pockets. He walked towards his parked scooter. He would always be one of those people in the wrong place at the wrong time. The rumours about his daughter were true. She wasn't just having an affair with the good-for-nothing knife sharpener fellow, but now he knew she was in love with him. Did this make her as bad as her husband? He had just seen his daughter and Vasudev with his own eyes – they were holding hands in a corner of Mapusa market for everyone to see.

Did Paavai know? He strongly doubted it, and once again he didn't feel he had the courage to tell her. His wife didn't want to see the bad side of Sandeep even after he had told her about the gambling. She definitely would not consider that her daughter was not the saint she had her marked out to be.

Neeraj rubbed his brow. This was the final piece of the puzzle. He knew it was his one chance to make it up to his wife and daughter. For the first time in a long while, he knew what he had to do.

CHAPTER THIRTY-FIVE

It was past midnight. Pankaj had never stayed so late in the office. Was this what detective work was like in the big cities? Having to work when everyone else was sleeping. His mother had brought some spicy *channa daal* and *parathas* and hot flask of *masala chai* for him and his boss. Chupplejeep had picked at the food, which was unlike him, but understandable given the stress he was under.

Inspector General Gosht had called earlier. 'You are supposed to be a big homicide detective,' Pankaj had overheard, despite the call not being put on loudspeaker. 'You want some recognition, solve the case, na?' The atmosphere in the office had changed after that phone call. So when the food arrived, Pankaj decided it was best to eat. Now that his belly was full, he wanted to go home and sleep. He was struggling to keep his eyes open.

'We're nearly there,' Chupplejeep said encouragingly. 'I've already booked my houseboat in Kerala. I can't afford to book new flights.' Chupplejeep smiled but Pankaj knew he was trying to make light of the situation. He may have been worried about losing money on his flights, but he was more worried about the Inspector General breathing down his neck.

~

Chupplejeep opened the Sandeep Shah file again. Inspector General Gosht had been very clear when he had called today. Solve the case by the end of the week, or he wouldn't be considered for a promotion for the next five years. He sighed. He had Christabel, he had an income and a small pot of savings. Did he really need to lose hair over this one small case?

Chupplejeep looked at Pankaj whose eyelids were drooping. What was he thinking? He had caught a serial killer when all the other detectives had given up. He had a very good success rate. At one time he had even thought of going to work in Mumbai. He wasn't going to be defeated by such a simple case. He was close to finding out the truth about how Shah met his end. He could fail himself, but he wouldn't fail Pankaj. Hadn't the boy said that he wanted to be just like him when he was in college? If he gave up now, what would Pankaj think of him?

The rural villages are what made Goa so special, Chupplejeep thought. Even Gandhi had said that 'India lives in her villages, not in her cities'. He had the job of keeping them safe and that was exactly what he was going to do. And forty was not the end of his career – forty was still young. To hell with young Detective Gupta and young Detective Fernandes. He wouldn't let

306

those young cops take over without a fight. A smile rose to his lips. It was high time they solved this case.

'Sir, we have been through everything at least five times. Lets go home, sleep on it and come back tomorrow,' Pankaj said, his face resting on his hands.

'Pankaj, a good detective never sleeps when they are on the brink of solving a case. Come on, let's go over it once more. The murderer has to be one of these people…' Chupplejeep took each of their suspects in turn and explained to Pankaj the reason he had excluded them as the culprit.

'Oi Pankaj!' Chupplejeep said loudly ten minutes later when he noticed Pankaj's head had dropped to the side, his eyes shut.

Pankaj woke with a start.

'You heard what I said?'

'Yes, sir,' Pankaj said confidently. At this time of night it was best to pretend he had heard every word. He didn't want to stay a moment longer than he had to.

Chupplejeep looked at his watch. 'Go home then, get some sleep, but tomorrow you meet me here at nine in the morning.' Then remembering how Poirot revealed the murderer at the end of a case he added, 'Before you leave your home tomorrow morning, Pankaj, call each of these people.' Chupplejeep stood up from behind his desk and walked over to Pankaj handing him a list of names. 'Tell them to meet us on the back veranda of the Lalji house next to the tallest coconut tree in Utol.'

'And if they ask why, sir?'

'Tell them that Detective Chupplejeep has solved the case.'

Pankaj eyes widened. He opened his mouth to say something.

'You said you were listening, didn't you?' Chupplejeep said with a smile. 'Now go home.'

'Sir...?' Pankaj asked.

Chupplejeep was silent.

Three minutes after Pankaj left the office, Chupplejeep heard a knock on the door. 'What have you forgotten, Pankaj?' he said as he stood up. Then he realised that Pankaj would have a key. He didn't need to knock. He looked at his watch. It was late for visitors. He looked through the window by the side of the police station door. He recognised the face instantly.

Chupplejeep opened the door. 'Mrs Dhaliwal, it's late.'

'Yes, Detective, but something is troubling me and I could not sleep.'

'You could have phoned. Why come here all the way from Kukurul?'

'I yave no phone, Detective,' she said. 'And anyway, it was something I do not wish my yusband to hear. Can I come in? It's cold.'

'Yes, yes,' Chupplejeep said as he ushered Paavai inside and closed the door. 'Tell me what is bothering you.'

CHAPTER THIRTY-SIX

'Good detective work is knowing when to trust your instinct and knowing when to trust the facts over those instincts,' Chupplejeep said, biting his lower lip. He had spoken to Kulkarni earlier. As suspected, no traces of anything suspicious had been found on Bala's ugly statue. He sighed. Chupplejeep had only ever made an arrest when the murder weapon could not be found and that was through the culprit's admission.

Both men got out of the car. They saw their original eight suspects there. Some alone like poor Neeraj, without his Paavai. Perhaps she had refused to be part of the public show. Also, Sanjog was there without Kamana. Pankaj breathed a sigh relief. He was glad the voluptuous woman, with her come-hither eyes, was not there to make him feel uncomfortable.

The two men walked through the gate of the Laljis' garden and through to the back of the house where Sandeep Shah's body had been found.

The guests were talking on the veranda, but there was silence as soon as they saw the detective. Granny Monji stared at him through the kitchen window, which overlooked the garden. Chupplejeep noticed that her smaller eye was slightly closed today. She looked at him for a moment and then went back to shelling peas.

The group started talking again as Pankaj and Chupplejeep thanked the Laljis for agreeing that all the suspects could meet at their house.

Mrs Lalji went back into the house to fetch the remaining Rasna Lavita had made for the guests.

'It's a bit worrying,' she said when she returned with a tray of glasses, 'having a murderer in your garden.'

'Tell me,' Chupplejeep said, ignoring Mrs Lalji's remark. 'There is one thing that is still puzzling me about this whole case and that is the murder weapon. You're sure you did not take anything from the garden before our guys searched it?'

'Sure, Detective. In fact, since that day, no one has been in the garden…only Baba to water the plants in the evenings. It's too scary, no? Knowing someone was murdered in your garden. You know this has changed my life. I have to lock the doors now. It's a good job Lavita is getting married. I worry about her the most. She is so scared, she won't even clean the chicken coop anymore.'

'That is understandable,' Chupplejeep said, his eyes drifting to the scene of the crime. 'Very understandable.'

'So let me begin,' Chupplejeep said, commanding the attention of the gathered crowd. The drongo cuckoo let out a high-pitched whistle and the vibrant blue kingfisher took flight.

The audience of suspects looked at the detective in anticipation. Lavita was playing with her *pallu,* shawl, while Bala had his arm around his bride to be. Utsa leaned on the railings on one side of the veranda before sitting next to her mother on a mat.

Sailesh stood near the door of the kitchen, standing straight with an air of confidence. Was he putting on a show for his parents who had accompanied him? Chupplejeep wondered if Pankaj had said something to Sailesh when he called him here this morning.

Sanjog was looking up at the coconut tree as if praying to the gods. Neeraj flicked his eyes between his daughter and her lover, Vasudev, who was standing at the farthest possible point from where Gita stood. He could see tears forming in Gita's eyes. It was time to tell them.

'Let me begin,' he said. He let his eyes scan his audience again, then he looked up at the house before letting his eyes wander to the place where Sandeep Shah's body was found. A couple of days ago he had wondered if he had considered all options and most importantly all persons who had reason to want Sandeep Shah dead. He had realised that he had missed someone; someone who had motive and opportunity was in front of him this whole time. If only he had the murder weapon. 'Wait here,' Chupplejeep said to Pankaj, whispering, 'Keep an eye on them,' as he wandered off into the garden.

~

311

Pankaj nodded following Chupplejeep with his eyes. Where was his boss going? He wondered if the sleepless nights were causing him to go a little mad.

Chupplejeep looked back at Pankaj and pointed to his own eyes.

Pankaj quickly looked back at the suspects. Sailesh talked with his mother and father. Occasionally he stole a glance at Utsa. Utsa sat next to her mother. She didn't look at Sailesh once, but she would have had to be brave to do this. Meenakshi was right behind her son, doling out evil looks at her. Pankaj's eyes focused on the culprit. He looked at the murderer with scorn. How could they? What a devil! No god would look kindly on what had been done. The murderer would come back in his new life as a cockroach for sure. Wouldn't it be nice if the Krazy Lines he used to rid their office of the insects could be used on people as well?

He mulled over what Chupplejeep had said to him before he nodded off at work last night. The female suspects had been discounted. Gita's height had ruled her out. Lavita's love for Sandeep and her ignorance about his wife meant she had no motive to kill. Utsa had lied and had been in Sandeep's room, but she had fallen in love with Sailesh and had put the driver and his false declarations of love behind her.

Sailesh, too, had been exonerated. Sailesh knew that Sandeep was married. This was his advantage. He could have threatened the driver with this knowledge at any time. He had in fact threatened the driver with this information and a left hook. That had been enough.

Neeraj was annoyed by the hurt he had caused his family by bringing Sandeep into their lives, but he had come clean about his failed attempt to scare his son-in-law and Pankaj had believed the old man.

Vasudev also had an alibi. The doctors and the nurses at the Daisy Chain charity had verified his mother's terrible condition. One of the nurses had even said she had noticed the sheets hanging out to dry on the morning of the eleventh November, giving Vasudev's alibi more weight. Still, Vasudev had his own conscience to live with, Pankaj thought. The man had betrayed his best friend by sleeping with his wife. Vasudev may not come back as a cockroach but he would definitely be reincarnated as something small and animal-like.

This had only left the loan shark, Sanjog, and Sandeep's friend from school, Bala. Kulkarni had confirmed that the ornament was definitely not the murder weapon, although it was the closest thing to a murder weapon they had. But it turned out that Bala had an alibi all along.

Bala's elder brother had stopped by to see Pankaj and Chupplejeep late yesterday evening. He had heard from his family that Bala was still under suspicion and so he had explained to Chupplejeep what he knew. On the night of the tenth November, he had gone to the family home at around eleven-thirty, to pick up his daughter's wooden toy that she often refused to go to school without. His mother always made plenty of food for the evening meal so he decided to have a small snack. Thirty minutes later he had his fill and was about to leave the house. But on his way out he had been tempted by the new television his father had recently purchased and stayed to watch three episodes of *Dance India Dance* before taking the wooden toy back to his daughter in the early hours of the morning. During his entre visit, Bala had been sleeping soundly in the old grandfather chair so he had to make sure that the television was not too loud.

'It was Sanjog Viraj,' Pankaj said, speaking his thoughts out loud.

The gathered crowd stopped talking and looked at Pankaj.

'You said Mr Viraj here was the murderer?' Mrs Lalji said, walking over to Bala and letting out a sigh. She put her arm around her future nephew-in-law.

Pankaj put his fingers to his lips. Had he said that out loud? Of course he had. He could see everybody's eyes on him. Each and every suspect, including an angry looking Sanjog, was looking at him waiting for an explanation. Pankaj looked towards the tallest coconut tree in Utol for his superior. Chupplejeep was nowhere to be found.

'Pankaj, you can't just make a statement like that and leave us waiting for more. Tell us how it happened,' Meenakshi said, holding on to her husband and her son, Sailesh, for support.

'I...er...please wait for the Detective,' Pankaj said. He wiped the sweat from his brow. Suddenly he felt hot.

'What are you saying? How can you say this?' Sanjog frowned. He was shaking his fist and walking towards the front of the crowd. There were whispers and sideways glances as he made his way through the people. 'I demand to know, right now, your explanation. You can't just make accusations like this. You will ruin my reputation and my good name. Explain yourself.'

Pankaj looked again for his boss. 'Sir, sir,' he called, but Chupplejeep was busy searching in one of the shrubs near to where Sandeep body was found.

Pankaj looked back at the house. Granny Monji, who was still shelling peas, stopped what she was doing, took a sip of water and looked at him whilst rubbing her chin.

'Here goes,' Pankaj whispered under his breath. He looked up at his audience. 'Sanjog Viraj, as you may know, lends money to desperate people.'

The crowd was silent. 'We know,' a voice from the back said.

'Sandeep Shah was a gambler.'

There was a collective gasp.

Neeraj buried his face in his hands.

Gita looked to the floor.

Pankaj's mouth was dry. He wished he could have a sip of water just to loosen his tongue. He raised his right hand to silence the gathering. He noticed his hand was shaking. The crowd was leaning in towards him, looking at him, waiting for him to say something more. He had no choice – he had to continue now. 'Sanjog had loaned a large sum of money to Sandeep. When Sandeep could not pay the money back, things got nasty. Sanjog has no alibi for the night of the murder. His wife was away.'

Another gasp from the crowd.

Pankaj looked over to Granny Monji. The old woman looked unimpressed. She shook her head from side to side, making Pankaj doubt himself even more. He looked back at the crowd in front of him. They were straining to see something behind him. Pankaj turned. He could see Sanjog's wife walking, quickly, towards him.

Kamana was wearing a purple sari, her bare round stomach poking out. She was waving a card in her hand and carrying a small green book.

'Here,' she said, desperately trying to catch her breath.

Pankaj noticed large sweat patches under her armpits as she handed the book to him. She didn't seem so attractive any more.

'I found it, my diary.'

This was not evidence, thought Pankaj. Anyone could have written this. He looked at Sanjog. The loan shark was wearing a broad smile.

Kamana handed Pankaj the card she was holding as well. 'My husband told you that he went to a wedding on the ninth November. I told you he has a memory like a bucket with a hole, na? The wedding was on the tenth. The tenth November. I found the invite with my diary. It had slipped behind my dresser. It's such an old antique it took two people to move it this morning. I only asked the servants to move it when my brooch fell behind it when I was getting ready for *puja*.'

Pankaj turned red. 'This is not evidence.'

'Check with the other guests at the wedding. My Sanjog was there.'

Pankaj swallowed hard. Kamana was right, if Sanjog Viraj went to the wedding, there would be many people who could vouch for his whereabouts. The invite said the wedding was in Margao. That was far. It would have taken several hours to go to Utol and back in-between.

Sanjog smiled and hit Pankaj on his back. 'Never mind, officer. We all make mistakes, sometimes. You're lucky you didn't wrongfully arrest me!'

Pankaj started to apologise but Sanjog stopped him.

'Detective,' Sanjog said looking behind Pankaj, 'as it is you who is leading this investigation and not your stupid assistant, please tell me, if I am not the murderer who is?'

Pankaj turned around to see his boss standing behind him. There was a loud murmuring from the gathered crowd.

'I have something to say,' Gita Shah said meekly, barely audible above the mutterings from the people on the veranda.

The audience fell silent again.

'It was me!' another voice from the crowd said. 'I'm the one who killed Sandeep Shah.'

CHAPTER THIRTY-SEVEN

The gathering parted to expose the voice.

It was Neeraj Dhaliwal.

Chupplejeep tilted his head to one side and looked at the tall man.

'Detective, it was I who took that man's life,' Neeraj said.

Behind him his daughter was crying.

There was tutting, head shaking and sucking of teeth from the crowd.

'What did you want me to do? I brought this gambling womaniser into my daughter's life. I knew from the Da Costas' *dhobi* that Sandeep was cheating on my daughter. What kind of man would I be if I just left him to break her heart? They had a child together, you know.'

Chupplejeep noticed that Vasudev had now walked over to Gita and was comforting her as she wept into his chest.

'I had to put things right,' Neeraj continued. 'I went to the village in the early hours of November eleventh and I hit him on the head with a round stone. Then somewhere between Utol and Kukurul I chucked the rock in a ditch.'

'What are you saying?' Ramesh said. 'Your daughter was having an affair with the knife sharpener. Your daughter and her husband's relationship was a dysfunctional one. It was not your place to take someone's life.'

Further disapproving sounds came from the gathering.

Neeraj's was silent. He looked at the ground as if he wanted it to open up and swallow him whole.

Suddenly a shrill cry pierced the air.

'Now what the hell is happening?' Chupplejeep said.

Gita Shah was walking quickly, towards her father. As she reached him, she started to punch his chest with her fists. 'What have you done, father? Look how old you are. You would not last a day in jail. I can't let you do this.'

Neeraj held his daughter's arms tightly.

'My father did nothing!' Gita Shah said boldly.

Neeraj gave his daughter a stern look. 'Let me do this,' he whispered. 'I was here in the village. Someone saw me.'

'It was me,' Gita Shah said. 'Even though my husband was cheating on me, I was racked with guilt for having an affair with my husband's best friend.'

'*Che*,' someone said from the gathering. Pankaj shook his head.

'I couldn't face my own husband anymore,' Gita said. 'I tried to make it up to him. I used to send him his favourite foods and pickles. It never made up for the guilt. Finally on that Saturday night, after Vasudev had dropped me home, I decided I had to do something. I snuck out of my room and went to visit Sandeep. I asked him for a divorce. He said he would never give me one. I could smell that another woman had been in his room. Something inside me snapped. I was the one feeling guilty even though he was deceiving me.'

'Lies,' Neeraj said.

Gita ignored her father and continued. 'He had no remorse for what he was doing. I lured him outside. That is why you found my hair on his body. It was me. I hit him with a rock and then got rid of it on my way back home. I threw it in a drain.'

'*Aacha*,' Chupplejeep said, nodding his understanding. 'And how did you get from Kukurul to Utol?'

Gita Shah stammered. 'I caught a rickshaw.'

'I see. You are much shorter than your husband, no?'

Gita nodded.

'From your height how did you hit him on top of his head? He is much taller than you. You just now agreed that.'

'Simple,' Gita Shah said. 'I asked him to sit down so we could discuss our relationship.'

'I see, very good. Would anyone else like to confess to the murder of Sandeep Shah?'

The crowd was silent.

Gita studied the mud beneath her feet.

'*Che*, Detective, I can assure you it was I who – ' Neeraj started.

'It was me,' Gita quickly interjected.

'And I love Utsa,' Sailesh said.

~

Pankaj gave his friend an incredulous look as Utsa's mother hit her daughter on the back of her head. Utsa smiled, but her smile soon disappeared as Meenakshi dramatically held the back of her hand to her forehead and fainted.

Sailesh's mother, caught by her husband, was saved any kind of bodily injury. 'Oh the shame!' Meenakshi said as she woke to find her husband sharing a smile with his son.

Sailesh strode over to Utsa and put his hand out for her to take. Utsa looked at her mother shaking her head in disapproval. Her eyes were wide and angry. Utsa took Sailesh's hand and rose to her feet whilst her mother buried her face in her *dupata*.

Chupplejeep put his hand up. 'Stop,' he said. 'Stop this nonsense. Sailesh, sorry, but no one cares about who you love. Work it out between your families in your own time. And you two,' he said looking at Gita and her father. 'It's time for the deceit and the lies to stop. Neither of you killed Sandeep Shah.'

~

321

Granny Monji, who had finished shelling peas, had started to eat them. Popping them in her mouth and swallowing them with large gulps of water like they were pills.

Mrs Lalji retrieved packs of *kul kuls,* grams and jugs full of Rasna from the kitchen and handed them out like they were in the cinema.

Chupplejeep sighed. These villagers had expected a little gossip, instead a soap opera was unravelling before their eyes. There were murmurings and laughing, it was like a *mela,* a festival, not at all like the final scenes in Poirot he had envisioned.

Gita and Neeraj were still looking at Chupplejeep in anticipation.

'Neither of these two people killed Sandeep Shah. Paavai Dhaliwal paid me a visit last night. She used what little money she had to get an auto-rick to bring her to my office and take her back in the dead of night.'

Neeraj and Gita exchanged a look.

'Neither of you knew?' Chupplejeep asked. 'Well she told me exactly what you two would say. She didn't know when, but she knew it would happen soon. She's a good woman, Paavai Dhaliwal. She could not be here today because she is looking after Ashu, no?'

Gita nodded.

'It seems your wife is not as ignorant as you believed, Neeraj. She knew that Sandeep was a gambler and she knew that you tried to arrange the marriage and then started to feel guilty for what you had brought into your home.'

322

'How?' Neeraj asked. 'How did my Paavai know all this?'

'The same way she knew what you would say today. In fact, she told me your confession almost word for word. Your wife said you would confess because you believed that your daughter had killed her husband. You thought this because, at the market, you saw your daughter and Vasudev together. You could see they were in love. You put two and two together and made five. You, Neeraj Dhaliwal, have confessed to a crime that you did not commit because you want to protect your daughter.'

The crowd was silent.

'It is understandable in the circumstances. You were seen in Utol. You intended to cause Sandeep physical pain with the rock but, like you told us previously, you couldn't do it.'

'I did kill him,' Neeraj said.

'No you didn't. You told your wife that this was what you were going to do to protect your daughter.'

'I never!' Neeraj said confidently. 'I have not spoken to my wife about this. This is all lies.'

'Oh yes you did. In fact, since your daughter's marriage, every night, you tell your wife everything you do.'

'I don't.'

'You do, sir. In your sleep.'

Chupplejeep noticed the sudden look of realisation on Neeraj's face. '*Aacha*, you understand.'

Neeraj stood with his mouth open, motionless.

The audience laughed.

Gita cocked her head to one side.

'Now Gita Shah, you are not quite sure what to do, are you?' Chupplejeep asked.

Gita was silent.

'Because you didn't kill your husband either, did you? You only said you did, because you were trying to protect your father.'

Gita pursed her lips.

'I could take you to the station for questioning, but we both know that would be a waste of our time. When you were first interviewed you did not lie to us. You were the only person who told us the truth. You had not been to Utol. Your father may have left the house, but you were at home sleeping in your bed that night.'

'How do you she was sleeping at home?' someone said from the gathering.

'What do you say, Gita?' Chupplejeep asked. 'Shall we drag this out further?'

Gita shook her head.

'We know Gita didn't kill Sandeep Shah, so who did?' Vasudev asked.

'*Ek minat*,' Chupplejeep said, as he disappeared back into the garden.

CHAPTER THIRTY-EIGHT

Pankaj followed Chupplejeep into the garden. The rest of the group trailed behind. Chupplejeep walked over to the rangoon creeper, which filled the space between the ixora and the curry-pak tree. The faint aroma of a well-seasoned curry filled Pankaj's nostrils as the breeze blew in his direction. He remembered this distraction the day he had been searching the Lalji's garden. What a beautiful smell the curry-pak leaves had.

Chupplejeep rooted around in the dark mass of the ixora. Several of the dark pink flowers fell to the ground. He could hear Mrs Lalji disapprovingly cluck her tongue against the roof of her mouth. Finally he found what he was looking for and stood up. The crowd noticed the large coconut that he was holding in his hand. 'This is the culprit,' Chupplejeep said with a smile.

'Really?' Sanjog said.

Chupplejeep nodded. 'I know it's rare for a coconut to kill. But it does happen. We all thought it at first. I mean the body was found under a coconut tree but then we started digging deeper. Why was Sandeep naked? And where was the coconut? We overlooked the obvious.

'Gita Shah revealed in an interview that her husband always slept naked. So his nakedness was not unusual. The question was why was he under the coconut tree. It seems that Sandeep Shah was on his way to the toilet. Mrs Lalji told me that Sandeep did this often in the night. Taking a leak on the bushes instead of using the lavatory. So it wasn't uncommon for him to be wandering around the garden at night, naked. Sandeep Shah was in the wrong place at the wrong time when the coconut fell, that is all.

'Let me assure you though, at the time my men were instructed to search the entire area and they did. I've been thinking for a couple of days now, ever since seeing the coconuts being protected by nets in the five-star resort, that nature may have played a part in Sandeep's death.

'I spoke to Kulkarni earlier. I asked him if it was possible that a coconut could have bounced of Sandeep's head and into a higher level in the bushes. My forensic pathologist said that if the coconut had hit Sandeep Shah with force whilst Sandeep was standing then it could easily have bounced like I had suggested. The coconut got tangled in the branches of the ixora, which were intertwined with the rangoon creeper. The coconut found itself in what you could call a nest of shrub branches, hidden from view.'

Chupplejeep pointed to the conical end of the coconut, which had what looked like dried fragments of skin and a few short hairs. 'Of course I will ask Kulkarni to check this coconut to see if it was what killed

Sandeep, but there is no doubt in my mind that this is what did it.'

'Are you sure?' Sailesh asked.

'Yes,' Chupplejeep said triumphantly.

'Bloody time waster!' Ramesh said taking out a *beedi* from his shirt pocket. Taking his wife's hand, he led her towards the main road. The rest of the group shrugged and began to leave also.

Pankaj looked to the ground. 'Sorry, sir. I was supposed to have checked those shrubs thoroughly.'

'Never mind, Pankaj.'

'I should have looked harder,' he said feeling guilty for being distracted from his search by the fragrant smell of the curry-pak tree at the time.

'Next time you will look harder, and not just on the ground.'

Chupplejeep and Pankaj walked back to the rear of the Laljis' house. The veranda was empty. Without any drama or something for people to gossip about, the villagers had drifted back to their own homes, keen to get out of the midday sun. Mrs Lalji was clearing empty cups. Granny Monji was still sitting by the window. She had stopped eating peas. Chupplejeep noticed a smile on her lips. 'Come with me,' Chupplejeep said to Pankaj. They walked up to the window and greeted Granny Monji.

'Well that got rid of the crowd, didn't it?' Chupplejeep said. For years he had wanted to reveal a murderer with all the suspects present. This case had presented the perfect opportunity. But as he had walked

327

into the waiting crowd, earlier today, he knew it was the wrong way to go about exposing a criminal.

Granny Monji smiled. 'Accidents happen.'

'You're a good shot,' Chupplejeep said. His eyes focused on the sports day certificate framed in the Laljis' kitchen, which he had previously seen when he had visited their house. Mrs Lalji had said that Granny was a keen sportswoman. Just how keen, he hadn't realised at the time. It was only afterwards when he saw the view from the landing window in the Lalji house, saw that the coconuts were so easily available and dangerous enough to be netted in that five-star, that he started to piece the puzzle together. 'First in shot-put. You haven't lost your touch.'

Granny Monji made a face. 'That was a long time ago. These old arms have no strength left in them anymore.' She lifted up her right arm to show the detective she had no muscle.

'I read the notes from the fire in Soco, the fire that killed your eldest daughter. You are not as old as you would like everyone to believe. You married at sixteen. You had your daughters soon after. I was suspicious when I was questioning Lavita and you casually walked into the kitchen carrying that heavy bag of rice. It must have been at least fifteen kilos. Yet you were not even out of breath. I knew then that you were younger than you look and you said it yourself, "village folk are stronger than you think."'

'Still. How could I have killed that man, he was so much taller than me.'

'When I visited this house last, I took a good look upstairs. From the front window on the upstairs landing it would be easy to throw a coconut out of the window. If you had a good aim it could easily land on an innocent driver taking a piss in the dead of night. Especially as you knew Sandeep woke up like clockwork at two in the morning to pee.'

Granny Monji made a face.

'I checked this with the forensic pathologist when I spoke to his earlier. He confirmed that if a coconut was thrown from a height it could cause death. The same way a coconut can kill if it falls from a tree.'

'Perhaps. But I had no reason to do that.'

'I think you had good enough reason.'

'I don't know what you are saying.'

'Firstly, you were angered that Sandeep had no respect for your property. He was pissing on all your plants. Mrs Lalji told me that your prized hibiscus had died because of it.'

'That's not a reason to kill someone.'

'Quite. But that was only my first point. Secondly, I read the interview transcripts from the Soco fire in which your eldest daughter died. She, too, was having an affair with a driver.'

'I wasn't even in Soco at the time. I was here in Utol. Are you trying to blame that fire on me, Detective?'

'You said in your statement, at that time, that you knew your daughter's affair would bring bad luck on her home. You warned her, in fact, didn't you? But she didn't listen and she died.'

'That much is true.'

'Your niece was following in her mother's footsteps, wasn't she? Lavita, like her mother, had fallen in love with a driver whose intentions were no good. Sandeep was bringing bad luck on your home. You said that to your daughter, but she thought nothing of it. It was only the other day when Mrs Lalji reminded me of your superstitions I began to look at this case differently.

'You are very superstitious, aren't you? You don't wash your hair on Saturdays or Thursdays. There is even a *totka* of lime and chillies hanging in the doorway of your home to ward off the goddess of poverty. I noticed this when we first came to inspect the crime scene. Because of what Lavita was doing, you were scared another fire would follow and your remaining daughter and niece would suffer the same fate. You already tried to get Lavita to wear that black marking on her forehead to ward off evil eye, but she would not listen and you were not going to let history repeat itself, were you?'

Granny Monji was silent.

'I'm sure if I have this coconut tested for fingerprints they will find yours on the fruit.'

Granny Monji let her shoulders drop. 'I wasn't going to let Sandeep bring bad luck into this house. I could smell the bad luck on him every night when he pissed under that tree. I had already tried speaking to him, but he did not listen. He thought I was a mad old woman.'

'We'll have to take you to the station.'

Granny Monji folded her arms across her chest. 'I did nothing wrong. I'll tell that to any judge. I was protecting my family, that is all.'

'Crimes must be punished. Don't you think?'

Granny Monji made a face. She looked over at her daughter who was still clearing up. 'I need to explain to my daughter.'

Chupplejeep nodded. As the old woman lifted herself off her seat and made her way into the garden, he turned to Pankaj.

Pankaj's eyes were wide with disbelief.

'Take the rest of the day off, Pankaj.' Chupplejeep passed the coconut to him, careful not to touch the hairs and the brown sticky substance on the one end of the fruit. 'I'll take Mrs Monji to the station and fill out the paperwork. And don't look so shocked, Pankaj. It was your first homicide.' Chupplejeep patted his colleague on his shoulder.

'I feel sorry for that grandma.'

Chupplejeep shrugged.

'I suppose the Inspector General will be happy.'

'I'll be sure to tell him your detection skills are coming along.'

Pankaj's face brightened. He put his arms out to hug his boss, but instantly retracted them. It was not appropriate. Instead he said, 'Christabel will be happy the case is closed. You can start planning for your trip to Kerala too. It's a big birthday. You need to have a big celebration.'

'Yes,' Chupplejeep said with a grin. He put his hands in his pockets. He felt the business card the jeweller, Mr Gopal, had given to him a couple of days ago. He rubbed the card between his thumb and forefinger. 'I think it'll be a big celebration, Pankaj. A big celebration indeed.'

Acknowledgements

Thank you to my friends and family, particularly my dad for sharing with me his heritage and beautiful ancestral home. Thanks also go to Urmi Kenia for her expansive knowledge on India. Any mistakes are my own. And of course a big thank you goes to Abingdon Writer's Fictional Adult Group for their continual support and critique.

About the Author

Marissa de Luna is an up-and-coming author with a passion for writing and travel. She grew up in Goa and now lives in Oxfordshire. 'Under The Coconut Tree' is her third novel.

Other novels by Marissa de Luna

Goa Traffic

The Bittersweet Vine

Coming soon

Poison in the Water

The Body in the Bath – A Chupplejeep Mystery

www.marissadeluna.com